DETROIT WHEELS

BOOK THREE OF THE MARSHA O'SHEA SERIES

JOHN A. HODA

CHAPTER 1

THE MEN SAT opposite FBI Agent Marsha O'Shea in the spacious conference room. No chit-chat while they all waited for their tea. She couldn't read their expressions. It surprised her that the imam had granted the meeting with such little notice and with even less explanation. The Arab-American Muslims in this solidly middle-class neighborhood west of Detroit had had an uneasy relationship with the FBI since 9/11 and more so in the last twelve years. The silence was heavy.

The glass tabletop allowed those seated to see the leg action of the others. Marsha was not a big fan of body language as emotional tells, but occasionally, she had watched liars calmly respond, while under the table, their legs told a different story. *Almost as good as Pinocchio's nose.*

Her dark blue pants and matching blazer over a white blouse buttoned to her throat showed respect to the cleric and professionalism to the attorney. *'Tis not the time, nor place for a skirt or teasing neckline.* Her cell phone remained in her purse along with her badge and credentials. She locked her gun in her car, a rented Mustang. She was in Dearborn, after all, the birthplace of Ford Motors.

She accepted a black tea and one sip told her it was hot, strong and aromatic. The men drank and set their cups on saucers, waiting. She moved her Rook's pawn first, but not aggressively. "Thank you both for meeting with me today. I am happy to discuss the purpose of my visit." This interview, like many others she conducted, resembled a game of chess and this was her opening move.

They nodded. *King's pawn out one square. Nothing aggressive about it.*

"It's difficult to explain why I am here. I have never been asked to speak to a spiritual leader as it relates to the welfare of their flock before." She moved the other Rook's pawn into play. "Forgive me, if I speak without sensitivity and I do not mean any disrespect."

"Thank you for desire to be considerate. That has not been the norm of late," the imam's attorney matched her move.

"Until last week, I only knew Detroit to be the home of the automotive industry and Motown music."

"And now?" The attorney could wait for her to discuss the actual reason they were there.

"And now I am assigned to look into your community's concern about what might happen *again* this year on the anniversary of 9/11."

The attorney looked to the imam for permission and pushed out his Bishop's pawn. He was playing defense. "What concerns are those and why would the FBI share those concerns?"

Looking at the imam, Marsha replied, "The concern surrounding the unnatural deaths of Muslim women on that exact date every year, going how far back?" Her question hung in the air.

The imam blinked, and the attorney leaned back and re-crossed his legs.

"Hate crimes and violation of civil rights falls under the FBI's jurisdiction," she continued.

"Your employer has extended no interest in the unwarranted mistreatment of our community since that fateful day. Why now?" The mouthpiece tapped his grounded leg.

"Once we stumbled over these anomalies, we became obligated to act." She pushed a Knight's pawn out.

"And how did you learn about those deaths, Agent O'Shea?" the imam asked. He mirrored her move.

She stared into his coal-black eyes. She had to be careful here. His headwear and spotless clerical garb framed his face; both she would have to learn the name of. His plain, round, black-rimmed glasses magnified his eyes, reminding her of the Mr. Magoo cartoons she watched as a kid, but she knew damn well that this spiritual leader was no nearsighted dummy. Marsha researched his impressive education both here and in Iraq.

"No one walked into the Bureau's Field Office, if that is what you're asking sir." Marsha reached for her cup, took a sip, peered over the rim and watched as both men did likewise. She put down her cup on the saucer after them to signal that she would give them more.

"I took this assignment at a location far away from prying eyes of FBI Headquarters and shredded the file I read before I left that meeting room." Queen pawn was out now.

"That sounds rather unusual. Is it?" the attorney asked, looking up from his notepad, matching her move with his Queen pawn by two squares.

"Very few people know that I am here acting alone in an official capacity."

They waited.

She moved another pawn. "I have seen nothing like that myself and it had me questioning all the secrecy," she replied.

"What are you not saying, Agent O'Shea?" the attorney pressed on. His background on local boards, fund-raisers, non-profits and private schools, in both here and Dearborn Heights, was well-documented, but he was not a former U.S. Attorney and his practice did not include criminal defense. This was not a zoning board variance he was asking about.

Shifting her attention back to the imam. "I'm not from the local field office . I have never worked hate crimes before, but in four months another member of your community may die a horrible death. From what I read, I agree with you," she said pointing at him, "that the women who died these premature deaths did not do so accidentally. I am not an actuary and I don't play one on TV, but I don't think for a minute these deaths were anything else but murder. The odds of that happening every year on that exact date are astronomical. You would have a better chance of hitting the moon with a rock." There it was.

She paused, took another sip and stared at the imam before speaking. "I have to determine what really happened to them, but I need to hear with my own ears, from someone here, before I can start my *official* investigation to prevent it from happening ever again."

"I have not talked to the FBI or anyone in authority about this," he replied calmly. He moved his Queen into check.

"You are correct, but so am I that I know you have *voiced* your concerns." She didn't block his move.

Immediately, the attorney began his protestations, but his client lifted his left hand from his lap and silenced him. "Agent O'Shea, I will take your concerns under advisement and pray on them." With that, he stood up and looked down on her. He might as well have knocked her King over. *Checkmate.*

Marsha calmly stood up and looked at him eye to eye. She then reached into her silver card case, presented to her by her father, a retired Philly PD captain of the Vice Squad on the day they swore her in as an agent. She retrieved two cards. "I am flying home tomorrow afternoon to retrieve my car and my clothes so I can drive back here to work this case." She handed each man a card. "Or I stay there until the Bureau gives me another assignment elsewhere."

She made her way to the door and opened it. She made a show of looking around the room as if scanning for something in particular. "It's your decision. Either way, we both know that the clock is ticking." She talked about the more deadly game happening on the streets and in the homes of his community.

Outside the room, the assistant who guided her through the maze of hallways back to her raincoat, immediately met her. The paintings and mounted photography along the way were vibrant, rich and steeped in history.

Growing up Catholic, the Stations of the Cross was about the only iconography that she was familiar with. This was all foreign to her. *Have I really led such a sheltered life?* Marsha had never been to Italy or the Vatican. Save the picture of the Pope and the Archbishop of Philadelphia, she had no remembrances of the artwork at Our Mother of Consolation in Chestnut Hill.

The assistant, a youthful woman dressed in soft pastels, wore a brown headscarf. She led Marsha to the exit door and opened it to heavy rains. Marsha returned her headscarf and slipped on her shoes. They exchanged gentle smiles. Marsha sighed. *Could she be the next victim?*

Out in the parking lot, Marsha looked back at the impressive domed mosque. It damn-near took up a square city block. Rain and wind pelted her face as she fobbed her way into the rental. The defrosters blasted her windshield clear.

A few turns later out of the expansive parking lot, she wound her way on side streets that brought her onto Michigan Avenue, the major drag of Dearborn.

She couldn't help but notice that the retail and commercial building signage were both in English and Arabic. Almost all the surnames of the dentists, chiropractors, lawyers, opticians, Realtors, and car dealers were Arab. Much of that signage was dual language if not totally in Arabic.

Why didn't I notice this on the way to the mosque? Her recent research told her that this area had the greatest concentration of Arab Americans. *Where was my head at?*

A short distance later, Marsha spotted Millers, a bar on the corner across the avenue from Bob Evans. Her Mustang found its way into the back-parking lot of the bar. *Happy hour?* She tapped the steering wheel and looked at her phone on the passenger seat. She took a deep breath. She made a promise. She would keep her promise, but in that moment, the urge passed just as quickly as it had been triggered. The Mustang found its way back onto the avenue and a few intersections later, Marsha spotted Sheeba's.

Through the full-length windows, she could see a brightly lit and decorated interior. She parked in their lot and walked through the entrance. The counter was already doing multiple take outs. Large brown paper bags were being assembled while cell phones were tucked between shoulders and ears as more orders were being taken. She had eaten Mediterranean before, so she wasn't totally out of her element. The smells of slowly heated meats and spices was a welcome relief to her empty stomach. She ordered a lamb stew. It quickly arrived in a bubbling cauldron too hot to touch, along with a piece of folded over flatbread, a foot in diameter. She wasted no time devouring her hot dinner.

After she finished swabbing the last of the stew from the bowl, she doubted whether the dishwasher needed to wash it, given how deftly she employed the last bits of her bread.

Yes, I want dessert. No, I don't need the sugar coma that would follow. She watched other diners as she waited for her check. Families with strollers and kids in high chairs filled most of the tables. Quiet conversations between husbands and wives and their well-minded kids were the norm. This is where the locals ate. She didn't have to be an investigator to deduce that.

Back at the Country Inn and Suites, she channels-surfed while deleting emails. She finally settled on the Tigers who were getting pummeled by the White Sox, but it didn't command her attention. She kept thinking about her brief meeting at the mosque; what was said, and what could have been said differently. She always was like this with the good, bad and ugly interviews. She wasn't sure which was which. She would sleep on it and it would come to her in the morning if she had done her best to get them to trust her.

Finally, as sleep was about to overtake her that night, alone in the expansive single king, her thoughts drifted to the imam. Illegal bugging by an unidentified three-letter agency, had surreptitiously recorded the imam fielding concerns from his flock about what would happen again this year. The bereaving family members of those who had died weighed heavily on him, he admitted to his inner circle. These were not phone intercepts. She wasn't sure where the bugging had occurred, but judging by his abrupt ending of the meeting, it was probably where no government agency had any business having a listening device or two or three.

Marsha didn't know much about praying. She hadn't prayed since confessing to Father Gallagher what she and Chad had done after the prom. She prayed then less for forgiveness and more for her late period to arrive.

For those grieving families of the dead women, she hoped that the imam had his Creator on speed dial.

CHAPTER 2

THE *MISSION: Impossible* ring tone launched her out of a very pleasant, lucid dream involving her favorite baseball player, Joe DiNatale. Twisting out of covers and rolling over overstuffed pillows, she swam half an ocean to the nightstand where an unknown caller waited for her to pick up.

"Yes?"

"Agent O'Shea?"

"Speaking."

"One moment please," the youthful male voice said.

This gave Marsha a chance to orient herself. It was still dark. Her alarm and back-up wake-up were not scheduled for another hour.

"Good morning, Ms. O'Shea, I hope I didn't wake you."

"You did, but that's okay. I was hoping you would call." She recognized the voice of the imam immediately.

"I would like to continue our conversation away from the mosque. Could we meet for breakfast in about forty-five minutes?"

"Absolutely. Where?"

"The restaurant where you had dinner last night won't

open for business for a few more hours and we will sit in a quiet room where we won't be overheard."

Word gets around fast. Marsha chuckled to herself. "Is it all right if I dress casual?"

"However you like. We will meet then."

"One more thing?"

"Yes?"

"Would I upset them if I brought my own coffee? Tea doesn't work for me at this hour."

It was the imam's turn to chuckle. "Yes, that would be fine."

"For lack of a better word, I just wanted to make sure it was kosher."

"It's kosher, Agent O'Shea," he assured her.

Stripping out of an extra-large Chase Utley Phillies Eighties throwback jersey and her panties, she figured out how to turn the shower on without scalding her arm and allowed the water to warm up while she peed and brushed her teeth.

He's gonna want to set the ground rules before he will talk to me. It was not exactly neutral turf, but she felt that if it makes him more comfortable, the better chance she would have of getting him to give her, legally, what they had gotten the other way. Food would help relax them both.

She went over the opening moves and how she visualized the first five minutes would go. Did she need to re-establish rapport? Was he that put off by the violation of his privacy and that of his sanctuary that she alluded to? Did she clarify that she was an outsider and not the unsmiling suits and black-clad ICE cadre making lives uncomfortable there since that most-memorable September day?

The day before, Marsha had kept her leave-behinds in her satchel in a manila folder of the few newspaper articles about the recent deaths, but she would use them as her "rescue questions" if she felt the imam's desire to meet was nothing more than a ploy to exact more information from her.

Blow-drying and brushing her longish chestnut blonde hair, she went over the conversation goals, almost like closing a sale. *Why do I want this case? Why I'm trying to sell this guy I want to work for it? Marsha O'Shea: Lone Ranger.*

She could soft-pedal it today or conversely piss off the imam so royally that she would leave Detroit without jacketing a case. A very simple email to the encrypted email address the number two guy in the Bureau, Grayson Stanfield, gave her would be all she needed to compose. The imam didn't want to make an official complaint, she would say in so many words. Case closed. She couldn't disclose that the Bureau had come into information from some three letter agency's illegal bugging of their house of holy.

She knew the City of Brotherly Love was still too hot for her to return to. The investigation that she and Mike Hollins of the Organized Crime Unit of the Philadelphia Police Department started had uncovered thirty years of bribery and corruption. The FBI and the PD's Internal Affairs unit were running separate and concurrent investigations. *The Philadelphia Sun* was avenging the death of their beloved crime beat reporter who had stumbled into the case. They were going balls out while conducting Pulitzer-Prize worthy investigative journalism. For too many reasons to count, she had to stay away from that case professionally and personally.

This case intrigued her and that she was hand-picked to work it. She didn't want to go to some backwater, low-priority squad or worse; to D.C. to die a slow death by paper-cuts.

Brown slacks and a cardigan sweater with matching flats completed her dress down look. As promised, the door to Sheeba's opened for her and they led her to a table setting across from the imam who was dressed similarly as the day before.

After greetings, he ordered for them in Arabic. Her Starbucks cup sat on the table like a fresh pimple on an adolescent's nose. It garnered a few glances from the server. The imam told her, in English, what he had ordered for them. Overripe bananas, fresh cream, raisins and honey were the major ingredients.

Both dishes arrived shortly, and she dug into her breakfast dessert with a tablespoon, savoring each bite. She took the time to profess her ignorance of all things Muslim and asked him basic questions about the Muslim expression in America. He suggested that she visit the Arab-American national museum before leaving town for her flight, if she had time. It was a hint of where the conversation might go. *Why bother to learn this stuff, if I will never need it?*

The dishes were removed, and they set a cup of tea before her. She moved the Grande paper cup aside for the server to take and moved the cup and saucer in front of her.

"I received answers to my prayers for guidance, Agent O'Shea," he began immediately when they were alone. "I understand why the local office of the FBI may not address these grievous attacks on our women and why outside agents may need to be brought in. Call it bias or prejudice, but your organization is a bureaucracy and it would be hard for them to see those women as innocent victims, after all these years of looking at our community as the fertile breeding ground for domestic terrorism." He sipped his cooling tea. "But you are alone in this matter, are you not, Agent O'Shea?"

"They will afford me an intelligence analyst of my choice, but essentially you are correct," she replied.

"Then I had to ask myself, of all the FBI agents working outside of this area, why this woman agent was picked to work alone."

Marsha knew that he was not being overtly sexist but was stating a simple fact that the Bureau was still a male-dominated culture. They would not send out a single agent to do a squad's work. That only happened in the movies. "I have to agree with you."

"Combine that with the secrecy of how you received the assignment, it would give your organization plausible deniability, would it not?"

"I see your point, but I look at it differently. By working alone and away from the field office, I would receive no interference and could proceed unencumbered by the bureaucracy." She then conceded, "But I can see where you think I am being set up to fail."

"To be truthful with you, Agent O'Shea, I was disinclined to assist you, but then we looked into your recent past," he said.

This should be interesting. She waited.

"Is it true that you and a detective proved that a man wanted for murder was innocent?"

She nodded, thinking of what her and Hollins had accomplished a few months earlier.

"And you and the detective were under investigation while your employers sorted out all the details?"

She wished the server hadn't taken her Grande cup and shrugged in the affirmative.

"I take it you didn't make many friends in your investigation, Agent O'Shea."

"Guilty as charged." Marsha managed a wry smile. He had all the control in the interview now and she didn't know where he was heading.

"Then you confronted an armed man while on vacation in Florida and got the best of him. Is that true?" he asked almost incredulously.

"I had help," Marsha replied.

"Part of me thinks you are being set up to fail, but maybe they are secretly wanting you to succeed because of who you are, Agent O'Shea."

"I thought that too, but I can also tell you that none of me wants to fail." That was the truth. Back in her Miami days with the Bureau, she was a gunslinger. Working bank robberies and fugitives, she worked on teams that went after the bad guys with gusto. After 9/11, the FBI's law enforcement mission took a backseat to investigating terrorism. She returned to her hometown to finish out her career when the organized crime scene exploded the past winter. She needed to prove that her work there was not a fluke and that she could play in the big leagues again.

"I am guided to believe you, but I, too, have to be careful how I proceed. People look to me for spiritual direction and strength as their leader during these troublesome times. How the information was gathered that your employer learned about is inexcusable and I hope that the truth will come out, but what is more important is that the killings stop. How can I be sure of your ability to stop the deaths?"

She nodded. "I plan to disclose as much as I can to you throughout the course of the investigation. You can judge for yourself." Here it was, she had no more moves to play. *Time to fish or cut bait.*

"I must take my leave now. Your bill is taken care of, Agent O'Shea. Thank you for meeting with me. My answer will come to you soon enough." He nodded to her, did not offer her his hand, whisked past her and was gone.

He left her sitting there staring into her cup. She didn't know how to read the tea leaves.

Marsha took a sweet from the tray and popped it into her mouth. It was hard for her to decide if the poppy seed or almonds or mincemeat was dominant. They all took turns swirling around in her mouth before she swallowed.

She would collect her bags, check out, skip the museum and see where her next assignment would take her. She felt that she did her best to convince the imam of her good intentions. She'd be sure to follow the news coming out of Detroit in four months to see if he'd have another sheep from his flock taken in some terrible way.

She finished her water and nodded to the server. She stood and made her way to the doorway. Outside, in the principal seating area, one table was occupied, and they all were staring at her with expectant eyes.

The host guided her to the only empty chair at the table. "Please sit here. Can I get you more tea?"

That is when it hit her. The imam gave her his response. She suppressed a smile seeing the gravity of the situation.

Over the next two hours, she talked to a sister, a mother and a husband of three loved ones who died unexpectedly and unnaturally on 9/11 over the last three years.

CHAPTER 3

SHE HAD to meet him at work for multiple reasons. She recalled being fixated on rubbing the dried blood from her hands and fingernails the last time she had been there. She and another cop cleared a wanted murder suspect. This also had a way of bringing out the scowls and shaking heads from the tight-lipped suits.

The official warning letter telling her, in no uncertain terms, to stay away from that case hadn't moved from where she placed it six weeks earlier, just hours before her world tilted in a bad way. Now Marsha stared at it like all those unfair marks on her report card from Sister Bernadette in third grade for "self-control." She used it now as a drink coaster for her iced triple-ristretto in a Venti cup with coconut milk.

After all that time on administrative leave, the Bureau had reluctantly concluded that she had acted bravely and properly. She was back in business.

Coming back into the Philadelphia Field Office was just as much about vindication as it was about validation. Her former office mates took turns walking by her cubicle, not to chat but to glance at her. She paid them no attention, as she made plans to have her mail forwarded to a PO box in Dearborn. Marsha cancelled her parking garage fees and her gym membership.

There wasn't much need for Krav Maga, the Israeli self-defense form of martial arts, in that town. She would find a kick-boxing studio somewhere out there. The physical release of stress and mental fatigue from practicing Krav Maga had been lifesaving in every sense of the word while she spent her paid-leave time in Clearwater, Florida, the spring training facility of the Philadelphia Phillies.

The morning flew by as she planned to be on the temporary long-term assignment. They would keep their record keeping separate from the Bureau's on Slack. *You would think somebody would have made a commercial app for tracking mass murderers by now?* Marsha mused.

She and her analyst would have read-only access to NCIC, VICAP and the Behavior Analysis Unit (BAU) files. She loaded her laptop with databases she used while working off the books for her former boss, Charlie Akers, now retired, who worked as a private investigator in Florida.

The American Express Gold card that Grayson Stanfield gave her was coming in handy for this project. She was instructed to work outside of normal channels and to have little or no interaction with the local field office. The little voice in her head told her to heed the imam's misgivings that she was being set up, but she relished the freedom to investigate this case how she saw fit with no interference or micro-managing. With it, however, came the awesome responsibility of finding and stopping the killer before he struck again. Until the evidence determined otherwise, she would operate under the assumption that it was a male *UNSUB*, short for an unknown subject acting alone.

She had avoided Ramit until lunchtime when they planned to grab food cart fare and sit on Independence Mall to gaze at the tourists. They had talked a few times when she was on leave; he always with hushed tones from the office. It gratified him to hear that she was no longer getting shit-faced on most days ending with the letter Y. He was her intelligence analyst in the biggest case of their careers and handled himself in the field with excellent results. Ramit was a good sounding board during those bitter winter days and then briefly afterwards before she went South, in more ways than one.

At noon on the dot, she tapped him on the shoulder, and he jumped half-way out of his seat, so intent he was on whatever he was working on. "Hey, Ramit, are you ready for lunch?" Marsha grinned. She enjoyed getting a rise out of him, literally and figuratively.

"Hi, Marsha. Yeah, yeah sure," he stammered, "let me shut things done here. I will meet you by the elevators."

She stopped at the little girl's room and then stood by the elevators. The traffic leaving cubicle hell for this brief respite was heavy. Agents from her old squad came and couldn't avoid her here and went by with a nod, but not much in the way of fist-bumping, back-slapping, way-to-go Marsha greetings. She had left under an ominous cloud and tripled their workload overnight. This bunch had always kept their heads down, worked just enough to keep the bosses happy and counted their days to retirement. She figured that she was still kryptonite. It would be this way forever.

Ramit looked different when he punched the down button. He dressed better and looked like he had been a regular at the gym. Marsha couldn't quite put her finger on it. He looked relaxed and more self-assured. *I go away for six weeks, and he grows up on me,* she mused. They were of equal height and the added muscle made him heavier than her.

"How does it feel to be back?" he asked.

"I can never work here again. Our case feels like an albatross around my neck."

"I feel that way too. As long as the agents are in town looking into what you uncovered, it's okay, but as soon as they leave, I think I may have to move on too."

"Anybody giving you a hard time?" she asked.

"No. I've been pretty much ignored since Jingles retired."

Jingles, as Daryl Stocker was called behind his back, had earned that nickname by insisting that his agents call in regularly back when pay phones were in use. He was a micro-manager even then. God help the agent who didn't keep a pocketful of dimes jingling in their pockets. When the facts came out about how he tried to shut Marsha's investigation down, they gave him the choice of a plum assignment in Guam or retirement.

Their favorite food cart had the best kielbasa and soft pretzels. They slathered mustard generously on both. She favored sweet iced tea, while Ramit grabbed a cold Orange Crush. They sat facing Carpenter's Hall.

"I take it you have had little fun since I went on 'vacation' either," she probed.

"That was the biggest case of my career. With you not around, I went back to running agent's queries and doing routine follow-ups. I was lying low. I wasn't sure what would happen to you," he said.

"And how much stink would stick to you if things went sour for me," she added.

"I wasn't worried with what would happen to me,

Marsha. I was just an IA following direction from an overzealous agent." He smiled.

"Not going down with the good ship O'Shea, huh, Ramit?"

"You kept me out of things. Remember, Marsha? I was pissed when you held me at arm's length, but as the days went on and you were in rehab — relaxing in Florida, I came to appreciate you watching out for me. For a while there, it looked terrible for you."

"I didn't know which way things were gonna go until last week when I met with Stanfield." She sipped her sweet iced tea through the straw.

"The number two guy in the Bureau?"

"Yep. I got reinstated, and they assigned me to a case that makes 'Bad Vlad' look like a choirboy." She let that sit for a minute while they watched a tourist haggle with the driver of horse-drawn carriage.

Borrowing one of her lines, he said, "You're shitting me."

"I shit you not," she replied as she had done a dozen times with him.

"You wanna know what's even better?" She balled up her wrappers and hit a three-pointer with her toss into the nearby barrel.

"What?" he asked.

"I demanded that I get my own analyst, or it was no deal."

"What did he say to that?"

"He knew I couldn't work this case alone, and that I needed somebody who I could trust and somebody willing to do what it took to break a case open like we did. Do you know anybody like that, Ramit?"

"Where is the case, Marsha?"

"Detroit."

"Detroit?"

"Yeah, Detroit."

"I don't know, Marsha. That's a long way from here."

"What's a matter, Ramit? We get this plum assignment handed to us by the Assistant Director of Field Operations and you have cold feet?"

"For how long?"

"Mid-September."

"Mid-September, that's a long time."

"What's the matter, Ramit? You haven't even asked me about the case."

Ramit was silent while the tour buses belched diesel fumes and lurched into traffic to the ire of four-wheelers trying to go about their business.

"It's just that...." he trailed off.

"What?" She looked at him now expectantly.

"I have a girlfriend. I think it's serious."

So that's it. He's in love and doesn't want to leave her. "What's her name?" she asked.

"Manju. She is in residency at HUP to become an eye surgeon."

"I take it you didn't meet at our country-western Karaoke bar." This had been one of their favorite things to do when they celebrated a rare win in their big case.

"No, no. My roommates had a party and one of their girlfriends brought one of her roommates. It was right after...." He circled his arms. "Everything and I told her I worked on the case and...."

She punched his arm and startled him. "Way to go, Ramit. You are the FBI guy that broke the case that was all over TV and the papers. What a turn-on that must have been for her."

"Marsha, it wasn't like that. We—" He was blushing now.

"Don't bullshit a bullshitter, mi amigo. It's not like you work in data analytics for some corporation in Center City. You work for the freakin' FBI. You are the man, Ramit! Just think what it will be like when you tell her about this case that you were hand-picked for by the number two hombre in the Bureau."

"I don't know, Marsha. I've got it good here. We— We are thinking about becoming a couple."

"I get that, but what I don't get is all this time you still haven't even bothered to ask what the case is about. My feelings are hurt, Ramit," she said it first as a sales ploy, but then felt it, like a tightening around her heart. *How could I work this case without him?* On the plane flight home and before falling into her own bed exhausted, she thought about how they would divide and conquer. She expected him to follow her like a faithful puppy dog into their next adventure.

They stared at the fife and drum corps parading by in three-pointed hats, blouses and leggings from the time of the upstart Colonies uprising against the king of England.

"Am I kryptonite to you too, Ramit?" Marsha quietly asked.

"We barely talked while you were away. You left me here to fend for myself. Now you want me to drop what I am doing and go to Michigan. It's easy for you to run away again on some quest, but I have reasons to stay here."

"Thank you for your response, Mr. Ravikant, but can you answer my question? Am I kryptonite to you?"

"No, you are not, Agent O'Shea," he shot back.

"Until last week, I didn't know I would still be employed in the only career I've ever had. My life was not always in control for several reasons. It was better that we waited until we knew what would happen to me. The more we talked, the more the headhunters could bend you over the table. That was unspoken. We had to wait. You know I had to sort a lot of my own crap out too. You thought it was a magnificent idea for me to get out of Dodge and even suggested it."

She threw her tea away and turned to face him on the park bench. "I am truly glad that you are in love. I am sorry that my brother is dead and that my parents blame me for his death. There is no love coming from my old squad either. So yes, I am happy to take off again. Work is all I have right now, and they have handed me another career case. I get to run a monster case my way with no assholes like Jingles looking over my shoulder or nit-picking my expense reports and you can be part of a big case."

It was a marvelous spring day, with puffy clouds, a warm sun shining on their faces with a gentle breeze and none of it mattered. Their friendship and working relationship hung in the balance.

"So, you are not going to ask me what the case is about?" she said.

"I am afraid if I do, I will say yes and go with you," he replied.

"I don't know many investigators worth their badge who would turn down this case if the bosses offered it to them."

He wasn't taking the bait.

She finally said, "We should get back to the office. I have to clean up some stuff before I go home and pack the car. I am driving out tomorrow. It's supposed to be a perfect day for the convertible."

* * *

She sat at a table away from the bar. She told the server she was the designated driver and asked for a fountain Coke. The server seemed more puzzled at that request as Marsha remained by herself after several refills. Alone, no Ramit tonight to sing country songs along with. No Ramit to help her in Detroit. She would have to waste valuable time getting a new intelligence analyst. Worse, who would voluntarily leave their familiar confines and go to Detroit to work long hours away on a temporary assignment. For some at the Bureau, it was a prestigious job and a vocation, but for many, it was a just a government paycheck.

Honestly, she had bounced between those poles. The gradual change from America's federal top alpha-dog in the fight against crime to the domestic terrorism intelligence gathering arm of the Department of Homeland Security left her without the adrenaline pumping work that she relished. Until that Russian gang case, she was happy to cruise into retirement. She wanted to prove that she could get back in the saddle again.

A year ago, would she have even considered this assignment? All those thoughts swirled through her head as the cowboys and their cowgirls twirled and two-stepped around the dance floor.

Her early dinner with Mike Hollins had been bittersweet. She caught up on his slow recovery from the gunshot wound, which left him partially paralyzed. They talked about their case and what he could glean about the ongoing probe. He wasn't sure what he wanted to do yet. The physical therapy was giving him incremental improvement. She told him about the Detroit case and he blew out a low whistle telling her she was jumping from the frying pan into the fire. No argument from her on that one. They promised to stay in touch.

After that, she had gone to her condo and loaded the back seat of her car with her clothes and toiletries. She debated stopping at her parent's house but decided against it. Too soon.

Feeling too jazzed to go to sleep, she found her way to her favorite urban cowboy bar. The last time here she was shit-faced and had a stare down with a bouncer while Ramit ushered her out the door into a freezing snowstorm.

"I thought you might be here."

She looked up to see Ramit standing there.

"Hey, pardner. Kick up your heels and set a spell." She lapsed into the corny country western movie talk that they both enjoyed.

He sat down and ordered a beer on tap. When it arrived, he toasted them and said, "I owe you an apology. You parachuted back into the office and laid this Detroit thing on me. I just needed time to process it. That's all."

"Yeah, I got thinking about it too and realized that I hit you with too much too fast."

He took another sip. "What are you drinking?"

"A Coke. I've got a twelve-hour drive ahead of me tomorrow and don't want to do that hungover."

He nodded. "What about the rest of the time?"

"I had a rough patch down there, but got it under control, if that's what you're asking."

He nodded again. "I was worried about you."

"I was worried about me too." She sighed. "It's gonna take me a lot of time to process what happened both up here and down there. I don't expect to figure it all out. I had to stop beating myself up with couldas and shouldas. I know now that I won't find the answers in a bottle."

They sat in comfortable silence while listening to the next song and people watching.

"If I am going to say no, I should know what I am saying no to. I owe you that much, Marsha."

She scooted her chair closer to his and talked into his ear when the music ended. "Every year on the anniversary of 9/11, a killer makes it look like a Muslim woman dies accidentally or from a suicide." She paused and pulled back to gauge his expression.

"In Detroit?"

"Detroit has the largest concentration of Arab-Americans in the country. Not all Arabs are Muslims and not all Muslims are Arabs, but if you want to hunt buffalo, you need to go where the buffalo roam." She saw that he was processing this.

"I didn't know that," he responded, then asked, "Why you?"

"I'd like to think I'm the baddest badass special agent in the country, but I'll say it has to do more with what we did here. We worked alone when everyone told us to back off. They need an outsider and somebody who can operate independently. I was on Headquarters' radar and it seemed like they could solve two problems at once. You know they could have just buried me somewhere, so there must be some political expediency for their actions, but I can't see it right now." She let that settle in.

"I won't be getting any boots on the ground from the Behavior Analysis Unit. The BAU are the experts for serial killers and their ilk." Marsha took a calculated step. "We have a ticking clock and not much to work with. On the plus side, we don't have Jingles-type to contend with. We are free to work it the way we see fit."

Ramit sat back as the music started up again. She could tell it intrigued him. He said, "Maybe they are hesitant to have it come out that there is a domestic terrorist trying to cover his tracks, and he isn't really a sicko."

"Some fringe white supremacist or ultra-nationalist?" She hadn't considered that.

"Because he is choosing to kill persons of that faith on that specific day."

"Imagine how that would play in the media if that got out," she said.

"What is about them being all female," he asked.

"If anybody caught on, then it would look like the work of a serial killer," she guessed.

Both their gears were turning now, just like when they worked their big case.

"We know about three for sure, maybe as many as five, but we don't know when it started and how many there really are," she added, hoping to add more fuel to the fire of his curiosity. "Whaddyathink? Is this something that would interest you if it was across the river in Camden? Something that would still have you home at night?"

"For sure. It sounds exciting. I would like to be part of the investigation."

"And if it was local, would you mind working with me on it? Do you think we could make an excellent team again, Ramit?" She was looking into his eyes.

"You were the only agent to trust me to work outside of the office and you listened to my ideas," he said.

"If you worked with me on this, you would have to do more field work. I can't do it alone. It has the makings of a massive project. It's not something that you would work on here and me there, we would have to work together out there I'm afraid." She waited.

He took another swig. Could he resist the siren's call of a big career case? She got her answer quickly.

"How often could I come home?"

"Every other weekend, maybe? It's just a two-hour direct flight."

His second beer arrived with her last Coke. He was mulling it over, she could tell.

"I have to make a call," he finally said.

"I have to go to the girl's room, when I come back, say yes. I could sure use your help on this one." She got up and left him staring at his mug, wondering what he would say to his girlfriend now.

His visit was unexpected. She played it well. She had planned to think about how she would find another IA on the ride out. This was truly a second bite of the apple. Walking back to the table between the boot-scooters kicking up sawdust on the barn flooring, Marsha saw him on his phone.

She loitered around the pool tables while she watched him in deep conversation. When he finished, he looked around for her. He finished the rest of his beer and signaled the server. He cleared his tab. She was hopeful now. He was standing when she appeared.

"What time do we saddle up, Marsha?" he asked.

She wanted to hug him, but, sensing the change in their relationship, didn't. They would ride off in her Mustang on their fresh adventure. "I'll pick you up at nine."

* * *

They took turns driving. She on the Schuylkill Expressway and then onto the PA Turnpike to Harrisburg. He cruised at the speed limit through the rest of Pennsylvania with her transversing the Buckeye State to Toledo before heading north on I-75 into Michigan.

Top down, they had to scream over truck traffic and fight sun glare on his laptop, but it was worth it. The rolling mountains gave way to the verdant green farmer's fields west of the Allegheny and made for a pleasant ride as they chased the sun. When she drove, he keystroked. When it was his turn behind the wheel, they talked about the case and got caught up in their lives. Stopping only for lunch, gas and bathroom breaks, they made pleasurable time. She favored the sweet iced tea, he the energy drinks. To the truckers, she was the foxy lady with the flowing blondish hair and aviator glasses, he, the nerdy co-pilot. Nobody would guess they were an FBI team going after a mass murderer.

It was near dusk when they pulled into the driveway of a stone cape cod just off the corner of Prospect and Woodworth in Dearborn. She handed the waiting Realtor two month's security deposit, and six months' rent in cash. She counted out the hundred-dollar bills like she was using Monopoly money to buy a hotel on Park Place.

Twenty minutes later, the furniture truck arrived, and burly Arab men unloaded two twin bed frames, box springs and mattresses. A pull-out couch, futon, coffee table, dining room table and chairs, a worktable and a large, smart flat screen TV completed the haul. They finished the installation while Marsha and Ramit sat on the back patio with Chinese delivery. In the morning they would pick up the tinted-window rental van for Ramit and raid the local Staples and Ikea before making a courtesy call on the FBI field office in Detroit. Tonight, they had sleeping bags, and their own pillows and two bath towels. They scheduled locksmiths and the cable guy for the early afternoon. By mid-afternoon, they hoped to be in business.

***

The administrative assistant had disappeared with their credentials forty-nine minutes earlier and five minutes before their confirmed noon appointment with the Area Supervisor in Charge. They located the FBI offices in the McNamara Federal Building, a tall rectangular concrete edifice with matching gray oversized planters; the kind that popped up around all federal buildings after the Oklahoma City bombing. These were empty of any trees, bushes or flowers as most were. Marsha guessed that the wide-open spigot of DHS funding paid for the planters as a security measure, but not for the plantings to go inside them.

Marsha knew why they left to chill in the waiting room. Just like when the trooper on the interstate held your license, registration and insurance cards, you couldn't go anywhere until you got them back. Finally, the receptionist received the call and led them to a compact interview room with cups of lukewarm coffee still on the table, not the Assistant Supervisor in Charge's office, nor a conference room. Once seated, the wait started all over again. These rooms were for "investigative interviews" or what interrogations were called nowadays. Luckily for both, they had been working their phones and kept laying the foundation for their case processes and systems.

Seventy-five minutes after their arrival, the ASIC made his way into the room and they rose to offer their greeting.

"Ravilant?" Looking at Ramit's credentials. "What nationality is that?"

"Indian and it's Ravikant," he replied.

"You born here, Ravilant?" He squinted at him.

"Yes." Ramit was puzzled by question.

"Good," came the terse reply. He handed Ramit his creds.

Finally addressing Marsha, "O'Shea, is it? What brings you here to our fair city from Filthy Delphia?" He hadn't invited them to sit back down.

Marsha smiled and reached for her credentials, and once safely tucked into her purse said, "I don't appreciate the game you're playing, Callahan." Dispensing with any semblance of politeness, she pressed on. "I duly note it that you made two FBI employees making a courtesy call cool their heels in your waiting area with no explanation or offer of coffee for nearly an hour. The next time I come here, it won't be by appointment. The last office jockey to cross swords with me was told to take an assignment in Guam or retire. I came here to tell you to stay on the sidelines while we do the job that Headquarters assigned us to do. Personally, I don't give a flying fuck if your nose is out of joint, just don't stick it in my business. Is that understood?" Without waiting for a reply, she added. "This courtesy call is over." She brusquely brushed past him and out the door with a shocked, mouth-agape Ramit trailing behind her.

They didn't talk until they both were breathing fresh air on Michigan Avenue.

Marsha looked at Ramit and said, "Do you think I am angry?"

He nodded cautiously. "Ah, yeah. Real angry."

She placed her hand on his arm and said, "I am not now and nor was I upstairs." She turned, and they walked to her car. "He wanted to let me know who was in charge. He did that, but do you think he will meddle in our investigation after what I just did?"

He shook his head. "No way."

"We are not here to make friends with the locals," she said, "Maybe I burnt a bridge back there, but I'd rather think we are like the ancient Greeks who arrived on their enemy's beach and burned their landing boats. We can't ask for help and we have only one way to go and that is forward."

They got in the car. Marsha was smiling. She pushed off from the curb.

"What?" Ramit asked, looking over at her as they sped down the avenue.

"God that felt good though." She glanced at him. "Was it good for you, Ramit?"

CHAPTER 4

"JAMILA HAD BEEN FOUND unresponsive in her bed." Marsha put Jamila's name on the white board. It was the most recent death. "According to her sister, she was a healthy young adult working full-time and going to night-school to get her MBA. The family became concerned when she didn't appear at their insurance and travel agency at 10 a.m. Wednesday morning, September 11. Her younger sister went to the townhouse, used the key code on the garage door and ran up to the second-floor bedroom above the garage. She tried shaking Jamila before calling 9-1-1."

"Cause of death?" Ramit asked.

"The EMTs were first at the scene. They were unsuccessful in resuscitating her. They couldn't get a pulse. Then fire department arrived and noticed that her Ford Escape was still running in the garage. They turned it off and opened up the all windows. That's when it was decided that she died of carbon monoxide poisoning."

"Was the car functioning properly," he asked.

"I don't know," she answered. She added a notation to the board and her laptop.

"Does that happen often?"

"When I googled it, I learned that carbon monoxide fatal poisoning occurs about 400 times a year in America — not even a blip on the radar screen."

"More than once a day though," he replied.

She nodded and said, "At first, the family wanted to take the body from the hospital to prepare it for immediate burial, but the Wayne County Medical Examiner's office strongly urged that autopsy be performed. Normally, when a death is suspicious, an ME can order it." Under the cause of death column, Marsha put a faint question mark.

"There was no evidence of foul play in the bedroom. There were no pills or a note found at the scene. The family had no indication of depression or self-harm," Marsha read from her notebook.

"Nothing to make it look like a homicide or suicide, got it," he said.

"Everybody just assumed that she was exhausted from working full-time and going to school at nights. She must have accidentally left the car on and went upstairs. The family finally agreed to a blood draw and it confirmed CO poisoning as the cause of death. The manner of death was deemed accidental," Marsha said and marked both columns that way.

The first name was on the board and they stared at what they had: 9/11, Muslim woman, CO poisoning, and accidental. They would concentrate on the last point.

"How did he know that she would be home that night?" she asked.

"He must have known her schedule," he said.

"It was a new school year. He had to make sure what her class schedule was," she said.

"Surveillance or GPS?" he asked.

"She wouldn't suspect a tail, especially if he has been doing it for years," she said.

"Have to put the GPS on and have to take it off. Car is garaged at night. Can only do that in broad daylight," he said.

She asked, "Did he even need to surveil her that night? How hard would it be to get her schedule from the school?"

"Pretty hard unless...."

"Right," Marsha agreed and made a note to profile each victim to see if any had a connection to the Wayne State.

"It would be an easy place to pick your next victim," he said.

"What about where she worked? Let's take a look at that and where she lived," Marsha made another note in their Slack. "What about the car?"

"Can it be started remotely?" he asked.

"Can you check with Ford?" she asked back.

"Sure." He made a note of it.

"But with a remote starter, he would need a fob," she pointed out.

"I can check to see if it has to be a factory install or after-market," he added. "We definitely need to inspect the car."

"If there is no remote package on the car, then how did he turn it on?" she asked.

"Her keys or a spare set." he said, then asked, "and how would he get them?"

"We need to talk to the family in more depth to see if she reported them stolen or had extra sets made," Marsha noted.

"Any signs of forced entry?" Ramit asked.

"Good question, everybody came and went through the garage," she said.

"If there was no remote starter, then he had to get access to the garage to be able to start the car."

"He had time to plan this. Maybe he broke in and stole her keys and that's how he would get access on D-Day."

"D-Day?" Ramit cocked an eyebrow.

"Death Day. We know it's 9/11, but it has to be that specific day he has to commit the killing."

"Unless she changed the locks," came his reply.

"Family would know about the break-in or if the locks were changed."

"Unless...." Ramit paused.

"Unless what? What are you thinking, mi amigo?" She could almost hear his wheels turning.

"He intercepts her at the school and somehow renders her unconscious," Ramit was talking his theory out. "He drives her to the house, uses the garage door opener, leaves the car running, takes her upstairs, undresses her and closes the garage door behind him."

"Why not just kill her and leave her in the car?" she asked.

"He has to make it look like an accident."

"So he's staging this, if he intercepts her elsewhere," she concluded.

"Is it easier than breaking in while she's asleep?"

"How did he knock her out?" she asked.

"How do we know that she was not dead on arrival to the house and the rest of the set up is to hide the murder?" he asked.

"The carbon monoxide would not be in her blood system," she replied.

"You're right, I forgot that," he answered.

The hypothetical hung between them. Neither of them thought for a minute that she died accidentally.

"How could he get her unconscious? What else was in her blood system," he asked.

"I was thinking the same thing. They find the CO and stop looking," she said, then quickly added, "I will get the full toxicology report — if one was even done."

They stared at the board. Next to it, the flat screen displayed Ramit's laptop, cataloguing their growing list of leads.

Marsha said, "I want to talk to all the responders in person and the ME after we talk to the family."

The locksmith and cable guy finished almost simultaneously. They tested the internet. The locks were changed, all manners of egress and exit were wired and the monitoring system was working. The cops would be notified about any intrusions. They went over the keypad instructions. The locksmith pointed out that the fire extinguishers and smoke detectors were located in the kitchen and hallways.

"Holy shit, we almost forgot to see if the townhouse had a CO detector," she said. Looking at the locksmith. "Do these detectors work for smoke and carbon monoxide?"

"Yes. You have gas heat? If you were on electric, we would only have to install a smoke detector."

"Why's that?" Ramit asked.

"Varies from state to state and whether a local ordinance takes precedent. Landlords only do what they are required to do to save a buck."

Turning to Marsha, Ramit said, "Wouldn't he have to know that too? If she had one, it would have gone off and woke her up."

"Makes me think that he had access to the townhouse

before that night. The first thing the fire department would have checked is what kind of detector did she have. We will need access to their report and the crime scene."

The locksmith shouldered his workbag and said, "Not sure what you are talking about, but the tax assessor will tell you what kind of heating source the property has."

Feeling like a couple of rookies, they nodded.

* * *

The victim's younger sister answered the door and ushered Marsha and Ramit down the hallway to the dining room. She had been the one to make the discovery. Steaming bowls of rice and seasoned vegetables sat on the table. They set additional place settings for them by prior agreement after weak protest. They were starved. Her notebook and his Chromebook stayed in their cases while their mother brought out the main chicken dish. Her father carried out the still-steaming bread and they sat down together.

The small talk was important. The parents talked proudly about being third generation Turks in America. Their grandparents settled in Dearborn and most of the extended family were still in the area; members in good-standing with the mosque. This family's story could easily be a copy of the Irish coming to Boston after the famine or of the Italians sailing into Ellis Island during the 1920s. Stories of whose kid was the first to go to college, which family got their first house in the suburbs, The first teachers, doctors, lawyers and elected officials all were displayed in old-fashioned photo albums. After they cleared the plates, they set hot tea and a tray of sweets out along with a Shutterfly album all about Jamila.

Lest we forget that she was a happy young lady with her

entire life in front of her. Welcome to homicide, Marsha thought.

With pride and tears, the family talked about how competitive she was growing up. "Jamila had to be first in everything: tag, board games, sports, grades. That never changed as she got older."

She was an honors student and a basketball player. In college, she worked nights and weekends while getting her accounting degree in the daytime and switched when she went to grad school. There were princess dances with her father and prom dates with boys her family approved of. Vacation trips with the family, a day at the beach and other outings completed the montage.

Ramit and Marsha learned that Jamila was fiercely independent and wanted to make it on her own. Marriage was somewhere out over the horizon and children would come later. There were two shots of her with her new car. She had bought on her own from a dealership the family didn't frequent. Her father was astounded with how she had gotten an impressive deal and 0% financing. It was her first big life purchase. She rented the townhouse from a family friend and was slowly decorating it with quality hand-me-downs from their large extended family.

The investigators had to get down to business eventually and didn't rush it. Earning the family's trust was more important, but gradually the conversation became a conversation with a purpose.

"Did she have any concerns she was being followed in the last year or so?" Marsha asked. They all shook their head no.

"Was her apartment ever broken into or did she ever notice any missing?"

Again, came the negative responses.

"Did she ever lose her keys or get extra car keys?"

Mom and Dad couldn't think of a time when their daughter lost or misplaced a thing. "She would yell at me if I borrowed something from her without telling her," the sister said.

"Do you know if the car came with a remote start?" Ramit asked.

"Winters can get cold here. She would always run out a few minutes before we would close the office and warm up her car before going to school," her dad offered, "She kept it in the garage when she was at her apartment."

"Do you know if she any problems with it?" It was Marsha's turn to ask.

"No, only oil changes and tire rotations. It was still under warranty at the dealership, and she took it there. They gave her a free car wash every time she brought it in," Dad said.

"I wish my dealership did that for me," Marsha said. Looking at the younger daughter. "When you came in through the garage. Did you hear the car running?"

"No, and I thought about that later. I think it was because the garage door was still making noise as it went up and I was in the apartment before it opened all the way."

"Was there anything different about her room or the way she was dressed for sleeping?" Marsha asked without letting on about their concerns that Jamila was placed in her bed unconscious.

"No, she was wearing her favorite nightgown. She always kept a glass of water on the bed stand. It was there. Half filled."

"How would you know that?" Ramit, an only child, asked.

"She would invite me over to stay some nights for

movies and pizza. I liked that she had her own place and we could have a girl's night in."

That perked the FBI team up. "Did you ever stay during the week?"

"No, no. Just Saturday nights and not that often and never again, I guess." Her eyes welled up.

"I know this is tough, but we just have a few more questions," Marsha said. She waited until the sister was ready and asked, "Did the firemen say anything to you about the car running?"

"Yes, they opened up the windows and put an exhaust fan in the garage. It was really noisy."

"Did they tell you about why the smoke detectors didn't work?"

"If they did, I don't remember, it was pretty crazy while they tried to wake her up."

"I understand," Marsha said. Looking at Dad. "Do you think your friend can show us the apartment?"

"He has rented it out again, but I can try." He got up and went to another room to place the call.

"Do you know where the car is now?" Ramit asked.

"You walked by it in the driveway," the daughter said, "I'm driving it now."

How could we miss the obvious? Marsha thought.

The father returned to the dining room and said that they could meet the landlord at the apartment in thirty minutes. It would still be daylight.

Ramit asked her for the keys. The Ford website determined that the car did not have a remote start. They saw that it was a keyless start, but the driver needed the fob close by. Marsha took pictures of the dealership information from the paperwork in the glove box. There was no mention of trouble with the exhaust system or recalls. Just the same, they would have an expert check out the car.

Marsha and Ramit said their goodbyes to the family and placed the crime scene in her GPS. On the way over, she said, "He would have had to access the apartment while she was sleeping or drive her into the garage unconscious. There is no way to start the car from outside."

They met the landlord outside of the building and before they walked in asked him three questions.

"Did you change the locks before renting the apartment to Jamila?" Ramit asked.

"No, but I did afterwards."

"Were the smoke detectors working when she lived there," Marsha asked.

"Yes."

"Did they include CO detection?"

"No, I didn't have to. The law required only smoke detectors as the unit is all electric, but it does now. I know it's too little, too late for Jamila. I feel bad for that poor young woman."

They nodded.

"Can you get me the names and contact information of the tenants before Jamila?" Marsha asked.

"There were none. I lived in it from the time it was built until I rented it to her. I am living in and rehabbing a house nearby and will do the same when it's complete."

"Was the unit broken into or did you ever lose your keys and had to have them replaced?" Ramit was catching on quickly to the follow-up questions that had to be asked.

"No, this is a wonderful neighborhood. I had no problems. The reason I changed the locks is that there was a key broken off in the front door deadbolt."

"Do you know how that happened?"

"No. I just assumed that her family was unfamiliar with the lock and twisted too hard."

"One second." Marsha got the younger daughter on the phone. "Hi, this is Agent O'Shea, I have a quick question for you. What do you know about the key broken off in the front door deadbolt?"

She listened and while waiting said to Ramit, "She knew nothing about it. She's checking with her parents." Then back to the phone. "Okay, thanks." Marsha said to Ramit and the landlord. "Jamila and her parents had a set of keys for both the doorknob and the deadbolt. They said they returned them both to you."

The landlord nodded and said, "Yes. That is correct."

Ramit asked, "Where did the extra key come from?"

She pulled him by the arm out of earshot of the landlord. "The actual question is, did he break it off accidentally or on purpose?"

"Leaving in a rush, he snaps it off?" he asked.

"Breaking it off on purpose forces her family to enter through the garage and discover the car running," she said.

Turning back to the landlord. "Do you know what happened to the deadbolt?"

"I was here when he installed the recent one. He said it was too much work to disassemble the lock, so he just threw it out."

Along with possible DNA. Marsha just shook her head and said, "Let's go in."

"I have a favor to ask. I did not tell my tenants that someone died here. I repainted and had the carpets steam cleaned. Can you not say anything in front of them?" the landlord asked with pleading eyes.

Ramit and Marsha shrugged their shoulders and said, "Sure."

They knocked on the door and the landlord made hasty introductions to the young couple who apologized that the clean and orderly apartment was not spotless. They clung to each other in nervousness that bordered on terror. There must have been something in the phone call to them that two FBI agents were coming.

"Hello, I am Agent O'Shea and this Ramit Ravikant. We need to do a walkthrough and take some pictures for an old case that we are working. Would that be all right with you?" The less said, the better.

Ramit still looked for signs of forced entry on the ground floor and took photos, while Marsha went upstairs and photographed the bedroom. Ramit ended up in the garage with the landlord opening and closing the garage door a few times. They asked the tenant to start his Subaru in the garage while they exited and entered as the door was still going up.

She was right, you can't hear the car running with all those gears meshing. Marsha went back upstairs, and they started the car and opened and closed the garage door again.

"Okay turn it off. Thank you for your help," she said to the husband whose eyes were getting red from the smoke fumes in the garage. *That's how fast it could happen.*

Once outside, Marsha said to Ramit and the landlord, "I couldn't hear the car start, but I could hear the garage door opening and closings. I could feel the opener vibrate while sitting on their bed."

"Thank you, Agent O'Shea for not saying anything to them."

"If we have to come back, I may have to," Marsha said as Ramit had already taken down their names and phone numbers. The couple's heart rates may return to normal before bedtime.

They shook hands and drove away in silence. Their gears were turning. Suddenly Marsha braked and parked at the curb. "Shit!" She whipped a U-turn, slamming Ramit against the passenger's window and sped back to the parking lot. She told Ramit to take pictures of the street signs and the entrance. She then had him take pictures facing the garage door and from the garage door outwards.

"What I know about CSI, I learned from the bank robbery detail, back in the day. I just can't remember all that they did." She waved around the parking lot and at the other townhouses. "This is a fishbowl. He had to be here to get into her townhouse. Where did he sit? Nobody asked the neighbors if there was anybody hanging around out here. Do the cops have any reports of suspicious persons or cars? I was ready to drive away and didn't think to do any of this. Shit! Fuck!"

* * *

Tamara finished the boy's lunches while their soccer uniforms were in the dryer. Both were on travel teams this spring and doing well at their charter school. It made for some interesting carpooling arrangements with the other moms. During the months of longer daylight, her husband Omar ran hard between his two crews doing masonry work. They were also building a house in Livonia where he was the general contractor and that's where he spent his evenings and weekends. His dinner was in the microwave. Their life together was hectic, but happy as they lived the American dream. Married for sixteen years, they had their share of ups and downs as most couples, but they lived their faith and didn't just show up at the mosque for prayers. They were active members of the community.

CHAPTER 5

THE IDIOT in front of Sean jammed on his brakes with no blinker to pull into the gas station entrance that must have come up on him too fast. Although not on his cell phone, Sean's mind was on the answering machine message of his wife Mary he played over breakfast twenty minutes earlier. He reacted too late and didn't even get his foot on the brake.

At 30 mph, his seatbelt tightened, and the airbag went off, punching him in the face and chest. He couldn't breathe. The wind was knocked out of him. He didn't hear the crunch of metal and glass between the rental he was using and the ratty pickup truck.

This must have been how Nura felt when she died.

Playing football in high school, he had the wind knocked out of him a few times and it was never pleasant. Finally, though, it came. The sweet whoosh of air rushed back into his lungs about the same time the airbag deflated. This is why he disconnected the airbag that other time.

He wondered what it was like for Nura to not get that relief. He recalled staring into her eyes as the panic set in.

He had her pinned on the kitchen floor, arms stretched above her head. His leather gloves kept her fingernails from scratching his hands. He had intercepted her at the rear of her car in the garage. He dragged her in the house before she had a chance to scream. His left knee was jammed down between her small breasts not allowing her to inflate her lungs. His other leg had her left leg splayed out wide.

She struggled. This mother of two teenagers and wife of a school principal had been surprised and acted involuntarily when she released her urine. He had felt the warm liquid saturate his crotch. He had recoiled slightly, and it only prolonged her agony. As that gasp of air in her lungs was not enough for her to even shriek. He had known that her family would not be home for several more hours. His careful planning was straightforward in his execution of his plan.

Try as she had, she couldn't use her free leg to lift him off of her and he had watched as the life drained from her face. He had stayed that way for some time until his breathing returned to normal. He dragged her upstairs and made sure not to scuff the hallway walls. She was petite, and he easily pulled her up the steps. He opened the tall wardrobe in the master bedroom and tipped it forward onto her body. It fell on her with a thud just below her throat.

He had measured the drop twice before. He used a wad of paper towels to blot his pants and then retrace his steps, dabbing the hard wood on the stairs and in the living room and finally the tile of the kitchen floor. Their cat was staring at him. He found the can of savory seafood in the fridge and a spoon. He returned to the bedroom and had remembered to dust the top of the wardrobe partially on the right side, leaving the feather duster by her right hand and the spray polish by her left. As a last gesture, he straightened her hijab.

The knocking on his window of his rental was becoming persistent. "Sir. Are you okay?" the police officer asked as he opened the driver's side door.

Sean nodded.

CHAPTER 6

HARD TO BELIEVE that every other overpass had the candy-cane shaped wire and steel-reinforced bridge railings to prevent jumpers from doing a swan dive onto I-94 except for this one, Marsha thought. They drove out of Detroit and rolled southwest to the outskirts of Detroit Metropolitan Wayne County Airport and back. They did the same on the other interstates. The morning was threatening rain, but it held off until they had to step into it. *Never fails.*

The Michigan State Police had done the fatal accident reconstruction investigation and deemed Nabila's death a suicide. Marsha had interviewed the trooper who did the reconstruction and the Dearborn Police detectives who caught the case. They worked with the trooper on the twenty-four hours of her life before she went over the railing.

Nabila's Tempo was found running on the opposite side of the road with the driver's door left ajar. They hypothesized that about two hours after midnight, into the morning of the eleventh. She crossed the roadway and waited until a tractor trailer came into view before she jumped. Her timing was near perfect as she hit the ground a moment before the eighteen-wheeler ran her over. The traumatized trucker reported seeing a blur and then heard the thumps of his tires going over her body. Nabila's cell phone was found on the passenger seat with a text sent minutes before her death to her mother. It read: *I'm sorry.*

The cover story Marsha told the law enforcement officers, LEOs for short, when she asked to meet them at the scene with their files was that a member of Nabila's extended family came up on a watch list and she wanted to know if the jump could have been staged as a suicide. The five of them stood in the drizzle on Rotunda Drive in Dearborn overlooking the interstate, not more than a foot from where she went for her plunge.

"Gentleman, if I wanted to make this look like a suicide, how would I do it?"

They looked at her and at each other. "Why?" came their collective response.

"Because I want her dead, but I don't want to make it look like a homicide," she patiently replied.

"Yes, I understand that," the trooper said, "Why do you want her dead?"

"I understand your question," Marsha replied, "but you didn't answer mine. How would you do it?"

It was the lead detective's turn. "If we knew the motive, it might explain the how."

"Why would the motive change how you would go about making this homicide look like a suicide?" she remained patient and unyielding, "I don't get it." She wiped the drizzle from her eyes while Ramit watched their tennis volley.

"If it was a vengeful ex-boyfriend or a street gang or a terrorist group, it might change how it was done. With all due respect, Agent O'Shea, we are curious why the FBI wants to look at a jumper from and a year and a half ago," the trooper asked.

"You mean like it was an act of passion or if it was premeditated?"

"Something like that," the trooper waffled.

Marsha might lose Smokey's cooperation and she needed it because of her and Ramit's absolute lack of training in these kinds of cases. The FBI could throw tons of expertise at jumbo jet crashes, but the locals were much better prepared to deal with this manner of death. *It was local government's job to keep the roadways clean.*

"Nabila was faithfully married to a second generation Palestinian. Her kids were in a private elementary school at the time and I don't think either were Bloods or Crips. She had no connection to terrorist groups, although she was pretty vocal in the PTA. I don't believe some road rage asshole would pull her from the car and throw her over the railing and then take the time to unlock her cell phone and type out a message to her mother." Looking at them, "You guys have a lot more experience with death cases than I do. It's rare, but people try to make homicides look like suicides. Can you throw me a bone here?"

"So, you will not tell us why you think it didn't happen the way we reported," the trooper persisted.

"It sounds like you fellows agreed to meet us here to find out about our investigation and why the Bureau would be interested in a jumper," Marsha said.

"Cooperation goes both ways, Agent O'Shea," the trooper said evenly.

"Yeah, too many times the Feebs have big-footed our cases," the senior detective chimed in, "and taken all the glory."

Marsha sighed. "Would you mind at least showing me the photo again where her Tempo was sitting so I can park my car there?"

The photo was produced and Ramit angled her Mustang to the exact spot and left the door ajar.

She took a photo of the 8x10 glossy and handed it back. "You know, guys, I would love to tell you, and someday I might, but I can't. I am sorry. I may be chasing my tail, but right now I am looking at a jigsaw puzzle. It's your experience and expertise that can help me understand what pieces I am holding."

Tip-lipped men shook their heads.

"Will you call me when copies of the files are available?"

"You can make a Freedom of Information request just like John Q. Citizen," the trooper said. With that, the detectives grinned.

"So, this was just a fishing expedition. Huh, guys? You wanted to find out what the Bureau is working on. You had no intention of helping me out on this."

"What are you working on, Agent O'Shea?" the trooper bluntly asked.

"Losing five pounds, keeping my calm, staying in the moment, and remaining compassionate for Nabila's family, whom we've all met, while I find her killer."

***

Omar's new accountant wanted his books done online. The previous accountant had a bookkeeper that swept up all the invoices, credit card receipts and check stubs weekly. Omar would call in payroll to them every other week. Now, Tamara was the bookkeeper, and they immediately hired a payroll firm. The savings were appreciable for his growing masonry company. Everybody had an I-9 on file in case the ICE agents paid them a visit, again. She would call in payroll now and kept both the paper records and entered the data into the cloud-based app. They didn't want to run afoul of the IRS again with their quarterly estimates, thanks to a costly mistake by the prior accountant. At year's end, they would also get a heads up from the CPA on how much they could set aside for their SEP IRA.

Housekeeping, bookkeeping, volunteering at the school and running two kids around for after-school activities kept her busy. Most days it was manageable, today it wasn't. The boys had been argumentative and with Omar up and out shortly after sunrise, it fell on her to settle them down during breakfast. Their bickering continued in the car and she raised her voice, threatening to make them walk to school and be late. Now she sat at the computer with a stack of credit card receipts to input. The computer froze, and while it rebooted, she stared at the Post-It where she wrote the time and date for her to bring the car in for its oil change. Normally, it would be in and out in less than an hour, but they had to do the free tire rotation and alignment which took the whole day. Maybe they would let her have a loaner for all the trips she had to make that day.

CHAPTER 7

"HEY, Sean, guess what? The dry cleaner didn't get the stain out of my dress. So they said that they will try again. I hope I will get it back in time for my training class. Your suits are hanging up on the rod in the laundry room." He replayed the message.

He had been proud of her, of what she had accomplished. The dress had been for the two-week training for new managers held in Los Angeles and she had been excited. She had only a high school diploma from where they graduated from in Charlestown and a smattering of credits from the Bunker Hill Community College.

"Mwah," he said, blowing a butterfly kiss across the breakfast table to her picture. He reached for his cheek to touch her return air kiss before draining his coffee cup in the sink with the leftover milk from his bowl of cereal, then placed both into the dishwasher.

Sean needed to focus on his day. He gingerly strapped into a demonstration model from the car dealership. Even though he had gotten a ticket for rear-ending the piece of shit pickup truck the other day, he convinced himself that he wasn't at fault. Unfortunately, he couldn't find any cameras pointed in the accident's area to prove it. It was a good thing it was one of his surveillance rentals. Try explaining to your boss how you're not at fault for destroying a demonstration model or a loaner. All the gas station's cameras were pointed at the pumps for drive-offs, on the cash registers or in the stockroom. The busy manager showed him the monitor in his cramped office. He had totaled it and was sore from head to toe. *Am I going to golf in the men's twilight league Wednesday night?*

Face-to-face car sales were becoming increasingly difficult with the internet and car-buying services. Places like Carvana and CarMax were decimating used car sales, so he stuck with both newer models and trucks. Margins were getting tighter with the emphasis on selling extended warranty packages and smart car options. He relied on being one of the best new car's salesmen at a high-volume Ford dealership in Greater Detroit. The plaques on the wall behind his desk gave the customers something to fixate on when he completed the numbers to get them into their dream ride. Earning those awards year after year meant working weekends and nights when regular folks were available.

He networked hard at the Rotary and Chamber of Commerce. He was always quick with tickets to the Tigers, Lions, Pistons and Red Wings home games. When a decent trade-in came in, he was first on the phone to a favorite customer with a son or daughter about to graduate. He made it his business to learn the kid's names. He'd breakeven on the sale, but he made customers for life. During quiet times on the showroom floor, he signed birthday cards and Thanksgiving cards to his prized customer list. He kept the receptionists busy addressing and stamping them. When special customers' cars were in for a full day, he would personally take them out for a full car wash. He worked the phones to convert leads into prospects and getting them to make appointments at the showroom. He was a consummate closer and didn't resort to gimmickry or high-pressure sales.

Noon came soon enough, and he called over to Service. They were waiting on parts for the Al-Rasheed EcoSport. He grabbed it, went through his favorite drive-thru, hit the hardware store, then ate while waiting for the car to be washed and vacuumed. He was back before one. A regular customer there, he had a great discount and would get free full wash every tenth one. It was at his expense. He made it his business to be at Service when the customer came in to pick up their car. He'd tell them he took their car to the car wash to make it look and smell like the day he sold it to them as a thank you for buying it from him.

Mondays were his favorite day at the office. He kept the sports talk radio on low while he finished the weekend's paperwork and readied his leads for the week ahead. Mary's message said that it would be his choice tonight between baked chicken or meatloaf, both with mashed potatoes.

When it was his turn, he greeted the tire-kicker looking at a Lion's blue leftover F-150 with the wife and kids in tow. Sean got up, straightened his tie and walked over to them. Shrugging on his blue blazer and growing his smile, the needs versus wants analysis began with. "Hi, folks. Go on, climb in, let's see how it feels?"

* * *

"Hey, Charlie, howzitgoin?"

"One day at a time, Marsha, howzitgoin with you?"

His response had more to do with his promise to be her unofficial sponsor than his usual phone patter. While in Clearwater, Florida earlier that spring, Marsha had a thing for drinking only on days that ended with the letter Y. Waking up from a blackout one morning with a stranger in her bed was enough for her to seek the help of her now-retired FBI supervisor from her Miami days. He had needed an "operative" to help with his private investigation business and she needed to dry out. He took her in while she tried to make sense of what sent her slumming in the Sunshine State.

A heavy drinker in college, she could hold her own with the brothers at the jock fraternities. As an agent, Marsha never missed a chance to go out after a successful case and be one of the gang. Her ability to drink most of the agents and task force cops under the table subsided when she met Mr. O'Shea, but resumed in a big way, like she was making up for lost time, after their childless divorce. She cooled it in Philly as the adrenaline-pumping cases were a thing of the past and she became a paper pusher content to ride off in the sunset with a cozy federal pension. That was until her last case. It pushed her over the edge from heavy drinking to binge drinking and black-outs.

"There's been times when the urge hits me to pick up a drink or two or ten and I look at my phone to call you, but then I think about what we talked about and the urge passes, at least for that moment. How's Shira?" she asked, moving on.

"Offer still stands, I am just a phone call away," he said, then added, "Shira's tougher than any special agent I ever knew."

"Tell me about it. That little ninja kicked my ass every day we sparred."

Referring to her Krav Maga teacher in Clearwater, a five-foot ball of coiled steel who took on a man with an AR-15 military-style assault rifle pointed at them in a tight upstairs bedroom of a battered women's shelter.

"I caught her cutting her pain pills in half. She's out of bed and scuffing my floors with her walker already," he replied.

"How's she handling it?" Marsha asked.

"Taciturn with a blush of ornery, I'd say," Charlie replied.

"Yeah, I know what you mean. The only time I saw her smile is when I snap-kicked my oversized sparring partner between the knees," Marsha said.

"When old Charlie Akers wants to complain, he just has to look at her recovering from a couple of gut-shot wounds and ask himself what is my silly ass problem again?"

"Yeah, you just made me realize that I have to stop whining about how stupid I feel working this case," Marsha agreed.

"Talk to me, O'Shea, what's on your mind?"

"Other than the *Battleship FBI* that set me and poor Ramit adrift in a rowboat and that I don't know shit from Shinola about homicide or how to properly work cold cases — not much."

"And?"

"I just dropped Ramit off at the airport so he can go home tonight and get jiggy with his girlfriend. I feel so stupid this time around. When we worked the Russian case, he looked up to me like I saw all and knew all, but now I'm telling him I've never walked these paths before."

"What else."

"Damn you, Charlie, I know what you're doing. You are making me figure things out like you made me back in Little Havana."

"What would your friend do?"

"Wha— What would who do?" She was confused.

"What would Shira do if she was up in the Motor City?" Charlie asked.

Marsha was silent for a more than a moment while she harkened back to the days after their workouts when both women were bathed in sweat. Shira was a former Israeli Defense Force and a badass in the truest sense of the word.

"She would find some meathead to spar with and take out all her aggression. She would say, 'It is what it is' and tell herself to 'suck it up, cupcake.' She would be honest with Ramit, but not question the possible success of the mission in his presence. She would be a leader and not a complainer. She would find a way to get the job done."

"Anything else?" Charlie asked.

"Nah, that's about it, Yoda."

* * *

After profusely shaking hands with his newest best friends, the tire kicker, his wife and the kids next to their clunker, he nodded to the sales manager through the showroom window and gave him a thumbs up. The sales manager just shook his head and laughed. Sean gave him a sign that he was going out for his late lunch break.

Having a different car each time he went out on his surveillance runs made him more comfortable that he wouldn't get "made."

He nestled into his spot by the charter school just in

time to see Tamara's kids get into her Edge. *Just like clockwork,* he noted the time in his notebook. He'd go back to the office, confirm some evening appointments and grab something to go. He always enjoyed cranking up the VHS player and watch family movies while he ate their favorite take out.

CHAPTER 8

THE EMPTY SINGLE-FAMILY dwelling on Majestic, a few doors down from Rangoon, had been in foreclosure. The elderly widow who had lived there passed away alone and her scattered family couldn't get their act together to probate the estate or keep up the mortgage, utilities and taxes. The bank moved swiftly to secure the property before it fell into disrepair, so it didn't stick out. The grass was being cut and scavengers hadn't broken in yet to rip out the copper piping, which made its demise even more mystifying.

Lila died between the time it collapsed and the arrival of the fire department, eight minutes after a neighbor had called 9-1-1. Frantic digging with heavy equipment and spotlights lifted layers of debris until she was found. She was pronounced dead at the scene at 10:19 p.m., a little over an hour and a half before the stroke of midnight into September 12. They would not have looked hard or urgent for a body, had it not been for her car parked in the driveway with her business cards in the cupholder. No other cars were seen in the area.

This time, the paper file was extensive. Marsha had obtained her death certificate, the bank's foreclosure paperwork, the bank's insurance company's claim file and experts report which included the complete Fire Marshall and Building Inspector reports.

Lila was a Realtor specializing in showing bank-owned properties. What was a part-time job when her kids were little, blossomed during the worst recession since the Great Depression. She and her husband, an IT professional for the Detroit School District, were empty nesters with both kids working as busy professionals. She worked mostly on distress sales with buyers willing to invest sweat equity into properties that they could pick up dirt cheap. The trick was getting the houses under contract before drug fiends vandalized or set them afire.

When the economy tanked, the number of derelict properties grew to alarming levels in the hardest hit sections of western Detroit. The banks had gotten better over the years, doing short sales with rehabbers willing to buy their foreclosures. These cash and carry remodelers and spec builders then did the cosmetic repairs while bringing them up to code, renting them out and eventually selling them off when the economy turned around. Neighborhood decay was slowing down, and some area were being rejuvenated by these enterprising folks making lemonade out of some serious lemons.

Marsha and Ramit met on the street in front of the caller's house, which faced the empty lot where the house had once sat. After Lila was pulled from the debris and the inspections were completed, the city knocked down rest of the structure, pushed it all into the basement and covered it over with dirt. The dandelions had taken over the property between clumps of grass shoots and tall prickle bushes. It was a clearing waiting for nature to take its course. Hard to believe that a murder had taken place at this spot not so long ago.

Accidental cause and blunt force trauma as the manner of death, the death certificate read. Case closed.

"She was to meet a rehabber at the site that Tuesday for a 7:15 p.m.," Ramit told Marsha. "I was able to get the IT guy at the realty firm to sit with me this morning and we pulled the records from a server they were no longer using." He was proud of both his persuasiveness and tech skills.

"Do we have a name?" Marsha asked.

"Yes, and no." He sighed, "The rehabber was Robert Orr, probably a fake name. His house number is non-existent, and the phone number was from a burner phone. The email address he gave came back to a Y-mail account under the name of William Russell and was set up at the main library according to the IP address. That account closed on 9/13."

Ramit enjoyed being able to work leads to a conclusion without having to ask permission. Marsha and he talked at length upon his return from his visit with Manju in Philadelphia about having greater responsibilities and more autonomy.

"That's superb work. Can you get the call records on the phone?"

He said, "It was never replenished. Must have been bought with cash. I will get the seller's location tomorrow. We will need a subpoena for the calls, the service provider's legal department informed me." He knew that with the demise of telephone booths, burner phones became the drug slingers phone of choice and the service provider on these phones bought for cash at mini-marts, dollar stores and gas stations were swamped with law enforcement requests. They had to get in line, like every other LEO. "We can get Lila's estate to ask their provider for all the calls from that number, yes?" he asked.

"No, we can't, and I will tell you why later, but that would have been a good work around, even though we are missing out on his other outgoing calls," she said, "it is what it is. We take what we can get." Changing the subject. "How many properties did they look at?" she asked.

Ramit was ready and expected the question. He pointed to the printout. "Just this one with her."

Both of them stared at the weed-strewn lot.

"Talk to me," Marsha said.

"What did you say?" Ramit looked at her.

She pointed to the lot. "I was telling the crime scene to talk to me. It knows the secret of what really happened."

The slight breeze rustled the grass, birds made their plans for the evening and the occasional truck banged gears on Livernois Street nearby.

As if he was channeling the spirit of the house, Ramit said, "He killed her in there with a 2x4 or something heavy from the basement and then pulled the house down on her. He got out before it collapsed."

"How do you collapse a freaking house and nobody sees you?" Marsha asked.

Ramit closed his eyes and imagined standing in the basement of an abandoned house with a lifeless body at his feet. He wanted to make the death look like an accident. How would he make the house topple onto the body? It came rushing to him, a blast from his childhood. "Jenga!" he blurted out.

"What did you say, Ramit?"

"Jenga! Did you ever play that block game as a child?"

She nodded. "More times when I was a drunk adult. He couldn't do this in one day. Could he?"

"Right, he would need time to weaken the structure a little at a time right to where he would only need to loosen one or two last pieces." Ramit was onto something.

"Get it to where a stiff wind could knock it over and nobody would know."

They were on the same wavelength. "That means—" He slapped his knee to Marsha's startled reaction. "With the game you remove a piece at a time. How could they find something that was taken away, something that wouldn't be there to be examined?"

"Right. Right. Unless they reconstructed the house, how would they know what was taken away? If they did a careful excavation, they would see signs of cut wood or maybe sheared bolts. He would have to remove the evidence that the collapse was intentional."

"Exactly." Ramit was proving his theory as they batted it back and forth. "He couldn't park out here and be seen walking in and out. Even at night. Maybe over a long weekend, he could weaken the structure and at nights drag the pieces out."

"To where?" Marsha asked.

Immediately, they jumped from his van and ran to the center of the lot. They began turning around in opposite directions and settled on the faint path through the backyard towards the adjoining street. It was like they were entering a forest. The houses appearing behind them had been abandoned for years. The path led to the rear of a burned-out shell of what was once the proud home, probably of a large family of an auto assembly-line worker from days gone by. The shroud of trees extended around the house and enveloped the driveway.

"He parked here at night. His car would be virtually hidden." Ramit was on a roll. They retraced their steps and saw that the path ended at the concrete cellar steps. Looking back through the dense overgrown foliage, he could trace the path to the middle of the lot. "Do you have the plot plans for the collapsed house?"

"Yeah it's on the computer back in the van. Why?"

"I am almost certain he dragged the pieces out at night, bit by bit from that cellar to this cellar."

Marsha cursed. There were no street lights. They were on Barton, which only had few houses on the block where the owners refused to move and they were clustered on the far end of the street. "How much do you want to bet that this house was torched after she died?"

They peered over the foundation into the fetid pool of blackened water where the evidence they were looking for had probably been turned into ashes and muck.

"There still has to be some clues out here." He said not wanting to believe that the killer was infallible.

Back at the van, they confirmed that the cellar door was where Ramit thought it to be.

"The insurance company's expert walked the scene with the Fire Marshall and came up with an undetermined cause." Marsha skimmed the report, and they passed photos back and forth. "There had been no recent renovations or structural changes done to the property in fifty years." Looking at Ramit. "Believe me, if they could pass the buck to some other entity, they would have. They had nobody else to go after for negligence."

Back to the report, Marsha summarized the summary. "The house was not occupied by vagrants or squatters. It was tight as a drum, according to interviews with the neighbors. It gets worse, Ramit." Marsha scrolled through her laptop. "By the time the family contacted a lawyer to see if they could sue the homeowner, the house had been demolished. The homeowner coverage had expired. The bank's force-placed insurance just covered the structure for replacement in case of fire or vandalism and minimal limits for liability too.

"Lila's husband told me originally that the attorney's expert could only comment on photos made by the Fire Marshall and the building inspector's office. They argued that the house was so decrepit that no one should have been allowed in it until a proper house inspection was done, otherwise it wouldn't have collapsed. They allowed the seller's agent to go into a dangerous situation, given that the elderly woman did no upkeep in the last decades of her life. That is the theory of liability." Raising her voice for emphasis, "But here is kicker, Ramit."

"It can't get much worse. Can it, Marsha?" he asked.

"The husband also was the one that voiced his concerns at the mosque after he heard about the other more recent deaths of the jumper and the girl that died from carbon monoxide. He told his lawyer he had talked to me and the lawyer had a shit-fit."

Ramit wasn't liking the sound of this. "Why?"

"I didn't know this either until he explained it to me and now it makes perfect sense. The lawyer for Lila's estate didn't come out and say it, but he doesn't want us to find the killer. As it stands now, she was in the course and scope of her employment as a Realtor at the time of her death. She was waiting for a no-show appointment at the house she was supposed to show on behalf of the realty firm's client when it fell on her and she died. The estate is entitled to a death benefit and a percentage of her future earnings. He gets a cut of that. He is looking to get more for the estate and a percentage of that, if he can prove negligence by the bank, which is a third party."

"I'm lost," he said, not pretending to understand civil law and its loopholes.

"If I prove that she was killed because she was Muslim like the others and they all were killed on the exact same day, year after year after year, her death would have nothing to do with her employment and therefore her death would not be...." she paused to get the legal term right, "compensable — they would be entitled to nothing. Nada. Nyet. Zippo. Squat."

Marsha stopped for a moment for effect. "She's dead, Ramit and we can't bring her back to life. The attorney is now talking about dropping his case against the bank. He knows he can't tell the FBI what to do, but he made it clear the family will not cooperate with us voluntarily from now on." To add insult to injury, Marsha added, "Lila was interred over three years ago and we cannot justify an exhumation based upon what we have, and even if we find more evidence, the family attorney will argue strenuously against it."

"Shit," he said.

"Double shit," she said.

* * *

"C'mon, Dad. The Tigers are home against the Yankees. You promised we would go to a game this season," his youngest said.

Tamara looked over her son's shoulder and caught her husband's eye with a shrug.

Omar said, "This is the first dry weekend in a month. I have to work on the house while my crews catch up." He had left their home that Saturday morning before dawn and fourteen hours later collapsed at the dining room table for their first family dinner all week.

She came around from the stove and stood between her sons. "Why don't we watch the game tonight and you can explain to me the parts I don't understand while I order tickets for the three of us to go tomorrow?"

"It's not the same, Mom, you know it," Omar Jr., her oldest chimed in.

"I promise when it gets slow this winter, I will watch the matches with you every Sunday morning," Omar said.

Both his boys played elite soccer and loved the English Premier League. No sports, and no church obligation, as their services were on Fridays, made an idyllic time for father and sons to lay about and root for their favorite teams on the cable feed.

"Can we get seats behind home plate, Mom?" Joseph asked.

CHAPTER 9

THEY STOOD in the bedroom staring at the wardrobe. She and Ramit had taken their shoes off at the door and were ushered into the house by Nura's husband Hassan. Her young adult children returned to the nest to meet with the FBI agents. It was crowded standing there.

Marsha had found out about her death from a small article in *The Detroit Free Press* written seven years ago. It was not reported to her through the mosque connection, but with a few smart search terms including 9/11, she realized now that she had yet another death. The list was growing.

Hassan said, "I thought it was strange that I was not able to reach her. I arrived at home and saw her car in the garage and called her name. 'Nura! Nura!' I went upstairs and found the wardrobe pinning her to the bedroom floor. I hurt my back trying to lift it off of her." He stopped.

"What happened next?" Marsha gently prodded.

Coming out of his trance. "I pushed it to the side with my legs and I tried to do mouth to mouth and CPR. I learned that in the Air Force and we get regular training at the school. After trying for about ten minutes, I knew my

Nura was dead. That is when I called for the paramedics. I sat there looking at her staring upwards. I saw that her skirt was wet. She must have wet herself struggling to get out from under it. I don't know how long it was, but I heard the sirens and then the paramedics arrived. They came to the same conclusion. Our neighbors came over and rushed upstairs and that is when I lost it. They asked me, 'Hassan what happened? What happened?' I told them that my Nura was dead." He broke down crying.

Marsha looked again at the death certificate which read:
Manner of Death: Asphyxiation.
Cause of Death: Accidental.

Was this an odd set of circumstances? Could it really have happened that away?

"I was having a meeting with my fellow editors of the high school newspaper." Daughter Stephanie said, explaining why she hadn't taken the early bus.

"I had football practice. I was trying out for varsity that year," Nura's son Ray recalled.

Hassan bleated out, "What I still don't understand after all these years is why she had to dust the wardrobe with a car full of groceries getting warm. When I followed the paramedics outside, I saw the trunk of her Taurus was still open with bags of groceries in the trunk. I touched the juice and it was hot and the frozen vegetables were getting warm. That is when I realized that she must have been lying there for hours. How long did she suffer for? Oh God." His sobbing increased.

Son and daughter comforted father, the FBI remained stoic.

Seven years and it still feels like yesterday for him,

Marsha thought. *How many more of these are we going to find? How many more grieving families do we get to question? Do I even tell them that I think it was a murder?*

It was Ramit who brought them all out of their private thoughts. "Had you ever seen her dust it before?"

Quizzical looks between the family answered that question.

"How do you know she was dusting it?" Marsha continued.

"After the paramedics left, my neighbors and my children lifted it back to its position and I saw the duster and polish by the dresser. It took four of them to tip it back up."

"How heavy do you think it is?" Ramit asked looking at the four-foot wide, seven-foot high, two-foot deep solid oak wardrobe.

"It took two guys to bring it in when we had the bedroom set delivered," Hassan said.

"Have you changed out the contents?" Marsha asked.

"I haven't had the heart. I wish I could remember what she looked like in those clothes. Someday the memories will return. I know it." Hassan sniffed.

While Stephanie comforted her father, Marsha and Ray tried dead lifting it from either side with Ramit reaching down from the front. The three of them struggled to bring it up six inches.

Ray was first. "Has to be over 200 pounds."

Marsha nodded. "Closer to 250, I imagine. I'm sorry, Hassan. How was she laying under it?"

"Her hands were near her head above the top of it. She was lying face up."

"When you got the wardrobe upright, how wet was the carpet below it?"

"Now that you mention it. I have to say, I don't

remember it being wet at all. Nobody said anything about their feet or socks getting wet when they pushed it back up."

Marsha asked the family to go back downstairs while she and Ramit measured the wardrobe and the room's dimensions. She read him the numbers and he recorded them. They created a photo log. Finally, they stood there listening to the scene.

Marsha looked at the family portrait taken a few years before Nura died, guessing by the ages of the kids and by Stephanie's braces, she wasn't much shorter than her mother then and looked to be about her mother's height and weight now.

She called down to the family and asked them to come back up to the room.

"Stephanie, I need to ask you a favor. If you were to climb up the wardrobe and try to dust the top of it, how would you do it?"

Stephanie opened the wardrobe, extending both doors to the sides and stood on the top of a bottom drawers about eighteen inches from the floor. She grabbed the pole that held all the hang-ups and lifted herself up. From that position, she mimed dusting, spraying and wiping. She changed hands and repeated the process. The wardrobe didn't budge. She got down and then the others each took turns. Marsha's socks slipped on the drawer's surface and she gripped the pole with both hands until she could gain her footing. "Wow, that was close."

Hassan blurted out, "Oh!"

"What, Daddy?" Stephanie asked.

"Your mother would always remind me to take off my shoes each time I came in from outside."

"Yeah, me too, Dad," Ray said.

Ramit and Marsha were equally puzzled.

"While I was waiting for the ambulance, I saw that she was still wearing her shoes. I never saw her with shoes in the house. I stared at my poor Nura and told her that she forgotten to take them off."

Ray and Ramit both climbed the wardrobe and got their arms over the top of it to grip it from the back, afraid that they would wrench the pole from its fixtures. Marsha and Stephanie grabbed them by the waist and pulled hard. Only then did the wardrobe start to tip.

"Whoa, that's enough," Marsha said and everybody disengaged.

"Hassan, was there a chair or a step stool here in the bedroom that day when you came home?"

"No," he replied.

"Can we talk downstairs?" Marsha asked.

The family filed out first, but Marsha held back Ramit. "Take photos of the wardrobe with the doors opened."

"I'll get pictures of the door hinges too, I know where you are going with this," he said.

Marsha waited until Ramit finished and they both walked down silently.

"You must be wondering why the FBI is looking into your mom's death from seven years ago." Marsha scanned the faces of the adult children. "With the doors opened, we realize that if the wardrobe had tipped, it would have broken the doors off at the hinges and your Mom's chest would have been able to inflate against her clothes on the hangers. Yes, she would have been trapped but no, she would not have asphyxiated.

"There was no chair or stool to stand on in the room. The wardrobe would have had to be open for her to dust the top as we just proved. Dusting the top of the wardrobe is something you never saw her do. My feet slipped in the wardrobe and that made us question her wearing shoes in the house which you never saw her do.

"Last thing I want to point out — her skirt was wet, but the carpet underneath wasn't."

Hassan looked at her. "Agent O'Shea, are you saying that my wife's death was not an accident?"

"What day did that happen, sir?" she answered back.

"A Monday."

"I meant, what date did this happen?" she corrected herself.

"September 11," he replied.

"9/11," she clarified.

"Given what we know about how it happened, what if I told you that this is the fourth death of a Muslim women on 9/11 to die from unnatural causes in the Detroit area that we have come across?"

The clock ticked on the mantle while the stunned family took this in.

"Oh, God," Ray talked first.

Stephanie looked back and forth between her father and Marsha. "Is this true? Somebody did this to Mommy?"

Hassan started bawling. Son and daughter put their arms around their father. They hugged and rocked.

Marsha opened up her notebook and Ramit opened his Chromebook. Both avoided eye contact with the family for a full minute. "We need to ask you more questions about the months leading up to your mom's death and we need to look at the garage as the crime scene. Is that okay with you?" she said.

CHAPTER 10

WATCHING the VHS tape of his blindfolded nephew whacking the piñata, Sean recalled another time years later, as the papier-mâché donkey took its *thwack, thwack, thwack* beating.

The sharp cracks of boot on bone slowly became more muffled as Aaliyah's fractured skull yielded and could no longer protect her brains. Sean tired and panted from all the effort to that point. Was it from the exertion or from the adrenaline coursing through his body as he carried out the murder that had taken much longer than he expected?

She lay motionless now in the stairwell of the University of Michigan student parking garage in Dearborn. Her long lashes over her pretty eyes were closed, and her lovely face was a battered pulp. Just a few minutes earlier, they had walked up the stairs together and chatted amiably. How funny was it they would bump into each other, he had said. He told her he was taking business classes. What classes was she taking that semester, he asked. He had promised his wife that he would get his degree someday.

Aaliyah would graduate in December and the end was almost in sight. He knew that she lived at home, worked for an architect in town, doing drafting mostly, and was studying to become an architect herself. The family would expect her in about twenty-five minutes. She always went straight home. If there was a boyfriend, he didn't know about one.

They climbed the stairs to the fourth floor where they parked both of their cars. He knew that because he followed her there that night. He lagged for a second, as she reached for the door. Up here, no one would hear her. This semester, she was one of that last students to access the garage. His surveillance work had paid off.

As she reached for the door, he set down his backpack and pulled hard on her leg from behind and below, throwing her off balance. He remembered the shock on her face. He kept pulling, and she fell to the ground. He then used both his hands to twist her leg, so she was face down and he dragged her down the stairs. On the landing between the third and fourth landing, she tried to kick him away and twist out of his grasp. He went down a few steps until she was hanging on to the metal grate of the landing. He brought her ankles up to his chest and her face crashed against each of the landing steps to the third floor. Her hands raked the stairs to gain a hold, and he pulled her face down on each step to the landing between second and third. She tried to cover her face with her arms. She was still breathing. He propped her stronger arm between the landing and the first step and stomped on her forearm. She passed out from the compound fracture.

He dragged her down to the second floor, and that is where he had kicked her face and head until she was dead.

He had stood over her body, breathing heavily when he heard the first-floor entrance door open.

This is taking too long, he groused. He pulled her computer backpack from her limp body and tossed it up to the next landing. He pitter-pattered down the remaining stairs and shielded his face with his arm while pointing over his shoulder and said excitedly, "Somebody fell down the stairs. Call 9-1-1. I am going for help." he said, in a husky voice, as he ran past the male student who barely looked up from his cell phone he was talking into. "Second Floor, hurry."

Sean ran to the other side of the garage and looked around, making sure no one saw him as he ran back in and up the rear stairwell. He fast-walked up the stairs, gulping for air. *This was not the plan. Why did we have to park on four?* His chest was heaving. He had to get out of there. He opened the door and cautiously looked both ways as he crossed their floor. He didn't see any cars or students moving and entered the stairwell where it all started as he gathered up his backpack filled with *National Geographic* magazines he had found in a box next to the dumpster where he lived. One came out of zippered top. Just then, he realized that he had not ripped the address labels off of the magazines and they would put the cops in his apartment building if he had left the bag there.

He made his way to the tinted Flex he was using. Slapping a Tiger's cap on his head, he drove carefully down and out of the garage with his heart pounding. He reached for the jumbo mini-mart slush cup and shielded his face as the campus police with lights whirling screamed by him.

This is the most excitement they will ever have, he thought.

He drove out past the former Ford Mansion and away

from where help would be summoned. He took his time driving aimlessly on suburban streets until he returned the Flex demo to the dealership, changed the plates back onto a car being sent to auction the next day, and walked into the dealership's men's room.

It was after hours and only the cleaners and floor polishers were there. He walked into a stall and changed out of his clothes and boots and into his salesman attire. The clothes and boots with their DNA, hair, skin and saliva went into the trash receptacle behind the clothing store next to the dealership. He drove home directly and finished listening to the baseball game in the parking lot. The Angels won it on a walk-off home run by a rookie pinch-hitter. It was almost midnight as the game was being played on the West Coast.

Walking to his front door, he noticed the waning crescent of the moon. It was a clear still night, cloudless and warm, almost the same as the night when his world turned upside down, except tonight there were airplanes high above, blinking silently as they traverse the clear moonlit night.

He walked straight to the kitchen. He played the answering machine message, and the cassette tape whirled. "Hey, Sean. If you're hungry, I have some leftovers from a party at work today. There are roast beef sandwiches and a meatball grinder. You can't eat all the cookies. You need to save a couple for me. I had to go back in because they screwed up payroll again."

He had been so proud of her. She had done well for herself working herself up from entry-level accounts payable to human resource manager and did so without having a college degree. They had liked Mary and had told him repeatedly at the company Christmas parties and summer picnics.

"Cookies," he said in his best Cookie Monster voice as he returned to the VHS tape which was now playing scenes from his other sister's backyard BBQ later that summer.

CHAPTER 11

"I NEVER THOUGHT it was a fall down. She was beaten to a bloody pulp," Dennis Horton said.

"So why weren't the State Police called in? All we have is your name from the family."

About then, the paramedic who had responded to this parking garage stairwell over five years ago walked up to Marsha, Ramit and the former campus cop. "Hi, I'm Fred Lolich, I remember you," he said looking at Horton.

"Hi, Fred, good to see you again. What have you been up to?" Dennis asked.

"Trauma Nurse at Detroit Receiving," Fred replied.

"That's the place to be for Trauma," Dennis added.

Fred nodded. "And you?"

"Oakland County Sheriff's office, patrol."

"Nice."

"Yeah, sure beats this place," Dennis said, "This is FBI Agent O'Shea and her assistant Mr. Ravikant."

"Nice to meet you both. It's about time somebody looked into it. This was no accident," Fred said.

"That's why I ask you both to come here. The University campus police don't know we are here. I hope that is okay with both of you," she said.

"Much better, I agree," Dennis said.

"First the school told me they didn't have a report, then they said that they didn't keep it. When I emailed them a copy of the girl's death certificate with the location of death circled, they finally said that their online records didn't have the incident, like it was erased. We had to find you both on our own on. We worked backwards from the hospital records to find you, Fred."

"It figures. Having a murder on a commuter college campus is bad for business," Dennis said.

"Yeah," Fred said, "I remember that they wanted me to say that she had a skull fracture from an accidental fall. I went along with it, but after what I now see regularly in the ER, I would have pushed back. What I saw was a beat down, pure and simple."

Dennis produced a manila folder. "I covered my ass. I knew someday somebody would want to learn the truth. Here is my original report. You can see where my supervisor changed it on this other one and made me sign it."

He showed everybody both reports. The 9-1-1 caller's name and telephone number were listed on the first and it included his written statement to Dennis. Both were missing from the second.

"I thought you might want these too. I snapped them, figuring that a Major Crimes Detective would want to see what the scene looked like before the EMTs got here and trampled all over it." Looking at Fred. "No offense meant."

Fred peered over Marsha's shoulder and said, "No offense taken."

"Were there security cameras at the time?" Marsha asked.

"Yes and no," Dennis explained, "We had cameras on the street entrances and exits of the campus and placed on the exteriors of some Halls. There were cameras on some interiors of the common areas where they held classes, but not on this garage. I guess they weren't too concerned about an active shooter in a parking garage."

"Damn," she said.

"What's worse is when I wanted to look at the security tapes to see when she entered the campus to see if she was followed. I was told to forget it. It was an accident. The tapes are long gone. They didn't want any record." Dennis was visibly pissed. "Campus police or not, I still swore an oath to uphold the law. Not just when it's convenient for my employer."

"And?" Marsha asked, knowing there was more.

"She had finished her class and was walking back to her car. Any cars leaving at or about the time of the 9-1-1 calls would have been my numero uno suspects. Hey, but what the fuck do I know? Pardon my French," he said.

In the photos, Dennis had done a decent job of photographing the scene. He even used his Maglite flashlight and aluminum ticket holder to give the viewer an idea of dimensions. He took pictures from the stairs above and below. He took close-ups of the body and a surreptitious photo of the witness. He kept a log of all the people on scene until they removed the body. It was the photos taken from ground level around her head at a distance of six inches that would be of most use to a forensic pathologist.

"Do you still have the phone that took these?" Ramit asked.

"No, but I downloaded those onto each phone I've had ever since." Dennis busied himself with the retrieval.

Fred looked at the photographs and shook his

head. "She would have had to roll down all the stairs and be able to make ninety-degree turns on the landings, while keeping her momentum up to end up down here."

"Here," Dennis said. He began selecting the photos to airdrop to Ramit standing next to him.

"Whaddyamean?" Marsha asked.

"Think about it," Fred said as he climbed the stairs, "the injuries were too severe from her to have fallen from here."

Fred stood on the top step before the third floor. He counted the steps back down to where she had died. "Look at the arm, how it's bent between the elbow and the wrist at that angle. She would have had to do a swan dive from up there to break her arm that way. *Multiple skull fracture, Cause of Death: Blunt Force Trauma. Manner of Death: Accidental,*" he read aloud from the death certificate. "Yes, and no."

Dennis finished his download to Ramit. "I agree. Her head looked like a melon somebody dropped from a second-floor window. This wasn't an 'oops, I fell down and can't get up' scenario."

"Look at her hands, how her nails were shredded," Fred said, "I remember this girl dressed like a professional and her hands looked like she slid down a rock pile."

"Wait a second," Ramit said. He transferred the digital photos from his phone to his Chromebook. "Look." He magnified the photos of her hand, the compound fracture of her arm, and of the lopsided face and head. They observed a jagged hole where a canine tooth should have been. The others stood around him where the body had been slain.

"Did you find the tooth?" Marsha asked.

Both men shrugged. Dennis was first to speak, "The next day, they had maintenance come out and hose it all down, I watched them. No crime scene tape, no crime, end of story." He shook his head in obvious disgust.

"Where was her car parked?" Marsha asked, looking at the two photos taken from opposite angles.

"Fourth floor," Dennis said, "No signs of struggle by the car. It was sad. I was here when the family came to retrieve it. I told them I was first to respond to the scene after the witness called in."

"That's when you gave them your card," Marsha said.

Dennis nodded. "I'll be darned. They kept it all this time."

"Let's go."

They walked up the stairwell four abreast looking for clues.

On the last step leading to the landing between the third and fourth, Fred was first to spot it. "There it is!"

They all took turns squinting at the metal tread lipping around the step. Marsha then moved in close and squinted. A tooth was embedded in the tread with its roots exposed to the elements. It was on the tread several inches from the hand rail post. *Off the beaten path,* she guessed that was why it was still there.

"Holy Freaking Christ," Dennis said, "I knew I was right."

"Dennis, show Ramit how to photograph it," Marsha said, realizing that if they taught her crime scene photography at Quantico, she forgot it from lack of use.

They all backed down the steps, and Dennis showed Ramit where to stand, squat and aim. Then he placed a dollar bill on the step between the side wall and tooth and a dime directly above it on the tread. "A dollar bill is six inches long, and the dime is... well, the standard size of a dime. The dollar gives you distance and the dime perspective," he said.

Ramit zoomed in as close as he could with the lens fitted on his iPhone. They would not remove the tooth until they finished the search. They then took one more step, and it was Ramit's turn. "Stop!" Look!"

A faded red fingernail was wedged into the grate of the steel tread on the landing.

It was Marsha who winced, shuddered and cursed, "Damn!" They all repeated the eye-level squint. While the others used their phones to shed extra light on the second ghastly discovery, Ramit recorded its locus.

They continued their search up to the doorway of the fourth-floor stairwell entrance to the parking garage, and then Ramit shot photos out into the garage and back down the stairs. Marsha came back to where they stood around the fingernail and tooth wondering how they would extricate both without removing or transferring their own DNA.

Fred walked out to his Jeep. He came back with an unopened pack of surgical gloves and a needle-nose set of pliers from the repair kit he kept in his car. Ramit filmed as Fred place a glove on his right hand and then used the pliers to cleanly remove both pieces of evidence from their hiding-in-plain-sight locations and he dropped them in separate fingers of the right glove. They all initialed and dated the evidence glove while Ramit did a running commentary on the recording.

They took as much care as they could for amateurs and Marsha reminded herself that they were cold case homicide investigators now and they needed to up-skill, lest some Criminal Defense attorney ream them a new body orifice.

Fred was first to play detective. "Hands drag here to try to grab a hold of something, maybe the handrail post." He motioned, both hands sweeping down the grated step. "Then she does a face plant here."

Marsha said, "Either her feet slipped out from beneath her or...."

Dennis chimed in, "Her feet were pulled out from underneath her causing to fall...."

"With such force as to cause her to rip a fingernail and lose a tooth...," Ramit said.

"But if that is the case, how does she end up two right turns and two flights lower? She'd be laying on the stairs here," Marsha said motioning to where they were standing.

"She could have gotten up in a daze and tripped down the stairs and fell where she died," Fred offered.

They all appeared in deep thought, trying to envision that sequence.

"On that last fall, she broke her arm," Fred added.

It was Dennis who finally said, "No, fuck that. She was dragged down the stairs face down like a sack of potatoes, and when that wasn't enough, he kicked the shit out of her right here."

The first responder and the FBI agreed. "Tru' dat," Marsha surmised. They finally had direct evidence of a crime.

* * *

They had met at a technical high school. She wanted to follow in her Grandmothers footstep in the culinary arts with a passion for baking, he in the construction trades. Today was quiet. The kids would be done with school next week and she allowed herself the pleasure of making several dozen cookies.

Tamara's man and boys attacked them like hungry

wolves, and she set aside a couple platters for the school's fundraiser. Her sweets were a highly contested auction item. She made gift platters of Namora or Namora with nuts, but both platters were piled high with petit fours, macaroons and gaibeh.

CHAPTER 12

"HEY, MIKE, HOWZITGOIN'?"

"It's goin', Marsha. 'Bout you?"

"Just another day in paradise."

"So, Detroit is paradise these days, huh?"

"It's so flat and wide open out here. Not like Philly at all and the mosquitos are nastier." She heard him chuckle over the phone connection.

She knew that she was out of her league on this case and reached out to the only cop she could trust. There was a time when she would have talked to her two favorite cops over Sunday night roast beef at the family home, but her brother was dead, and her father blamed her for it. It had been years since she worked the mean streets of Miami with the locals and didn't feel she had the connections to ask them Homicide 101 questions.

"I'm over my head here, Mike. The guy we are looking at out here is making these deaths look like accidents or suicides."

"No shit!" he answered.

"What makes it worse is that not only were they initially investigated that way, save one, none of the locals want to even consider the possibility of them being murders now. I am getting no cooperation from them at all. When I took this case on, I was told to leave the Detroit field office out of it completely. To top it off, I have read-only rights to most of the FBI databases, but not all, and can't even use our lab. Those were the rules I had to play by if I wanted to work the case."

"You certainly have a way with the locals. As I recall, Philly Homicide will not invite you to the summer FOP pig roast soon."

She said, "To top it off, I am probably staring at two decades of cases. That is a ton of cold cases. Ramit and I have to figure this all out before he strikes again."

Mike cut her short, "So you didn't call me up to complain, Marsha. What's up?"

Marsha drew a deep breath. "We need you to come out here and give us a crash course in homicide investigation for a long weekend. You were 'murder police' back in the day. Ramit can send you what we've done to date, so we can run and gun while you're out here."

"I dunno, Marsh."

"Be the expert consultant, fly in, get us on the right track and fly out."

Silence.

"All expenses paid courtesy of the FBI. Whaddya say?"
Silence.

Sensing the need to twist his good arm a little bit. Marsha went to Plan B. "Hold on a second, Mike. Ramit wants to say hi."

"Hi, Mike. It's Ramit, how are you?"

"Doing about as good as expected, Ramit, how are you?"

"Working for a slave-driver, what can I say?"

"Marsha tells me you have a girlfriend, is that right?"

"Yes, can I introduce her to you the next time I'm back home? Her name is Manju."

"I'd like that," Mike said.

"Marsha tells me she wants you to teach us how to better investigate these cases. I've learned a new phrase from her: She says that we don't know shit from Shinola. What does that mean, Mike? She's always muttering that."

"That means she doesn't know her butt from her elbow."

Marsha moved over near the speakerphone. "See you said it yourself, your favorite FBI agent doesn't know her butt from her elbow with the stuff that you know like the back of your hand."

"C'mon, Marsha, you're putting words in my mouth."

"Still it's true, what would it hurt? We fly you out and back direct. We chauffeur you around while you show us the ropes. Whaddyathink?"

"How about my time?" he asked.

"Two thou a day plus expenses sound okay to you?" She had a nibble.

"When?"

Looking not to conflict with Ramit's conjugal visits. "Second Thursday of June?"

"And a day to look over what you got so far?"

"It's a deal. Thanks, Mike. You're the best."

"You're the second woman to tell me that in twenty-four hours, O'Shea."

"Now you're making me blush, Hollins. Ramit will work the details out for getting your flights arranged and sending you everything in Slack. Thanks a bunch. It will be good to see you again."

"Thanks, Mike," Ramit said, "I need your personal identifiers to book the flight."

* * *

"Hi, I am calling for Myles Hanski, please," Marsha asked.

The polite older woman on the other end asked, "Whom shall I say is calling?"

"Special Agent Marsha O'Shea. He taught me at Quantico and I had a quick question for him?"

"Hold on a second, I think he's taking a nap. If that's the case, he will have to call you back."

A gruff voice answered the phone, "I don't remember teaching an O'Shea, who is this?"

"What a memory you have. You are correct, sir. My maiden name was Drummond. I married Mr. O'Shea after I graduated from the academy."

"Marsha Drummond?" he paused, "Rings a bell. What can I do for you?"

"Grayson Stanfield said it would be okay to call you. I need to reach outside of the bureau and away from BAU on a special assignment."

"He did, did he? Why should I do a favor for him? He stepped on many people on the way up the ladder," Hanski shot back.

"Um." Marsha laid her first figurative card on the table. "Because he said you are the best. Not were the best but *are* the best."

"Did he now? What else did he say?"

She flipped her second card over now. "If I had to consult with anybody on this case, that I should talk to you.

You had a lot of cases where you discovered things about the UNSUBS for the first time. Lot of seminal cases that we still rely on for profiling today."

"Well, he was always slick as a seal's ass when throwing around the praise."

"I agree with you. That's probably how he got me to work this case." She waited a beat, "To tell you the truth, I am having a hard time keeping my head above water on this one."

"Been retired for nineteen years now. Did my wife tell you I was about to take my nap?"

"Yes, sir."

"I'll let you in on a secret, O'Shea, that was my favorite period in Kindergarten. Nap time. Why did they take that away from us in elementary school?"

"I don't know, sir. You said nineteen years. This guy I'm looking at would have started after you retired. You wouldn't have seen him on your watch." She had two cards left after this one.

"You'd think I could retire in peace. Every true-crime show wanted to re-enact my cases. Then the cable networks wanted me to comment every time another loser got caught. Now these damn podcasters are popping up like the crabgrass in my yard and they want me to consult with them too. Hell, I had to put my foot down. You have to walk away some day. I said *no more* as my New Year resolution."

"So, you haven't taken on anything this year so far?" One card left.

"Yep, and couldn't be happier," he said.

"Well then, Myles, you should be fresh. I thought I'd give you first crack at this one. Unless you want me to pass it on to somebody else?" She used his first name and waited.

"Give me a brief synopsis, O'Shea."

She turned over her last card. "He strikes only one day a year, the same date every year, 9/11. He lives in a target-rich environment for his prey: Greater Detroit, home of the largest Arab-American population in the United States. He's only targeting Muslim women only."

"That explains why that political animal has you operating outside of normal channels."

"Yes, sir. I hope you didn't mind me calling you by your first name."

"Marsha, right?"

"Right." She waited. If she could hear the brilliant man's mind turning, she knew that it was still a well-oiled machine that was humming along and she prayed that he had one last chase left in him. *Did he still have the gas in the tank, the fire in his belly?*

"Myles is fine, Marsha. Send me the stuff overnight. I want paper and individual photos, 8x10s glossy. No discs or links. Paper, just paper. I will tell you what I think. Make sure you fill out the protocols as extensively as you can. Guess work is allowed. I remember you were a pretty smart rookie."

"We will send it out by tomorrow afternoon and thank you. Thank you very much."

* * *

"I hope you don't mind me bringing in reinforcements, Ramit?" Marsha said over her slice of pepperoni pizza.

He set his slice down and leaned back in the Adirondack chairs by the fire pit on the tiny patio behind their rental. He stared into the flames. Citronella candles marked the four corners of the patio and gave off their unique scent. Many times, bitten, now shy.

"I am glad you did, and we will need even more help. We are the eyes and ears, but we need to know what we are looking at and understand what we are hearing, so we know what to ask."

"We are about a third into it so far, but we've only picked the low-hanging fruit. Five cases out and who knows how many more out there and we still don't know when he started. We've got to find the rest. We have to build the puzzle with as many pieces as we can. I sure he made mistakes, especially in the beginning. I am sure of it."

She had to keep up her flagging spirit. Ramit, with the boundless energy of a puppy dog, was running circles around her when it came to good ideas and boring data entry. They needed technical expertise, so that they could work the cases once without worrying about dropping leads.

"Without the newspapers publishing obituaries, we have come up with another way of finding prospective cases," he said, "I'll put my thinking cap on that."

"We can ask the mosque's attorney when we meet him and the contractor tomorrow at the neighbor's house across from the collapse," Marsha added.

She, too, stared into the fire now, thinking about how that would play out.

It pleased Marsha that Ramit's energy was still good. The regularly promised trips back to Philly seemed to keep him from becoming too homesick.

He went to the gym every morning before she had her first coffee. She went to the Kick-boxing place every other day to blow off steam. They ate like foraging bears after the sunset most nights like tonight. The work kept her drinking urges manageable. Charlie was right about that. She noticed every day that they were less frequent and less severe, but tonight, after talking to Hollins during the day, the craving for a six-pack or two made her thirsty in the wrong way. Talking about what went down in the Philly 'burbs where he got shot stirred up the memories and the guilt. After a life-saving operation, he came away with a partial paralysis of the muscles controlling his upper left arm.

The pizza and sweet tea would not cut it.

"Hey, Ramit, if you don't mind, I will call Charlie Akers and see if he can think about anything we might be missing."

"Goodnight, Marsha, I'll knock on your door when I leave for the gym."

That had become her alarm clock. With Ramit out of the house for a good chunk of time, she could walk about without worries of him seeing her in various stages of undress.

She gathered up her empties and pizza crusts and slipped back into the house.

"Hi, Charlie. Hope it's not too late to call," Marsha said.

"Nope, just listening to the Red Sox taking another shellacking. What's up?"

"Well, I connected with Mike Hollins today and also Myles Hanski, they both said they would lend me a hand. Mike's coming out in a couple of weeks and Myles will consult from home."

"Myles Hanski, Jesus, I haven't heard that name in a dog's age. He's still kicking around, huh?"

"Yep. Sounds sharp as a tack too. It didn't take much to get him interested in this case."

"Wouldn't think so. You got a real humdinger there, Marsha," Charlie said.

"Talking to Hollins stirred up some shit, and with things not going really great here, the six-pack sirens were sweetly serenading me. I thought I'd give you a ring." She realized that was all she needed. "Thanks for taking my call, Charlie. I am good now, going to bed. Good night, give my best to Shira."

"Call me anytime, any hour. G'night, Marsha. Sleep tight."

CHAPTER 13

SEAN TOYED with the child-resistant lid of cough syrup with codeine in his desk drawer. The large economy-sized bottle was nearly empty, and he had never taken a drop before or after that day. He had bought it over the counter in nearby Canada and smuggled it back across the border. It never got dusty as he handled it often to relive the moment. His prints were all over it, but hers were not. He smiled as he looked at the expiration date from over a decade ago. He relived the memory now of jumping from the bedroom closet with a knife in one gloved hand. He had talked to her calmly with his other gloved hand firmly on her throat as he backed her unto the bed. She was about the same age as Mary when she and Sean married. She was heavier and shorter than Mary.

He had watched Qadira's fear grow as he made her chug from the cough syrup repeatedly after forcing her to gulp a handful of high dose acetaminophen fast-acting PM tablets. He had poured them into her hand like candy-corn. He told her he didn't want her to be awake while he did what he wanted to do since the day they met. It would make it easier for both of them, he had reasoned with her. She had fixated on the knife and her eyes told him that she understood what the consequence would be if she resisted. He assured her it would be over quickly, and she wouldn't feel a thing. He was being truthful. She probably thought he meant he would rape her, which was god-awful, terrible, but he had something different in mind.

Qadira's husband worked four p.m. to midnight as the night manager of his family's restaurant cross town. She taught fifth graders at an elementary school near to the restaurant. They weren't ready to give in to both their parent's incessant pleadings for grandchildren just yet. Her slightly used Mustang convertible in the driveway was proof of that. They both enjoyed their work and worked long hours. Their quiet residence sat back from the road in a tree-lined neighborhood of raised ranchers. This neighborhood had seen seventy years of tree growth and vegetation, giving the post-war baby-boomer suburban tract a rural feel.

Their half-acre backed up to a factory that had been shuttered sometime in the last millennium. He had parked there, walked through their yard and let himself in with his spare key as he had done on his trial runs that summer.

Then he had sat next to her and said nothing as he handed her the cough syrup again and again, keeping the serrated hunting knife to the ready. He glanced about the room and saw that the knick-knacks and wall prints had not changed since the last time he was there. As she began to drift into drowsiness, he told her to lay back and to close her eyes. He promised not to touch her while she was awake, but would hurt her if she tried to escape or scream. He still couldn't imagine what feelings she had as the drug cocktail took effect.

The old-fashioned movies had the nasty guy grab the

damsel in distress from behind and cover her mouth and face with an ether-soaked handkerchief. Boom. Out like a light. Except ether in Qadira's bloodstream, if they even went that far in an autopsy, would be a red flag.

She had fallen deeply asleep. An overdose or a suicide note with an overdose would have been too easy to fake and it would not fit the plan. The plan was getting harder to fulfill every year. They had to die in a certain fashion or else he was just another run-of-the-mill killer. He had a purpose. He had many ways to kill his victims, but not unlimited. It was becoming more difficult for him not to duplicate what worked and still make it look like a suicide or an accident.

Making things happen on that date every year, whether it fell on a weekday or a weekend, made it even more challenging. He was becoming better at planning and had two plans in case something unexpected happened, like what had happened two years previously.

He had made sure all of her windows were closed. He had practiced at a rented hunting cabin during the summer. It didn't take him long to create the culinary concoctions which gave him the results he was looking for. He was part of his training for that day.

It had slowly become darker on that warm, rainy night. Qadira's breathing was slow and regular. He had left her alone upstairs with a bell on her chest and got everything cooking.

Using her largest pot on the right front burner, medium-sized pot on left front and a sheet pan in the oven, he had quickly assembled the ingredients and piled the exact portions into both and set the stove flame and oven heat at medium and high, respectively. The house was tight. No outside air seeped in and very little interior air exhaled from the dwelling.

He returned to his perch next to the sleeping schoolteacher. When the smoke poured out of the kitchen, it funneled upward and into the hallways and finally the young couple's bedroom. He turned on the portable police scanner and plugged in his headphones. As the smoke filled the room, Qadira still hadn't woken from her deadly slumber. He had carefully placed the Self-Rescuer respirator over his lower face and breathed in the oxygen as the room became dense with smoke. The hardhat with the headlight finished his ensemble, and he closed up his backpack. Her wedding photos on the nightstand had become blurrier as the smoke swirled and settled about the room. She became more difficult to see. He had known that he took a big chance. What if the elderly couple next door had become heroes, or a passerby had busted down the front door? He would have had to use the knife once, maybe twice to make his hurried escape.

He had gone downstairs and fed the medium pot again. It hadn't taken long for the smoke to billow once more. He had learned the hard way during the summer not to open the oven. His co-workers had much fun at his expense while his eye-brows grew back in.

Twenty-two minutes of heavy smoke in the house and she hadn't moved a muscle. Not so much as a cough. The police scanner chirped with a fire response to the house. He had calmly walked over to Qadira and tried to feel for a pulse. There was none.

He had walked down the stairs and quickly locked the back door behind him. The air sucking into the house had only fed the fire in the oven and on the stove more. From that spot, he was not seen from the front of the street or the side neighbors as he had slinked back to the factory parking lot. Through the woods, he had observed the flashing lights and heard the sirens penetrate the rain and gloom. Next, two district police cars had come and then finally an ambulance.

He drove slowly around the streets and parked on her street and watched as they ventilated the house quickly. The gurney went in empty, and it came out the same way. The call had gone out to the Medical Examiner's on-duty attendant. They summoned no detectives.

If he was a fly on the wall that survived all that smoke, he would have probably heard them talking about how she fell asleep while cooking and had become overcome by the smoke. They probably had observed that there was no sign of a struggle, no sexual contact, no sign of a break-in and nothing to be suspicious about. It had been a sad accident. *She was so young.* He had imagined them lamenting.

He had pulled away carefully. Having a police scanner on his front seat would have taken some explaining if he had gotten caught. If questioned, he would have told them he was a siren junkie and followed all the calls as a hobby. The smoky jumpsuit and respirator in the trunk would have different consequences.

Knowing that the cops and firemen watched for firebugs hanging around fire scenes, he hadn't loitered and then drove away. He had showered at the gym before grabbing some takeout. His jumpsuit and gear found a nearby dumpster. Mary had always liked dim sum, and he brought some home that night.

Sean put the bottle back in his desk drawer when he got the call from Service. He walked over to the service writer and grabbed the invoice from the printer, made it look like he took the customer's keys from the wall hook and brought the customer's black Edge around to the Service bay.

"Hello, Tamara, here is your bill. The oil change and

tire rotation is part of the free service package I was able to arrange for you. The alignment wasn't, unfortunately."

"Thank you, Mr. Kelly. I always appreciate how you take care of my car, you didn't have to wash it for me." She took her keys from him, and he walked her to the cashier.

"It is my pleasure. I want you to be a lifetime customer," he said, as he jingled the extra set of her keys in his pocket.

CHAPTER 14

OMAR TABRIZI STOOD in the dank basement and shined his flashlight around the room. The walls were half-century old cinderblocks and had just two openings for casement windows musty from years of coal-fired soot and cobwebs. Ancient wooden steps led to Bilco doors at the rear of the house.

Two steel I-beams set in the center of the floor held up side-by-side 8x8x12s that ran the width of the house and acted as the spine for the 4x8x16s that served as the rib-like joists holding up the flooring of the Dutch Colonial's lower level. "You say that this is the exact layout of the house that collapsed?" he asked.

The mosque's attorney and Ramit rolled out the original plans for both houses on a sheet of plywood supported by two sawhorses.

The elderly woman who owned the standing house nodded and was first to speak. "We kept each other company and folded clothes in our basements when it was too cold or raining out. I was over to her house almost every week until the day she passed away."

"What kind of condition was the rest of the house?" the attorney asked.

She didn't seem willing to say anything bad about her friend. "After her husband died, she let the house...," phrasing her polite answer, "get tired. It was hard for her to be alone, and her kids were nowhere to be seen. If fact, I only saw them the day after the funeral when they threw everything into the dumpster they didn't want."

Omar nodded as he looked at the plot plans the attorney had pulled from the building department. He walked up the interior stairs followed by the group, lest anyone be left in the basement of a house that was a carbon copy of the one that was no longer. "The interior walls of the first floor contained the load bearing studs that support the second floor. Same for the second floor going to the attic. It's called balloon construction," he said, "Come with me."

They returned to the basement. "It's very simple to do what you suggest happened. Loosen these bolts from each joist at the main crossbeam running the width of the house. The joists will stay in place as long as we do not remove the bolts. Then raise up two 8x8s on tire jacks here and here." He pointed to the outside of each I-beam bolted to the Center beams.

"Then you loosen the bolts on the steel beams top and bottom. This is where it gets tricky. Jack up the 8x8s until they support the cross beams and slowly remove the steel beams. Now everything is resting on the 8x8s sitting on tire jacks. Collapse the jacks and the temporary beams fall down and away. There is nothing to hold the crossbeam up, and it pulls down all the joists. All the weight from above drops down in the center of the house, pulling the walls in. Then the roof tips into the center. The upper floors fall down into the basement."

The women shuddered and crossed her arms, hugging them into her chest. "I heard this loud crack and looked out my window and saw exactly that. It went down like a house of cards."

"It was probably the crossbeams breaking that you heard," he said tapping the 8x8x12s with his flashlight. "They were the backbone of the house. Everything fell into the basement."

Ramit spoke next, "When the old, vacant house collapsed on the Realtor, they probably pulled debris out as fast as they could until they found her."

"There was no mention of loosened bolts or I-beams that were intact or missing," Marsha said.

"Nobody noted hydraulic jacks or tire jacks in the basements. The photos don't show any in the debris," Ramit chimed in.

The attorney added his observations, "It was an old, vacant house just like thousands around here over the past twenty years. He made to look like an unfortunate accident."

"What are you saying?" Omar asked.

The woman stood there hugging herself more tightly. "Oh my God."

"Mr. Tabrizi, several families have come to the FBI to tell us that their wives, daughters or mothers died under strange circumstance, each on the exact same date on different years. We are seeing a pattern. We think the woman Realtor was lured to the house, and either killed or knocked unconscious before the house was pulled down on her to make it look like an accident," Marsha said.

Ramit asked, "Do you have an excavator?"

"Yes, why?" Omar replied.

Looking at the attorney, he asked, "It wouldn't be very

expensive to buy the property and the one behind it for back taxes. How long would it take to convey title?"

Marsha was catching on.

The attorney said, "The City of Detroit would love to clear the delinquencies and get them back on the tax rolls again. I'm sure we can expedite a cash closing. No house inspection, no mortgage. They would be simple title searches. Forty-five days, maybe sixty at the latest."

Turning to Omar, Marsha said, "I know this is your busy season, but do you think you could spare a weekend in July or August and dig out the basement of the collapsed house and the one right behind it on Barton that burned under suspicious circumstances?"

"Why the other house?" the attorney asked.

"We think that he dragged the I-beams and other structural elements there in the weeks preceding the collapse," Ramit said.

Omar glanced at the attorney, who nodded and faced Marsha. "Just give me as much notice as you can. What are you looking for?"

"Intact I-beams in either house, and if we are lucky, the jacks that held up the temporary supports. We will want to be there when you do the digging," Ramit answered.

They walked out of the woman's house and into the driveway. They offered heartfelt goodbyes to the owner of Tabrizi Masonry. Marsha then thanked the attorney for the introduction and the purchase of the two properties. He would create an LLC for them, just to keep their names off the tax rolls. As owners, they could do what they wanted, and it didn't require a search warrant.

"We have another question for you if you have a minute?" she asked.

Ramit was first to speak, "We are having a hard time

finding more cases. Your community doesn't put obituaries in the local papers."

"Yes, our tradition is to prepare the bodies for burial the next day. We are a tight-knit group. We spread the word differently."

"Is it true that they inter the bodies without a casket or vault?" Marsha asked.

"Yes, there are only a few funeral parlors that know our customs and abide by them. The burials are done without embalming. Most of the towns in the area do not enforce the antiquated burial laws," he added.

"Can you ask them about burials of Muslim woman on 9/12 or 9/13 since 2001? If they could have the death certificates and family contact information for us that would be great."

"What if they become suspicious and start asking questions?" he asked.

Marsha thought for a minute and remembered some work she had done for Charlie down in Florida at the Hillsborough County Probate office. "Tell them that your client is a Missing Heir Researcher and that your client will pay them for their time. Make it since 1999 so we don't tip them off."

Back in Ramit's van, they began their trip over to Dearborn Heights for their appointment with the Fire Department and Police Department. Marsha checked her email. "Just as we figured, there was nothing wrong with Jamila's Ford Escape. It was working properly. No tampering with the exhaust system to throw out more carbon monoxide. The catalytic converter was connected on both ends and was doing its job."

They both knew their growing number of cases by the

victim's name and had the facts memorized. Ramit replied, "The locksmith hasn't called me back yet about the broken key in the deadbolt."

"How many times have you tried him?" she asked.

"Twice."

She looked at her watch. "We've got time for a quick visit and we'll badge his ass." She looked up the to-do list in their Slack and entered the address into the van's GPS.

They arrived in short order at the locksmith's address. It was a storefront in a row of stores on Michigan Avenue in Dearborn just across the Detroit border, tucked between a pawnshop and a nail salon. It stared across the street at a gas station that had been converted into low-end titty bar. One of her favorite phrases came to mind: Downtown Shabby. The neon light shone PEN missing the O and welcomed them in.

"Hank Klippstein?"

The owner squinted across the counter at them. His rheumy eyes and sallow cheeks spoke volumes of his lifestyle. He chain-smoked unfiltered Camels and had one burning. "Who's asking?"

"Special Agent Marsha O'Shea, FBI." She thrust her credentials with a force of karate punch towards his face, much like the kick boxing classes she was taking a half-mile down the street.

"My associate called you twice," she said, pointing towards Ramit, "I'm sure you had a good reason for not calling him back."

He backed away from the counter and stood at a more comfortable distance from the stern-faced chestnut blonde wearing a Tigers cap and sunglasses.

"I'm busy. I get lots of calls. I can't remember everyone."

"I'm sorry, Hank, you don't mind if I call you Hank?" Steamrolling along, "That shit don't flush with me. How many people call you up about jobs where you have to change the locks after somebody dies?"

"Quite a few, Agent.... What did you say your last name was?"

"O'Shea, but how many where a girl dies from CO poisoning while she slept?" She detected something in his non-verbals. It was a mixture of awareness and apprehension.

"Just go get the deadbolt and hand it to us and we won't bother you again."

"What makes you think I still have it? That was over a year ago."

She had him now. "Because you would pull the key out of it and sell it like it was new and charge for it."

"No law against that," he said.

"Looking around here, I figure you know to squeeze a buck. Let's stop playing around. We can put Fifty on my card for your time and I will buy it from you. How does that sound?"

His eyebrows arched with surprise. "This isn't some kind of gag?"

She laid her credentials on the grimy glass countertop displaying ancient key chain pepper sprays and threw her AMEX card on the table. "Do I look like I'm kidding?"

"I don't take American Express," he said.

She sighed and pulled the bills from her wallet.

He disappeared behind the curtain to a cluttered back room that hadn't probably changed since the day he moved in.

Ramit said sotto voce, "All he had to do was return my call and tell me he tossed it. I would have believed him."

"Me too," Marsha said, "but because he didn't call you back after two calls became a red flag for me. That's why I played bad guy from the get-go."

He shook his head. "I have a lot to learn."

She turned to him as they listened to the locksmith rummaging around. "And you are, Ramit. Just think, if you were stuck in the bat cave back in Philly, you wouldn't be getting any of this experience. You've gotta step in shit sometimes before you can step around it, and guess what? Sometimes you step in shit and come out smelling like a rose. A long time ago, Charlie Akers told me GOYAKOD."

"GOYAKOD?"

"Get off your ass and knock on doors."

Like appearing from behind door number three in a game show with the prize in hand, Hank asked, "I suppose you want me to take it out for you too?"

Marsha brightened up, and for the first time smiled at him. "That would be very nice of you, Mr. Klippstein. Just use tweezers or pliers when you extract the key. We don't want your DNA on it."

"DNA?" He set it down like it was radioactive.

"Your hands have already been all over the lock. We will test the key only. Don't worry."

Marsha and Ramit learned how a dead-bolt came apart, the key was extracted with no transfer of DNA. The locksmith shook his head as he stuffed the cash in his shirt pocket, and everybody was smiling.

"That was easy." Marsha said as she marked the evidence bag as they nosed out of the parking space and finished their U-turn in the titty bar parking lot. They would find out which laboratories that Criminal Defense attorneys use for testing and FedEx it out the next day. "Too bad I used all my cash. We don't have enough for a couple of lap dances."

Ramit smiled and turned red. "Next time."

CHAPTER 15

IT WAS the middle of the week, no special to run this month after Memorial Day and before the Fourth of July. Sean decided to work on Tamara. September 11 fell on the same day of the week as today, and he wanted to nail down her schedule. Omar had left before dawn in his F-350 super duty. He had waited at the nearest cross street to watch him pass before moving closer. The tints on his dealer's demo Fusion Hybrid obscured him from nosey neighbors. If a cop pulled up, he would say that the dealership wanted him to do a repo because he didn't copy the buyer's driver's license when he filled out the credit app. He would hate to lose Tamara, but if the cops got his information, he'd have to go to his back-up victim. Closer to the Tabrizi home now, he could see her car with the morning dew slowly evaporating off of it.

Its amber lights front and back twinkled once. He checked his watch. It was 7:16 a.m. They were running a minute late. Tamara would test the yellow traffic signals by gunning through them and it would leave Sean stuck with a red light. School buses were another pain in the ass. If one got between them, forget about it. He would lose her for sure. But on a school day, he knew exactly where they were headed. It would a school day in September as well. They could go on a field trip on a nice sunny day, but his pleasant banter with the school secretary from a burner phone guaranteed that no such event was scheduled for this day.

The youngest was first to bound out of the house with a juice pack. The school uniform and backpack completed the picture. They had sent their boys to private school. It had an excellent reputation for academics and sports. He accessed their newsletter from the library computers. Competition to get into the best prep schools started with admission to these private elementary schools. A wonderful prep school with an excellent soccer program was the ticket to athletic scholarships offered by top tier colleges. He had seen this play out for the nearly twenty years he lived here as he learned by making it his business to be everybody's friend.

Tamara pushed their oldest out ahead of her as she locked the house. *Now that I have the key, I will get to see the inside when the house is empty.*

They all put on their seat belts and she backed to the end of the drive and looked both ways before backing into their street. He watched from his side mirror as they passed him. With the John Deere cap and oversized wraparound sunglasses, he would look like any other retiree bouncing around the highways and bi-ways of Dearborn Heights. The license plate on his car was borrowed from an exact make and model from his dealer's overflow car lot. Unless the cop looked at the VIN on the dashboard, he wouldn't get made. Besides, dealers always played games with plates. A mea culpa and a couple of box seats would usually take care of the cop.

What he was most concerned about was another way for cops and repo companies to identify cars. He learned about LPR or license plate readers from his anonymous trolling of Private Investigator Facebook groups. They were quickly replacing list serves and message boards as the way to get inside information on how to conduct surveillance and what the latest tools were.

The drive was a brisk fifteen minutes. No construction, torrential rainstorms or petulant crossing guards to slow them down. He stayed a car or sometimes two back when they got closer to the school. The "spacers" kept the target from seeing the same vehicle behind them. He pulled into his favorite spot to watch her car disgorge the two boys who raced up to the school door entrance.

She could only turn right out of the school and continued on back in the direction they had traveled. He tightened up on his follow with no spacers until he saw her put her blinker on for her street. He passed her on the right as she waited for traffic to clear. He watched in his rearview as she made her turn and he whipped a U-turn making sure the local cops were not lurking about and sped to her street.

He passed her house just as she was unlocking her front door and entering. He set up this time with their house in front of him, but he was three hundred yards away and had only the eyeball on her driveway entrance and curb line. He'd see anything rolling in or out. He doubted that he would see a repairman, but on one previous target years ago, he watched a regular male visitor to his target's apartment.

He fantasized about bursting in on them while they were in post-coital bliss and dispatching them both. He thought about putting the untraceable gun in the husband's car and have grieving cuckold explain the homicide to the unsmiling detectives how he didn't kill his cheating wife and her lover. He had shaken himself out of the reverie with a reminder that killing was not the plan. He had strict rules about the date and the manner of death. Only once, he was desperate and committed an obvious homicide just before Cinderella's carriage turned into a pumpkin.

He eased back the seat, put the visor down and cracked the windows about an inch. He could run the AC on the car's hybrid battery if it got too hot and humid. He was careful to switch cars up, lest some neighbors, years apart, would write down his license plate. As usual, he would pee in a bottle and eat nutrition bars while in stealth mode. He would not leave unless he had to move his bowels. His light dinner and forgoing greasy breakfast sandwiches helped to keep those rumblings from happening.

He was on his third consecutive motivational podcast when he saw her back out and drive away from his position. Seat up, ignition on, punch it into drive, Lions cap on head and Big Gulp in front of his face. He saw her make a turn away from the direction of the school.

Where are you taking me, Tamara?

It didn't take him long to get his answer. She pulled into the big box store which put all the Main Street hardware stores out of business back in the '80s.

Interesting. She's going into the contractor's entrance.

She knew him by face and he didn't want to take a chance of getting made. He sat in the lot near the exit. Twenty-five minutes later, she walked out with a store clerk pushing a flat pallet carriage on squeaky wobbly wheels. From the picture on the box, it looked like a heavy-duty tool of some sort. She opened the hatch and collapsed the back seats down, and he hoisted the box into the rear compartment of her small SUV. It fit, but the rear wheels sagged under the weight.

She drove out of the lot and began making her way away from her home and the one they were building. She got onto the expressway heading toward downtown Detroit and got off three exits later. He allowed a tractor trailer to get between them and spotted her veering to the exit.

She must be using her phone's GPS and not the car's.

At the end of the ramp, she turned left and then he approached the stop sign. He had to wait an agonizing thirty or forty seconds for traffic to clear. A guy laid on the horn and shot him the finger as he bolted in front of the irate man's car coming from his left. Sean sped up and couldn't acquire her car. He drove down that cross street as far as he thought necessary to have caught up with her.

Damn!

It was days like this that he wished he slapped a GPS on his target's cars and put a camera and microphone in their houses. He had to balance stealth, and knowledge against getting caught. So far, nobody had stumbled onto his ingenious plan of just one death by accident or suicide every year on the same date. He had to place caution over total control of the situation any day he was out stalking or hunting.

He worked his way back toward the exit by doing a grid search of all the residential side streets. Craning his neck left or right into driveways, he almost missed her car parked ahead of Omar's truck in the road. She stood in the driveway taking to Omar as his workers moved the box up the lawn to a brick walkway and steps.

He quickly averted his gaze back to the street, just in time to see a dog running from his left disappear below his hood.

Out of instinct, he jammed on the brakes and caused a sickening screech, but to his relief, he saw the pooch skitter to his right, tail tucked low. The dog was running away without a limp. The adrenaline coursing through his body tingled like the rush he felt when he confronted his victims on 9/11.

He sat there for a second and realized that everyone at the work site was staring at him. He slowly proceeded and realized that his car was burnt, as the surveillance operatives were fond of saying when they had to beat feet as cautiously as possible to get away.

Better than getting made, he thought.

He would call it a day. There would be a few more school days this semester for him to come back. He decided not to get another surveillance vehicle for the after-school pickup.

CHAPTER 16

"MARSHA, it took me awhile, but I think I found another one."

She swung from her workstation on the roller wheels of her desk chair and bumped up against his. "A gas explosion. Detroit. Kamaria?"

"Arabic for *the moon*," Ramit said.

Marsha scanned the Newspaper Archives article. "It says it was her apartment. Who was the owner back in '06?"

"TempleZ Properties. Do you want to jacket it?"

Finishing the article, she looked at the big board and back at Ramit. "Does a bear go poopy in the woods?" She swung across the floor to the whiteboard. Adding the data with an erasable marker and talking aloud. "*Kamaria Amir, Employer Blank, Age 26, Detroit, Apt 2R 1245 Mt. Elliott St., Manner of Death, blank, Cause of Death, Gas Explosion.*"

Ramit pulled from Assessor records and Secretary of State records, the registered agent and principals for TempleZ Properties.

Using Social Media aggregators and databases Charlie Akers turned her on to, Marsha began finding about Kamaria and her family. LinkedIn still showed a profile for her. She had been a title abstractor for a downtown Title company. Marsha added that info to the whiteboard.

Both were busy adding the notes and leads into Slack. Then came the requests to Vital Statistics for the death certificate, FOIA requests to the Police Department for "any and all" responses to the property for the Spring and Summer of '06. Ditto, the Fire Department. Medical Examiners would have been called — had to get that file too.

Given the nature of the death, Marsha pulled the info from the collapse case with Qadira and sent a request to the mosque's attorney's paralegal to go to Building and Inspections to pull records. Warnings and contractor permits would be important. She was better at that than either Ramit or herself and it would raise less suspicion. They were also learning what to outsource and what to do themselves.

On the phone now, "Hello, may I speak to Mr. Rothstein please," Marsha asked.

"Whom shall I say is calling?" the pleasant matronly sounding receptionist asked.

"Marsha O'Shea, this is not a sales call, I had a quick question for him."

"One moment, please."

Marsha looked at the board. It was getting filled up. They were over a third of the way now and expected to get more from the funeral directors within the next couple of weeks.

"I'm sorry, Ms. O'Shea, may I take a message? Mr. Rothstein is not available now. May I take a message?"

Something about her repeating wanting to take a message gave Marsha pause. "No voicemail?"

"No, no. We are pretty old-fashioned here."

"What is your name, dear," Marsha asked.

"Hilda."

"Thank you, Hilda. Can you interrupt Mr. Rothstein and tell him I am a Special Agent with the FBI and that I am looking into a gas explosion at a property back in 2006. I'll hold."

Raising her voice, Hilda said, "Did you say FBI, Ms. O'Shea?"

"Yes."

"And that it was about the gas explosion where that poor girl died back a while ago."

"Yep, that's the one."

A new nervous male voice appeared on the line. "Hyman Rothstein here. How can I help you?"

"Thank you for speaking with me, Mr. Rothstein. I wanted to ask you about the gas explosion at 1245 Mt. Elliott Street."

"That was a long time ago," he said.

"As Hilda reminded you, a young woman died that day. How many gas explosions do your properties have? Is it a matter of having so many that you can't tell them apart?"

"No, I meant, I mean," he stammered, "We only had that one."

"Can you tell me what caused the explosion?"

"Why?" he asked.

"Why what?" she replied.

"Why would you want to know what caused the explosion?"

"Why would you question why an FBI agent is calling about a death from a gas explosion?"

Ramit stopped key stroking and arched an eyebrow towards Marsha who was scowling now.

"DTE said that their gas lines into the building were working fine and blamed it on her stove." He sighed verbally.

"What did your insurance company say?" she asked.

"They tried saying that the connections were crimped and whoever installed it, didn't do so properly."

"Where'd they get with that argument?"

"Not far. The prior owner installed it at least twenty years earlier and he was dead by the time they sued. Nobody to go after. I never got my deductible back."

Oh, poor baby. A tenant died, and you're worried about getting your fucking deductible back. "Your memory is pretty good, Mr. Rothstein. Can I call your agent and say that we spoke?"

"Why — oh never mind. How about I have them call you?"

"That would be swell, but can I have their name for the file. So I know who to expect a call from?"

"Michael Scott, Scott Insurance on 3rd Street."

"Michael Scott?" She gave Ramit the high sign to get the number before she disconnected with Rothstein. "Is that 3rd Street in Detroit?"

"Yes."

"It that with two Ts or one?"

"Two."

"Again, thank you Mr. Rothstein for your assistance. My number is 215-555-1234 in case you have any additional information that you think would be helpful." Ramit keyed the numbers on his phone. It was ringing. "And make sure to tell Hilda...." Ramit handed his phone to Marsha. "Oh, sorry, I have another call coming in." She disconnected with Rothstein and answered, "Hello, Michael Scott?"

"This is he."

"Thank you for taking my call, I just got off the phone with Hyman Rothstein who suggested that you would be able to help me."

"How do you know Hyman?"

"Well, you see, Mr. Scott, my name is Marsha O'Shea and I am an FBI agent looking into that awful gas explosion back in '06 that claimed the life of a young girl. There is something about it that has us wanting to learn as much about it as we can as fast as we can." Steamrolling along. "We want to stop by later this afternoon around 2 p.m. and pick up a copy of your file. Hyman said that you would help us out."

"Agent O'Shea. The file is in limbo right now, I am sorry to say."

"Why's that, sir?"

He replied, "We went paperless a few years ago and started going backwards through the years at our offsite storage to move the paper files to digital. The company doing the scanning is working on those years as we speak."

"I see. Can you tell me who Hyman was insured with for the loss? While you are getting your file back from the scanner, I can talk to them direct."

"The bastards, I am looking at their fire mark on my wall right now. They dropped TempleZ Properties right after they paid the claim. I had to scramble and put him into the assigned risk pool. It cost Hyman a lot of money and they cut my commissions while we waited for his loss history to become old news. It was five years before another underwriter would touch them." He supplied the commercial property carrier's name and pulled up Hyman's account to supply her with the policy and claim number for the 9/11/2006 date of loss.

"Thank you for your assistance, Mr. Scott."

"No problem, you weren't kidding. My secretary just pushed a note under my nose saying that Hyman was waiting on the phone and that the FBI was looking into this claim. Can you give me a little hint why you are looking at this?"

"I make it my business to share what I can with people who help me. We saw a pattern of fires at properties where the mortgages had been refinanced and the pay-offs were well above what the properties were worth," Marsha lied, "Of course, this shit went on well before the housing bubble burst a few years later. We are just now catching up with them. This one jumped to the top of the list, because that poor girl died, but it was different in that it was a gas explosion and not a suspicious fire." *Let Rothstein stew on the other line.* "I hope you understand why it is so important. Please don't mention this to Hyman, I don't want it getting back to his lenders."

Ramit started tracking down the claims department and getting someone to pull their file out of storage.

"I won't." He probably was lying now too. "If there is anything I can help you with, Agent O'Shea, please call me."

"It's Marsha," she flirted with the septuagenarian.

"Please call me Michael," he replied.

Rothstein was probably bursting a blood vessel on the other line. "Thank you, Michael," she hung up.

They continued to work side by side gathering what they could about this latest one. They made an appointment with her family that weekend. Hollins was flying in Thursday night and they wanted to save a family interview for him to be present. She and Ramit talked about the possibility of having to redo some interviews once Hollins showed them how he worked cold cases.

Ramit had pulled up a Google Maps image of the building and did a 360-degree of the street view and nudged Marsha.

"That's interesting," she said.

CHAPTER 17

RAMIT AND MARSHA waited for Mike by the white grand piano on the main concourse of the Detroit Metro Airport. The sun streamed in from across the tarmac, glinting off of the jets arriving and departing. The support vehicles for aviation fuel, baggage handling, and food concessions darted about like bees buzzing around a flower garden.

They talked about the loose ends they tied up on some of their cases that day. Their progress was painfully slow. In one month, they had only uncovered four probables on top of the three handed to them. They had discounted many of the deaths of the elderly by natural causes. The killer so far had focused on younger to middle-aged Muslim women from Middle Eastern Heritage. They would assume that was the *modus operandi*.

Mike texted them on touchdown and they found their way to his gate.

"Hi, Mike, it's good to see you, how was the flight?" Marsha asked.

"Painless." He hugged her with his good arm and surprised Ramit with a hug too. Almost reading their minds, he said, "Why Muslims and why women? There are a lot of Arab Christians. How does he know which is which? This goes to motive. What motivates our boy to target only one faith? The question is further complicated by why only women. I don't think he is picking on them for how he is killing them. With his methods, he could just as easily kill men. A clue and an enormous clue are that he only strikes on 9/11. He's getting back at Muslims after 9/11, I get that, but why just women? Find that answer and you will get his motive."

Out the doors to short-term parking and into Ramit's van, the one-sided conversation continued. He had done his homework and was bringing them up to speed. The up-tempo approach did not abate as Mike sat in the back behind them and kept delivering his findings and opinions on their work.

Once they cleared the interminable construction around the terminals, Ramit navigated them back to their short-term house rental.

Leaving his weekender by the door, Mike surveyed the scene before him. The living room had taken on the appearance of a safe house situation room and it is there that three motivated investigators from varied backgrounds would focus on a single mission.

He said, "I like what you did with the place, Marsha. What's that I smell in the oven?"

"They do ribs out here pretty good. I thought you might be hungry. We have some corn on the cob and coleslaw to go with it. Sweet tea, energy drinks, or bottled water?" she asked.

"Sweet tea is fine. Can we talk and eat?" he replied. They made their plates and sat down facing the big board.

Marsha noticed that he had held the plate low across his stomach with his not-so-good arm and over-compensated with his right. The nerve damage from the gunshot in his upper chest allowed only a limited range of motion and strength in his left. She couldn't believe that Mike had been shot only several months earlier and here he was, working another case with her.

Was it unreasonable to ask for his help so soon? No, she concluded that this case, away from all the baggage and BS in Philly, was the best thing for him.

Wiping the sauce from his mouth with the back of his good hand and pointing a gnarled rib at the board, he said, "The good news is that you captured a lot of data from each death but each one is sitting in their own solo. Names, dates, addresses, telephone numbers, and witness names have to go in a relational database. We both have been spoiled by the tools given to us by our employers for this."

Ramit nodded. "It was becoming unwieldy going back and forth cross-checking names."

"You have a timeline spanning three decades. Where is your timeline for all the cases and each case?"

Silence.

"I know you had to hit the ground running, and the good news is that we can move all of that data with very little key stroking into a better program. Ramit, can you bring up the website for *CaseSoft*? They are owned by LexisNexis."

Ramit clicked across the homepage, then into the embedded YouTube video.

"You lost nothing by having an off-the-shelf program for

sharing and collaborating, but you wouldn't be able to see the forest from the trees when the case explodes.

"The other thing is we can bring some data into the program by OCR. If you have tons of documents, the scanning can take minutes instead of hours of key stroking. The more work you do, the more need for data entry you will have."

"You should be one of their salesmen, Mike," Marsha said, "but you are absolutely right. We've been running and gunning all day and evening and then we coming home and entering our reports until midnight."

"You two might still have to do that, but at least you will get the power of analytic tools besides just having a repository for collection, retrieval and sharing."

Both nodded as Mike attacked his corn. He had to lift his left arm in front of his face with his right hand and then place the corn into the left hand while turning the cob with his right.

Ramit said, "I'm on it. If we need help on the transfer, I will figure something out. Mike's right, we can't get bogged down in key stroking. I am excited how the timeline software works."

"Watching this joker grow and change from year to year will be interesting," Marsha added.

Mike said, "Way back in the day when I worked detectives out in the districts, we worked swing shifts. On the midnights when it was quiet, and we weren't getting called out, you'd see twenty detectives typing away all night. We'd work the cases on day and evening shift, keep good notes and type everything up on the graveyard shift. Everything except search warrants and arrest warrants. It's amazing how we got anything done. Between typing reports and court time, we spent less than half our time on the street."

Marsha disappeared from the war room to the kitchen and returned with a pie tin in each hand. "Pecan or apple?"

"Yes." Mike smiled.

She knew he had a sweet tooth. When she topped the pies slices with whipped cream, she handed them around and sat down. "You can never get enough whipped cream. So, Mike, let's hear the bad news."

"From now on, you should be recording all of your interviews." He reached into his blazer and produced identical pens for each of them.

"You want us to write down what the people are saying verbatim?" Ramit asked.

Mike reached into his side coat pocket. "No. You push this and put it in your shirt pocket or on the table and it will record your conversation. They think it's your spare pen."

Handing the packaging to them next. "Here are the download instructions. This app works best for transcription." He pointed to the app on his phone. "Same goes for phone calls. You never know when someone will tell you something over the phone that at the time seemed insignificant but became important later and you forgot it. You should read the transcriptions in twenty-four hours, so you don't forget what they said. It will help you immensely for follow-up questions. Then you feed them into your case files. Your memory and your notes won't be enough for these interviews, I'm afraid."

Next, Mike walked them through his notes on each specific case. First, he talked about what they did and holes they needed to fill, then he walked them through additional leads that they had not even contemplated, explaining why those leads were important.

Marsha realized that she and Ramit were the pupils. This is the education that they were paying for. Mike was patient with their questions and gave examples from his casework to explain why they needed to cover this ground.

Once he explained it to them, the obvious smacked them in the forehead, but both had no ego about learning how to investigate cold case homicides disguised to look like something else. Neither had that experience.

Marsha was seeing a broad checklist of how to look at people, places and things specific to each case. This was Homicide 101 with an outstanding teacher.

Her job was simple, but not easy. They had one suspect and one mission. It was to stop him before he struck again. They had the luxury of three months to put the puzzle together before he struck again but needed to act with urgency to find the pieces. The clues would come from how the pieces fit together from one case to the next to the next. This raised a question for Marsha.

"Mike, are we going about this the wrong way? Should we spend more time trying to find the first murders and try to build on the oldest cases first?"

Looking at the board, he said, "I know you are invested with all these leads from the most recent cases, and I think you have to run them in case our boy made a mistake, but 9/11 triggered this rampage, I would venture to guess."

Ramit asked, "Could he have been doing this before 9/11 randomly?"

"Sorta doubt it. Otherwise, why would he restrict his killings to one date a year?" Mike said, "This is how the Muslim community stumbled onto the deaths in the first place. If we spread out them on different dates over the years, we wouldn't be sitting here."

"Makes me think he wasn't a killer before 9/11 and learned from each year afterwards. Gotta wonder if he made any rookie mistakes," Marsha said.

"Exactly," Mike agreed, "He's learning from each one as he goes along."

"I will ask our profiler what he thinks is significant about our boy using 9/11 as the anniversary to act on." Marsha made a note.

"That was smart getting a profiler on this case, as soon as you saw that these weren't statistically probable accidents or suicides," Mike said, "How is that coming along?"

"He keeps asking me more questions on each case. I think he's trying to get a better handle on this bird."

"He's a rare bird for sure," Mike added.

Ramit asked, "Forgive me if I do not have a command of my American history...."

"For Christ's sake, you were born in New Jersey, they didn't teach history in the Garden State?" Marsha shot him a wry look.

Ramit turned red, but continued, "What I mean to say, is that I had no family members who were part of the military; who had their own personal recollections during war time. I was more interested in the sciences."

"Go on, Ramit," Mike encouraged him.

"Do you know of anyone killing Japanese on the anniversary of Pearl Harbor in the Forties?"

None of them had that answer, and Marsha made another note.

"Or Germans after U-boats sunk passenger ships like the *Lusitania*?" Mike added.

"Were there any date specific atrocities in Vietnam or Korea?" Marsha asked.

"When you look at it that way," Mike said, "The villains were out there, not here." Mike waved his good arm to make his point. "Men enlisted by the millions to kill Nips, Krauts or Gooks — not my language you understand."

"But not their women," Ramit said.

"And not in the United States," Marsha added.

"So, what does that make this guy?" Mike added.

The clock struck midnight as they pondered that question.

CHAPTER 18

THE BACK CORNER of Bob Evans was empty early Friday morning, save for the three guests quietly talking and enjoying their breakfast specials. Marsha didn't need the side of pancakes to go along with her bacon and eggs, but it would be an extensive field day, she reasoned. She laughed at Mike's waffles with the toppling tower of whipped cream. Ramit had acquired a taste for soft-boiled eggs and grits.

When the plates were cleared, Mike had Ramit and Marsha plan their extended weekend. He said that the geographic location of the leads was secondary to their importance. Take advantage of his skills while he was in town, he told them.

They would crisscross Dearborn, Detroit and Dearborn Heights many times before depositing him at the airport Sunday night. Mostly, he reinforced why each case was part of a larger puzzle. They nicknamed the killer Mr. Orr from his fake name given to the slain Realtor. They had to call him something. The UNSUB moniker was not working for them.

* * *

"Where would you sit, if you were watching the apartment?" Mike asked.

At the scene of the Carbon Monoxide poisoning, they stared at Jamila's apartment.

"Did the cops get any calls of suspicious vehicles?" he asked.

Ramit checked that lead in Slack. "No calls."

"Tomorrow morning, first thing — like eight o'clock on the button — we will knock on doors and see what the neighbors have to say. You can call the ones that moved away later at night, while you are between your stops, when you are not dictating reports. You gotta maximize your dead time to make sure you do a complete canvass on this one. Letter carrier had to put mail in each door slot, FedEx, and UPS would be in and out of this place all the time. Did he park in their favorite spots? We okay so far?"

They both nodded.

Mike rolled on, "Mr. Orr probably knew her car, so he didn't have to sit in this fishbowl of apartments to follow her out. Let's go back to secondary locations where he could sit to watch her leave."

They stopped at the single entrance and exit onto a road with commercial and retail establishments. He said, "You only need a couple hours of surveillance video from last 9/11 of movement between Midnight and three to catch him leaving. What time did the family say that she usually went to sleep?"

Ramit wrote down that question. They realized that Mike needed to see things for himself to plan more questions.

"The later she went to sleep on the tenth, the later he

would have to sneak into her apartment to start her car on the eleventh to be sure she was asleep. Remember, she wouldn't count if she died on the tenth."

"We got the Tox report, and she had nothing else in her system to knock her out," Marsha said.

* * *

By prior arrangement, they met with the specialists who had both Nura's and Nabila's cars in for examination. Both families had come that day to get fingerprinted and give DNA swabs. Charlie had found the experts who did CSI for high-profile criminal defense attorneys and well-heeled attorneys involved in high-stakes litigation. The FBI retiree network came through. They repurposed one of Detroit's many empty warehouses for the day. They even brought their own stanchion lights. While they did their CSI thing, Mike began interviewing the families separately.

"We have to think that whoever did this to Nura, might have intercepted her in the garage and forced her into the house."

Hassan, her husband, said, "She never would have worn her shoes inside the house."

"With your permission, those experts will follow you home and they will check the garage, kitchen and bedroom for fingerprints and DNA."

"After so many years, what do you hope to find?" the daughter Stephanie asked.

Ramit said, "Had we known about this killer then, we would have treated those areas as a crime scene. With the advances in DNA testing both by Law Enforcement and commercial family history firms, we might find him and stop him before he strikes again."

Marsha added, "Walk me through that summer again. Leave nothing out, no matter how insignificant you think it might be. Talk about birthdays, anniversaries, weddings, funerals, things at school for all of you. Rather than have you talk to me individually, you may fill in each other's blanks."

Ramit clicked his pen, and all of them began taking copious notes.

An uninterrupted ninety minutes later, they all answered Mike with a "That's it."

Every note where Mike made a circle, he clarified what they said with open-ended questions, then put a check mark in the circle. That led to more remembrances and more clarifications. The former homicide detective then asked direct questions outside of their memories.

"Did Nura ever complain about a strange man stalking her or talking to her?"

They shook their heads.

"No. Okay. How about seeing the same vehicle following her?"

"No. We told Agent O'Shea that already."

"Yes, I know, but sometimes this type of questioning may jog your memory. Was she noticeably angry about any drivers or persons enough to tell you about them?"

They all shook their heads.

"No. Okay," Mike repeated for the tape recorder their silent replies.

"Do you think we can talk to your neighbors who came over when they saw the ambulance and fire trucks?"

"I can arrange that," Hassan said, "I will see them at the mosque after prayers today."

"Today?"

"Yes. Friday is our day of Worship."

"I'm sorry," Mike said, "Maybe I should have known that. Why did I think it was either Saturday or Sunday?" He stole a glance to his associates.

"Some mosques broadcast their call to worship and other don't. It's not always obvious," Hassan said.

"If we can meet them afterwards, that would be great. Please text us," Mike said. With that, he stood up, and the meeting was over.

While Nura's family collected her car, Nabila's husband came to be interviewed again and slumped into the chair. He just as heavily burdened by his wife's death as the day he met her at the restaurant, Marsha thought.

Marsha was first to speak, "Thank you for waiting, Kamal. This is Mike Hollins and Ramit Ravikant." The men nodded.

Addressing Marsha, "I told you that the State Police paid me a visit again along with the Dearborn Police after you talked to them. At first they acted like they were interested in why Nabila would jump from that overpass."

"And?" Mike asked.

"Just as you said, Agent O'Shea, they acted sympathetic and began to ask me who might have pushed her over."

"As I did," Marsha said.

"Yes, but then their questions focused on me. As if I would do that to my wife who I loved with all my heart." He looked at his feet as his eyes watered. "They wanted to know where I was that night."

"What did you tell them?" Mike leaned in.

"I was home like I am every night. My children were asleep. It was a school night. She was late and not answering my calls. It seems they didn't bother to record or write my messages when they had her phone. She worked until eleven and I got worried around eleven forty-five.

"Sometimes, she would stop and pick up some needed groceries for the next day, but usually, she would tell me to pick them up so she could come right home. Then I told them that when I received their phone call at home and I heard that it was the police, I knew something bad happened to her."

"Was there anything in the weeks or months leading up to her death, where she suspected being followed?"

"No." Kamal shook his head.

"Did you notice her acting any differently?"

"No, and I told them that. Nabila would have no reason to kill — jump off that overpass. She was healthy, she didn't take any pills for depression, the kids had just started a new school year and everybody was excited."

"Her job?" Mike changed gears.

Kamal said, "She worked in-patient services at the hospital and handled all the emergency room registrations on the evening shift. All her work friends made a point to tell me how sad and shocked they were. None of them said she was having problems. She would tell me sometimes about when the Flu season was starting or some of the strange ways people got hurt, but her employer left her alone to do her job. They all liked her."

"Friends outside of work?"

"Our friends. We were a couple with young children. Our world revolved around the house, their activities and worship."

"Your wife was pretty, Kamal, any men make unwanted advances to her?" Mike asked.

"She would have told me."

"How about welcome advances?" Mike prodded.

Both Ramit and Marsha shifted uncomfortably as they watched Kamal stiffen.

"No! The cops didn't even ask me that question," Kamal answered.

"Kamal, they weren't doing their job the first time or the second time. A lover, maybe a lover that spurned her and possibly the father of the child she was carrying didn't want her and she felt she had no other options. The shame would have sent her over the railing, Kamal."

"She wasn't pregnant. She took care of that after our second child. It was her choice. Ovarian cancer ran in her family. I was willing to have a vasectomy. She gave me no reason to suspect another man."

"Or woman?" Mike had to ask.

"NO!"

"Did she get high on drugs?"

"No." Kamal's anger was settling.

"Did she like beer or wine?"

"We didn't drink."

Mike looked at Ramit.

"We received the Medical Examiner's report as part of the State Police report from our Freedom of Information request," he said glancing at Marsha.

Mike sat back as Marsha took a deep breath, "Kamal, her blood alcohol was three times the legal limit. She would have been nearly unconscious."

"She didn't drink, and she didn't secretly drink. I kissed her every night and told her I loved her."

Mike, pointing over his shoulder, said, "That's why we have them going over your wife's car with a fine-toothed comb."

"The killer forced her to drink in her car, then made her open her text messages and he entered the message to her mother just before dragging her from the car and over the railing," Marsha said.

"I never believed that she killed herself. She would never do that to her children," Kamal said.

"Or to you, Kamal. She would not have done this to you," Marsha added. She was playing good cop to Mike's bad cop act.

Mike asked, "Did the cops ask you about her blood-alcohol or if she even drank."

"No. Not a word." He sniffled.

"Or why she would text her mother?"

The three investigators waited.

"The killer made a mistake." Kamal sat up and wiped his eyes. "Her mother died from ovarian cancer the year before."

Everyone now looked at the car and hoped that it would tell them something about that early morning dead-of-night happening on the overpass.

Marsha spoke first, "If it's any consolation to you, Kamal. She was probably unconscious when she went over the railing. She probably didn't know what — was happening." *Asking tough questions of the victim's survivors were not going to get easier, but I have couch the questions with empathy,* she noted. Mike was brutally honest in asking what they had been tip-toeing around.

"Thank you for your kind words. I am glad that we met. I know you will find the man who did this." Kamal stood up and said. "Before I forget, you were right, Agent O'Shea. After you spoke to the police, they started following me around in Black Chevrolet Suburbans. They stop following me when I drove into the Dearborn Police Station parking lot each time I spotted them."

CHAPTER 19

THE INTERVIEWS and site visits continued on Saturday and Sunday. They now sat before the whiteboard and the large flat screen, both displaying all the accepted cases to their two invited visitors. Mike's luggage sat in the room's corner. Monday, Ramit would get started on transitioning the data and records over to *CaseSoft*. They had to end this meeting in under two hours or Mike would miss his flight back to Philly.

Marsha felt better about their inroads and the dizzying number of leads they generated after going back over all the cases with Mike. The crash course on how to work a mass murderer, how to work cold cases, and understanding the basics of homicide investigation was well worth it to all of them. She was glad that she had invited him to the Motor City.

In the kingdom of the blind, the one-eyed man is king, but at least I can see blurry shapes now. She wasn't the blind leading the blind anymore.

Marsha watched Mike come alive as he dove into the work. For the weekend, she had her old partner in crime back, and she enjoyed it. Two fourteen-hour days of banging out leads, shoulder to injured shoulder proved that. After their last adventure, neither were sure that they wanted to play the cops and robbers game anymore. Her time in Clearwater convinced her that being an investigator was her calling. She was grateful to do what she loved and to be given this top-secret high-profile case.

Grayson Stanfield, the number two honcho in the Bureau was sure that she had the "right stuff." Sure, she had gotten smarter over the years, but now she felt she was getting her mojo back. If she couldn't get jazzed by a case like this, she had no business calling her herself a criminal investigator. She felt the best compliment she had gotten in a year was from Mike. He called her "natural police" over sweet tea the previous night after Ramit went to bed.

After all the running around chasing bank robbers and fugitives in Miami, she mused that maybe she needed the time in Philly on a ho-hum eight-to-five backwater squad working non-traditional organized crime to recharge her batteries. Little did she know when she came back to Philly, that her life would change forever.

She remembered feeling totally out of her comfort zone when she took on this case. She realized that she still had so much more growing to do as an investigator and as a project leader, especially if she wanted to catch this dude.

In the brief time that she worked closely with Ramit, she watched how he grew by each challenge thrown at him. Marsha thought about all the agents she worked with over the years and would not hesitate to match his growing skills against most of them. His work ethic made her feel like a slacker sometimes.

Today, she felt firsthand, for the first time in a long time, what it meant to be part of a highly motivated team.

Ramit was summarizing for the other attendees by going backwards in time from the most recent to the oldest known case.

There were gaps in the years. The years immediately following 9/11 were still blank. Marsha was certain that Mr. Orr's rookie mistakes would lead to his undoing.

The funeral directors who worked with the Arab American community would supply them with more deaths to look at. Those would fill up some gaps for sure.

This was a smart time to bring their visitors in for a look-see. Mike had suggested it after their visit to the mosque to interview Nura's neighbors. They needed outside eyes. Muslim eyes, to be exact. His reasoning was simple. If the Amish community outside of Philadelphia was being targeted, wouldn't it make sense to consult with an Amish leader to get their point of view on what was happening and why?

"He has a year to select his victim," the imam said.

"Or maybe even more, if he is that methodical. We are not sure how he selects his victims or what criteria he is using," Marsha offered.

"The date is important as it falls on different days every year, so he needs to find a victim that can be killed on that specific day of the week," Ramit said, "We don't have proof of it, but we think he may also have an alternate choice in case the victim deviates from the known routine on that day."

"But none of the deaths are on their face considered by the authorities to be homicides," the mosque's attorney stated.

"The planning and how they are carried out are made to look like they are accidental or suicidal," Marsha said, "His profile is to stay under the radar."

"What does your profiler say about him," the attorney asked.

"Myles Hanski has written the book on serial killers. He tells me that the motivation is not clear. He doesn't have a large enough sampling to figure this guy out. Why Muslim women on only one day and that day being exactly 9/11 fits nothing he has seen in his entire career. He keeps asking for more observations and data. Mr. Orr is unique," Marsha said.

Before the question was asked, Ramit said, "Robert Orr is the name the unknown subject gave the Realtor to schedule the appointment at the building collapse."

"Car left running, food burning on the stove, heavy object falling, building collapsing, jumping off a bridge, falling on a concrete stairway, gas explosion," the attorney read down the causes of death.

"Very resourceful," Mike said, "These deaths were not meant to attract the attention of law enforcement or arson investigators."

"If it weren't for the fact that they all occurred on the anniversary of 9/11, they would have stayed off the radar scope," Marsha added.

"And to Muslims," the imam reminded them.

"And only to women," the attorney added.

The investigators nodded.

"We have been wracking our brains on those facts," Marsha said, "We hoped that you might add your perspective."

"We watched in horror that day when the planes hit the towers. The broadcast images of planes crashing and the towers catching fire and then people jumping to their deaths rather than perish in the flames have been seared into our brains," the imam said.

Marsha quickly looked up from her notes to the screen, then over to the chart and back. She stood up.

"It was only a short time later we learned that most of the hijackers were Al-Qaeda. That is when our safety and privacy in America took a turn for the worse," the attorney added, "It didn't matter that most of the hijackers were Saudi, it painted all Arabs with the same brush."

"Indians in New Jersey caught some backlash too. I watched as they were dragged out of gas stations and beaten along Route 1," Ramit said.

Marsha walked over to Ramit and whispered to him. Ramit quickly sought video on his Chromebook.

"This is what you were talking about, imam," Marsha said as she nodded to Ramit.

The images of the burning tower as the second plane flew past it and struck the second tower filled the screen. The scene was then replayed in slow-motion with a voice-over of New York radio host, Howard Stern, talking to his listeners when callers began calling in with eyewitness accounts. Brooklynites called in as the billowing black smoke from the ignited jet fuel billowed toward them on that crystal-blue cloudless day.

Police cars and fire trucks racing to the towers while traumatized occupants fled them now filled the screen. Agonizing shots of people tottering on the ledges of the tallest buildings in Manhattan gave way to one person after another falling to their deaths.

Clips of survivors coated with asbestos-laden concrete dust as they staggered uptown from ground zero followed the video of the building collapses.

"Go back and start at the beginning and mute the sound. Stop right there, Ramit. Freeze it. Now go back to the spreadsheet and copy the cause of death column onto a separate spreadsheet. Expand that column and fill the entire screen. Play the video again and toggle back and forth between the cause of death column and what happened that day."

"Agent O'Shea, you are on to something," the imam said.

"You're getting inside Robert Orr's head," Mike was next on the uptake.

"He's killing Muslin women on that date every year in the same manner as many of the people who died that terrible day," the attorney said it out loud for all their benefit.

"One of the hijacked planes crashed in the Pennsylvania farmlands ostensibly headed to D.C.," Ramit said.

"Cause of death would be considered Blunt Force Trauma," Mike said.

"Do we know if any of the passengers died fighting the terrorists on the plane before it went down," Marsha asked.

"If they did, it would be by knife or by box-cutter," Ramit suggested.

"What about the plane that hit the Pentagon," the attorney asked.

"Blunt Force Trauma, Burning, Smoke inhalation, CO poisoning," Marsha said.

"Building collapse," Ramit added.

"Asphyxiation — trapped under debris and not being able to breathe," Mike said.

"Being trampled on the stairs of either tower — like Aaliyah," Ramit said.

"Were any of the responders killed driving to the scenes or taking injured to the hospital," the attorney asked.

"Good question," Marsha said.

"Heart attack from climbing the stairs with all that equipment on?" Marsha asked.

Marsha, Mike, and Ramit threw out ideas and quickly discarded many but not all. The conversation between investigators was a signal to their guests. The imam and attorney rose to leave the investigators to explore all the causes of death on 9/11.

"Thank you for coming. We appreciate your input and we will update you regularly on our progress," Marsha said.

"Thank you for all your hard work, Agent O'Shea," the imam said, "I see that you have made substantial progress in the scant time you have been in our community."

There were no atta-girl praise coming from Washington. She didn't have her father or deceased brother to talk to about this case, the way she did at Sunday dinner back in Philly. Not that she needed praise for doing her job, but knowing the imam took a chance on helping her made his recognition sweet. She nodded her silent response to him.

Ramit walked them out to their car and returned. "I will have several college students working evenings on the data entry into the new system by the end of the week. They will need their own encrypted laptops, Marsha."

She nodded. "Ask the attorney if we can get twice as many. There is another project I have in mind."

They now had a template to follow. The brainstorming worked. Crowdsourcing with civilians was new to her, but they had admitted that they weren't knowledgeable of the turf or the culture and weren't afraid to ask for help.

The clock was ticking.

CHAPTER 20

THE HOUR and a half ride to downtown Lansing was pleasant. The tracks of suburban sprawl were replaced with farmland and undulating hills.

Driving away the rush hour traffic heading into Detroit and arriving at the state capitol just as the Michigan Vital Statistics office on Kalamazoo Street opened right on time for Ramit Ravikant, FBI Intelligence Analyst.

They ushered him through a maze of corridors to rooms containing the vital records. Introductions were made, and coffee or tea were offered and declined. When they settled in around a small conference table, he asked, "Can you sort by date of death?"

"How far back?" the office manager asked.

"1999," he replied.

"Yes," she answered.

"Will I be able to print out death certificates that far back?"

"It's a little cumbersome, but yes. We have so many family history genealogists, we needed to charge for copies.

The latest ones are digitized, but the older ones may be on microfilm."

"Can I filter by geography? I only need deaths in Detroit and the surrounding counties," he asked.

"That's about half of the population, you know," she said.

"I considered that might be an issue."

"The records can be sorted numerically by zip code, but not filtered."

"Can they be further sorted by gender?" He hoped to divide his search by half.

She posed him a quizzical look. "By gender?"

He nodded.

"I suppose so," she replied.

"We are looking for a woman that died in the last few decades in Metro Detroit around Labor Day. We were told that she died sometime after the school year started," he fibbed.

She showed him how to open the program. When he felt comfortable with the filtering by a date in 1999 and by female, he said, "Show me how to print."

From a few of the names on the printouts, he learned that the actual death records were digital.

He asked, "How much do I owe you?"

"Normally, we charge for each page." Pointing to the people in the lobby, she added, "We have Genealogists lined up outside the door every morning, we've never had an FBI Agent in here before."

"Thank you. Here is my card. Anytime someone does me a favor, I make sure that I can do so in kind," he said.

They exchanged cards with smiles, and they left Ramit to work the Vitals database on a read-only basis. He quickly shifted to last year and found Jamila's death as one of the

500 in the female subset for the exact date of September 11. Next, he sorted by zip code and reduced that number in half to the first three digits which included Detroit and the surrounding counties. It was worth it, as he only had to skim about 250 names for Muslim-sounding names.

That is when the fun really started. He had a population of about fifty deaths that he had to pull up and analyze. He printed any suicides or cause of deaths that mimicked how people perished that fateful day on the planes and in the twin towers. He texted Marsha:

Last year 9/11, round numbers, about 1,000 died in the state, half women, a quarter in our target area, a tenth with last names in our cohort. Guess how many by suicide or by 9/11 causes of death?

She answered: *Count them on one hand?*

Two. Jamila and an eighty-eight-year-old from Grosse Pointe who fell down the stairs in her home.

Hot damn! You are onto to something, my dear Watson. She texted back.

Watson?

It's a compliment. Explain later.

Going backward to 1999 to keep up the ruse, Ramit found candidates for every year except 2009. He would test them against what the funeral directors found. Marsha was meeting them that same day. She and Ramit would now have solid leads which will triple their caseload and give them almost all of Orr's killings.

Next he checked deaths for 2002 and 2009 on 9-12 and 9-13 with the thinking the victims somehow survived for a day or two more. He found one that was classified as a homicide in 2009. Amber was her first name and she perished in an arson fire. When he saw ones they knew about, they jumped off the page and that same intuitive feelings happened for the other years. He went over 2009 twice and was tempted to print off all the deaths for that year before he left the building, but felt strongly about the homicide.

They held the front doors open for Ramit right at closing time. *God forbid that a state agency serving the public would stay open a minute later.*

He had gotten through all the years, and if it wasn't for the photocopier running out of toner, he would have departed sooner. He was brain fried from scanning two decades worth of death certificates; separating the wheat from the chaff. As he drove back to Dearborn, he knew this day's effort was worth it.

With two-and-a-half months to go, they'd have to pick up their marathon pace. They were getting more inside help to assist with seat work and data input. He would have to handle some street interviews and official visits on his own.

Marsha promised that he would get more experience in this case than he would stuck on the intel desk back in Philly and she was right. She was relying on him more and more to shoulder a heavier load. His days were long, and he knew that his visits home would have to be less frequent. Put this puzzle together and catch a killer before he strikes again. He had to admit; the hunt excited him. Knowing that the next puzzle piece that he found might be the one that solved the case kept him focused on running quick, but not rushing.

Pulling into the driveway behind her Mustang, Ramit was elated to show her the death certificates and to ask her if she found anything for 2009.

Marsha had their worktable half-filled with death certificates sorted by year she had received that day and previously. "Put your findings on top of any I received," she said, "Use a marker to differentiate them from what we had and what I picked up today."

He noticed she was subdued. For all his excitement, he felt a letdown as he quietly laid down most of the years they didn't know about before today. He saw that he covered twice as many years as what she harvested from the funeral directors.

"That's good, Ramit. Your idea to go there was something we should have done from the start," she said.

"We didn't know then how hard it would be to find them," he replied. Not one to pry, he asked, "Is everything okay, Marsha?"

"Look at the table, Ramit, every death certificate is a woman who died solely because she was Muslim. None of them had to die that way. They were mothers, daughters, sisters, travel agents, teachers, Realtors, housewives, students...." Her voice trailed off. "That sick fuck destroyed how many families?"

They nearly filled the table with death certificates. The women ranged in age from eighteen to sixty-two. Ramit looked at names, the horrible way they died, and knew that it was not by disease, nor by catastrophe. It was the work of a single killer. A guy that had planned carefully to cover his tracks and was planning another grisly death this year. Standing there while Marsha quietly sipped a sweet tea, he wondered, *Are we going to stop him in time?*

She interrupted his worried concerns with, "The funeral directors gave me the personal identifiers for their next of kin on some of our probables. I have a slush pile over there of other deaths that day that didn't meet our criteria. Can you scan all of them in, just to be safe?"

"Sure, Marsha," he said.

"We have seen autopsy photos where the locals saw fit

to question the manner of death, but the funeral directors took their own photos of the bodies for identification purposes," she said as she handed him the stack of glossies.

He was about to open them, and she put her hand on the manila folder.

"Eat first. I couldn't after I left the meeting," she said.

CHAPTER 21

THE TWO WOMEN were clearly enjoying the late afternoon sunshine on their lawn chairs next to the playing field. Sean recognized them both immediately. Aisha had gotten a little heavier over the years, but Tamara looked to be her usual trim self. That both their kids would end up at the same private elementary school would not be uncommon, he figured. That both their oldest kids would be on the same travel soccer team did not seem coincidental at all. He found it humorous that one was spared the fate the other was to receive.

He used his binoculars sparingly, lest some nosey-body spotted him sitting in a tinted-window SUV peering at pre-teen boys practicing soccer drills. A couple box seats at the Tigers game and the ruse he was trying to recover a car before his boss at the dealership went bat shit was a pre-text he had yet to use. He could never be too cautious.

The years had trained him in all manners of skills that he never imagined when he graduated from high school. Each death presented him with new and exacting challenges. How could he be different and original, yet stick to his rules? He never printed his research on the public library computers using a simple incognito browser, given that the printers' cache could reproduce his macabre findings. William Russell was the name on his library card with a non-existent address in Detroit. He could spend hours in the stacks learning his craft from those that preceded him but somehow got caught. Most times than not, it was a dumb, stupid mistake and not ingenious police work that tripped them up.

He learned to never taunt the cops or take a souvenir from his victims. He was meticulous about minimizing the transfer of fiber, hair or DNA. There were nights when he dozed off listening to true crime podcasts. He had to laugh sometimes.

How many listeners were rooting for the bad guy NOT to get caught?

* * *

"Omar did a favor for the imam a couple of weeks ago," Tamara said.

"He needed some improvements at the mosque," Aisha asked.

"I wish. He came home that night and was pretty upset."

"What happened?"

"He met with an FBI agent at a woman's house in Detroit and they asked how he would collapse the house without making it obvious," Tamara said.

"Really," Aisha replied.

"The house was identical to a house that collapsed across the street years ago. There was a person who was killed in the house. She was a Realtor who was there to show it to a buyer," Tamara said.

"That's so sad,"

"What upset Omar was that the FBI thinks she was killed there and then the house was brought down on her, and what's worse, she was one of several women who died on the same day every year from suspicious causes. The killer's pattern is to make them look like accidents."

"I've never heard of that. Not even in the movies," Aisha said.

"He promised to do some excavation work to see if they can find any clues. The FBI will buy the property and have him dig out the basement."

"I hope they will pay him."

"Yes, they know it's his busy season," Tamara answered.

The boys were practicing corner kicks and Tamara's oldest, Omar Jr., headed the ball past Aisha's son's outstretched goalie gloves.

Tamara stood and cheered.

Aisha good-naturedly called it luck.

* * *

Practice was over, and the women collected their children. Both drove away in vehicles sold to them by Sean. The dealer's license plate frame was distinctive even at that distance. He followed Tamara as she drove to fetch her youngest at a play date and then on to her home where he noted the time of her arrival. Her husband was still working and would not come home until later that night.

Have to make hay while the sun shines.

* * *

"Hi, honey, I just received a call from Aisha. Her son plays on the same travel team as Omar. She had a question for me I didn't have the answer to. Do you remember when you told me about a meeting with the FBI in the basement of an old house," Tamara asked.

"I thought I told you that was private. That's sensitive information," he replied.

"I didn't realize that, but maybe it's a wise thing I told her about it," she answered.

"Why's that?" he asked.

"Was the day that woman and the other women died 9/11?"

"Yes. How would she know that?" he asked.

"Because she may have been one of them if not for a last-minute change of plans."

* * *

This isn't the first time she has thrown me a curveball, Sean thought. He followed Tamara to the Arab restaurant where she was then met by Omar. To his surprise, he watched as Aisha and her husband arrived in their car. Tamara and Omar never went out to eat on a weeknight. He didn't know that the couples were friendly with each other, just the women.

The parking at Sheeba's was tight alongside of their building and he didn't want to be seen by any of them when they left. He drove away and was almost hit by a red Mustang convertible with Pennsylvania plates pulling in too fast. A woman with blonde hair and a Starbucks cup in her face cut the turn too tight drove it.

Stupid bitch, he thought as he gave her the stink eye.

* * *

"What's that asshole looking at?" Marsha said to Ramit.

* * *

"Whoa, slow down, Aisha," Marsha said.

The hastily called meeting in the backroom of Sheeba's was crowded. Omar, Tamara, and Ramit were there as well. Aisha sat with her husband. She had the look that Marsha and Ramit came to recognize. It was that of reliving a tragedy while learning about the added twist that their loved one's death may not have been an accident or suicide.

Old feelings are dredged up again with the possibility of what they had been told was wrong and something worse had happened. The truth would not bring the victims back to life, but now it would reframe the deaths as being caused by more sinister means. Marsha realized the grieving for an accident differed from that of a homicide for which blame, vengeance, and justice is sought and many times denied.

Would we care about the world's first homicide if Cain said that Abel had fallen down a well instead? Marsha sighed.

They provided tea and sweets. They forgave Marsha her indiscretion of her triple ristretto iced with coconut milk in a Grande cup from Starbucks.

Omar had called Marsha. Marsha's living room would be the last place to bring the un-nerved woman. Seeing all the names on the board and a gaping hole for 2009 was the last thing Marsha needed Aisha to see. Just because she was alive didn't mean there was a happy ending to this story.

"My brother borrowed my van that afternoon to pick up some doors at Home Depot. He was doing some remodeling at his home and I got worried when he didn't call me." Aisha stopped in mid-memory of an event from over a decade ago. She had trouble collecting her thoughts.

No one filled the silence for a few minutes until Ramit gently prompted her with, "Please continue."

"The police found my registration in the glove compartment and sent an officer to my door."

"Okay," Marsha added.

"My husband answered the door and asked them why they needed to speak to me."

"The policeman said that an accident involved my van and asked him if we knew who was driving it."

"I came to the door then and told the policeman it was my brother. That is when he said he was sorry that he had bad news; that my brother had died in an accident," Aisha continued, "I asked him how and he said that he veered off the road and down a steep embankment. The van was totaled."

"Is there more?" Marsha prodded.

"A few days later, another policeman came and asked me how the van was handling," she replied. "I told him it was running fine. I had owned it for several years and never had a problem."

Aisha's husband now spoke for the first time. "He showed us our maintenance records from the glove compartment and asked us about a bill from March and was that the last time anyone worked on the brakes. I told him yes."

"He asked me if I had any problems with stopping," Aisha piped up. "I told him I felt nothing different."

"He said that they couldn't inspect the brake lines closer, because they were so badly damaged in the accident, but he thought the brakes gave out," her husband said.

"That makes little sense," Omar said and then looked at Marsha for permission to ask it. "Did it make sense to you?"

Aisha shook her head and her husband answered, "No. The van was not old, we used it to run errands and take the kids to their activities. It was working just fine."

"We took care of it. We had all the work done at the Ford dealership where we bought it." Aisha added.

"It's where we buy our cars too," Tamara said.

Marsha was staring at the brother's death certificate one of the funeral directors had faxed to them. *Multiple internal injuries, blunt force trauma, accidental.* She then circled the word "dealership" on her notepad and put a question mark next to it to ask a direct question about it later.

"You think this accident was meant for you," Marsha stated.

"I had visited my aunt every Friday. She was in a nursing home in Auburn Hills. She has since passed. It was a lengthy drive on I-75. I did that every Friday. She liked me to comb her hair while we talked. She knew who I was and liked to reminisce about when she lived in Lebanon as a child. It made her feel happy. I didn't care how many times I heard the same stories repeatedly." Aisha sobbed. "My brother knew that was my schedule and offered to switch cars with me that day. He died so I that can live. I firmly believe that now."

A lengthy silence settled on the table before Ramit asked, "How long had you been visiting your aunt at that point?"

Aisha and her husband looked at each other while they did the mental calculations. She shrugged. "Two to three years. I wouldn't go if it was icy, or the roads were not plowed, but I went every Friday, I am sure of that."

And so was Robert Orr, Marsha thought.

The questioning continued with more open-ended questions. Direct clarification questions which arose from Aisha's original offering followed that. The conversation was recorded by Ramit and their hand-written notes would be scanned into the new system as well. They continued to talk over dinner after the others had departed. The homicide on September 12, 2009, now looked promising as a way to catch the 9/11 mass killer.

Mr. Orr was desperate.

CHAPTER 22

SEEING Aisha twice on the day he was surveilling Tamara brought him back to the day he had tampered with Aisha's brakes. It was the night before her regularly scheduled trip to Auburn Hills.

He knew the route like the back of his hand. Just for that day, many years ago, he planned to follow her using an F-150 pickup truck with the honey badger front bumper. He had "borrowed it" from a customer the previous weekend and had kept it hidden in a garage. He secured thick rubberized mats over the heavy chrome extended front bumper assembly for Plan B.

If the brakes didn't fail, he had selected several spots along the high-speed interstate to give her a little bump when the road curved between steep ravines. Should some do-gooder have witnessed it, they would call in the stolen truck and the cops would have to investigate a fatal hit-and-run. Technically, it would have still been considered accidental. He reasoned why would somebody just decide to ram another car off the road? He would get rid of the mats and torch the truck later if it came to that. So be it.

He had wanted Aisha to die in a crash. Nowadays, he couldn't wait for the time when the smart car technology came out and he would be able to commandeer a car electronically and steer the occupants to their death.

On that morning years ago, the sun had risen in blazing reds and oranges, having given way to a beautiful cloudless day. He had waited with an eyeball on her van in the driveway only to have seen a man pull up in a car and go through the unlocked front door of her home. Minutes later, he had exited her house and then had walked up to her minivan and unlocked it.

He had been parked down the street, but he could make out the man opening the sliding door of the Windstar on the other side and take out the back seats and set them on the front lawn.

To this day, he didn't know why he followed the van. Had it been it to see if the brakes failed? He wouldn't have risked bumping the van off the road with a man in it. That would have broken the rules. Sean had followed the man, as they had driven quickly to Home Depot several miles away.

Every time the minivan braked; the brake lights had turned on. The man had gone into the store and came out with a helper trailing him, dragging a sled full of interior doors. The van had sagged under the weight and Sean had been afraid that the driver would have maneuvered it more carefully. Instead, the man had driven the scant distance to the interstate, and the minivan had lumbered up to the speed limit. He did not return to Aisha's home and had been probably driving the van to a job site.

Sean had seen traffic slowing ahead. The minivan's brake lights had flickered, and he had watched as it began closing the distance with no sign of slowing down. Instinctually, he had gripped the steering wheel tighter with his gloved hands. The brake lights had not illuminated, and the minivan had quickly come up on top of all three lanes of stopped traffic. The minivan had swerved left, striking another work-van which had probably been the man's blind spot. Sean had stared intently as the minivan swerved right across the middle and right lanes and through the guardrail, just missing a car that had stopped in the breakdown lane. Aisha's heavily loaded minivan had tipped sideways on the steep grade and it had barrel-rolled down into the dry creek bed below.

The Ford Windstar had lain smoking upside down. First there had been wisps of flames from the engine compartment. He had watched as the flames began to spread. He recalled feeling bitter as that was supposed to be the fate for Aisha. Why had such an excellent plan been wasted on this anonymous guy?

People had stopped and gotten out of their cars with phones glued to their ears. They had walked about trying to acquire the mile markers. The struck work-van had pulled over, and the tradesman had walked back to where the twisted metal of the guardrail marked the impromptu exit of Aisha's vehicle.

Sean had stared in fascination as the minivan slowly had become engulfed in flames. He had a clean license plate on his stolen truck, so he hadn't minded lingering there. A trucker with a fire extinguisher had slip-slided down the slope and had tried directing the nozzle into the engine compartment. It had slowed down the spread of the flames only momentarily.

Another brave witness had tried to pull the unresponsive minivan's driver from the passenger compartment but had been unsuccessful. The trucker's extinguisher had emptied impotently as the flames had continued to spread.

Both would be rescuers had looked on helplessly. They had stepped back, fearing an explosion. Black smoke wafted upwards. The smell of burning oil and rubber had mixed with the sweet sickly release of steaming antifreeze. In the distance, coming towards them, Sean had heard the sound of sirens. His satisfaction that the plan had worked had been quickly replaced with dread. He had maneuvered around traffic, not wanting to get stuck there. He had cleared the scene; his racing thoughts had played out the options. He had wondered how he would he kill Aisha after another mouse had sprung his carefully laid out trap.

He remembered cursing and slamming his hands on the steering wheel. He had no Plan B, nor a back-up victim. Not since his first almost-bungled attempt in 2002 had he had such a setback. He had needed to hatch an alternative plan. He recalled returning the truck to his garage rented in the name of Theodore Williams. He had changed back into his regular clothes, backed out the dealer's loaner, pulled the truck in and returned to the dealership. He had waved hello to everyone in his cheery way and then had dove straight to his file with his prized customer list. He had twelve hours to select another victim and kill her.

He had gotten frantic as the day wore on. He had gone back to the garage and swapped vehicles and clothing again. It had been a unique vehicle, but he hadn't the time to remove the honey badger bumper assembly. He had home addresses and employers. His victim's credit applications supplied him with everything he needed. He had crisscrossed Dearborn, Dearborn Heights and West Detroit. Rule One: It had to happen before midnight on September 11. Rule Two: They had to die the same way people died back on 9/11. Rule Three: They had to be Muslim. Rule

Four: They had to be women. These rules were solid as commandments.

Who would die, how she would die, where she would die and what gear he needed to pull it off was still eluding him as afternoon had turned to evening. He had gotten frantic as the day had turned into night. The single women had not been at their residences. The married ones had been home with family — too many witnesses.

What about ones that had worked the evening shift? He had tried their cell phones from his burner phone. If he had been caught doing the deed with the list in his truck and their phone numbers on his burner, it would have given an overworked homicide cop something to play with.

The Tick-Tock Motel on the border of Dearborn in Detroit had been busy that Friday night. With free in-room movies and room rates as low as $39.99, it hadn't taken long to figure out who they had catered to. He had caught glimpses of Amber in the office. The parking lot of the double-decker motel had filled up quickly as the cheaters, who had to get home, had given way to the one-night stands. He had figured that business would have been brisk until after the bars had closed. Housekeeping had been long gone and was confirmed when he had seen her carry ice bags to the upstairs far corner stairwell.

Broken ice machine, imagine that.

He had to get close enough to see where the security cameras were pointed. Most likely they had one over the front desk pointing over the clerk's shoulder to catch both the person registering and the register. Her family-owned motel couldn't handle the front desk 24-7. There had been more of a threat of the lowly paid desk clerk pocketing cash, than of a stick-up.

What about guest security? Anything pointing out to

the parking lot? How about a camera shooting the length of the exterior walkways? He couldn't take a chance of showing his face. He had an idea, but needed to practice. He had only one shot at it and had less than two hours to pull it off.

Sweating nervously and smelling like gasoline, he had pulled up the entrance door right after a drunk couple staggered in. *Oh yes, they would have a hot time tonight,* he remembered chuckling to himself.

Using his over-sized pickup truck as a shield from the cameras, he had lit the rag stuffed in the smaller wine bottle to get it to catch fire, then he had thrown a brick through the office window like a football pass. He had followed it with the Molotov cocktail and immediately heaved the larger two-liter wine bottle of high-octane fuel through the gaping hole in the window. The fireball had blown out the rest of the broken window and the entrance doors for good measure as well.

The crossing traffic on Michigan Avenue at ten minutes before midnight had been light as he had made his way into the dilapidated neighborhood across the street. He had stayed away from the major roads and eventually had torched the truck and his football uniform in the interior courtyard of an abandoned factory, a brief walk from his garage where the dealership loaner had sat.

While he waited for the Fire Department to put out the flames of the truck and depart the scene, he realized that the gods divining such things as fate and coincidence had given Aisha a pass but rolled snake-eyes for Amber.

CHAPTER 23

"9-1-1 CALLERS AND CAD REPORTS?"

"Yes, Lieutenant Harris, I was told they kept those separate from the Detroit homicide case file," Marsha said, "Communications would have to download them."

"How far back?"

"We need September 11 into September 12, 2009," Ramit knew the dates from memory.

Harris gave a low whistle. "There's no disc in the case file?"

Both feds shook their heads.

"I can tell you we've changed systems after the Homeland Security grant back in 2015. We kept a few years back to 2013 on archives, but not that far back. I'm sorry."

Both of them looked down at their hands in their laps in the spacious comm-center conference room.

Marsha looked up at Lt. Harris and asked, "Can you tell us if any other agency has made a request of those files?"

It was Harris's turn to shake his head. "Wouldn't know before the changeover. There have been none since," he said, scanning the results of his query on a tableside PC.

They looked out the floor to ceiling glass panels on three sides facing out at a high-tech low-lighting bank of communications display panels and soundboards. Everything was now dispatched out of this fusion-center, they had been told. Above the display stations were dozens of flat screen monitors, each with eight separate camera feeds rotating real-time shots of Detroit intersections and areas of interest. Marsha nudged Ramit when one view of the planters from outside of the Federal Building flashed across the screen.

Ramit looked at Marsha, then Harris. "Who else gets these feeds real time?"

Harris stiffened. "What do you mean?"

"What didn't you understand?" Ramit was learning from Marsha, "Who else gets these feeds real time?"

"DHS."

Marsha chimed in, "Anybody else?"

"Nope. That's it," he said.

"What about all the social media posts to the PD on Facebook, Twitter, Pinterest, Instagram, email and text messages?" Marsha kept her pen hovering over her notebook.

"It takes a screen capture with every screen change," Harris said.

"I imagine the requested data is retrieved by time and date," Marsha said.

"Yes, but we can also do it by keyword search within the time and date parameters," the lieutenant replied.

"GEO tracking?"

"The Bureau should know the answer to the question," Harris said, "Anything else I can help you with?"

"No, sir. Thank you for your hospitality," Marsha said. She and Ramit stood, signaling the end of their meeting.

Harris stood. "Can I ask what this is all about?"

"We are looking into a homicide at a hot-sheets motel as a hate crime."

"Your requested date is so many years ago, why are you looking now?"

Marsha answered, "Didn't realize it might be a hate crime until the last couple of weeks."

They left him to go about his business and walked out into the brilliant sunshine of downtown Detroit. It was a glorious early summer noontime. Workers from the Comm Center and surrounding buildings were out on every available park bench, with others walking briskly in twos or threes in their multi-colored running shoes. It reminded Marsha of Independence Mall around the Liberty Bell.

Both had come back energized from a mini-vacation over the Fourth of July weekend, Ramit back home to Philly and Marsha with a visit to Clearwater, Florida to see the gang. Luckily, she stayed with Charlie Akers and Shira and stuck to the sweet tea. Seeing her adopted family and Joe DiNatale gave her a big boost, but it did stir up lots of feelings. Feelings that were buried while she was running and gunning fourteen hours a day without a break in Detroit. Joe and she had a magical night when she was a sorority sister and he was a fraternity pledge at a jock frat on the Penn State campus. Their lives got complicated after that, but the vibe was still there and it was strong.

It was not lost on Ramit either that in a few days they would be staring at a two-month countdown to the next killing. They were hoping this particular case would yield some clues. While they were away, Ramit's team assembled the previous week, made of college students on break, worked twelve-hour shifts to finish the input they had begun shortly after the meeting with the imam and the mosque's attorney. Marsha would announce a new project to run concurrent with the input.

The email to Grayson's encrypted account told him she was going to Detroit Homicide and would play it straight up. She would say the Bureau's involvement in this cold case of Amber's death at the Tick-Tock was a hate crime. She would not mention the others. She also mentioned her plan to search for Mr. Orr a little differently. Her friend, Shira, recovering from the gut-shot wounds at Charlie's house, called her idea the "long-way short-way."

To that point in the investigation, she had only once gotten a response to any of her email status reports; it was a question mark and an attachment of the AMEX bill with a few transactions circled.

The Bureau was a Bureaucracy after all. Some bean counter had to be having a hissy-fit over some of my charges, Marsha thought.

Today, she had needed to see what the cops had. The file was thicker than she expected. The original detectives and responding officers had retired or left the PD, ditto for the FD's arson investigator. All three occupants of the motel office, Amber and the unlucky couple looking to hook up, died in the fireball. The motel register was totally destroyed, and since most of the guests paid by cash, there were no credit card registrants. The security camera monitoring system in the back room melted from the heat, so video of the check-ins or their cars went up like smoke. The parking lot of the Tick-Tock was nearly deserted by the time the first responding fire trucks arrived.

Try explaining to your betrothed why you were a witness to a fatal fire at a no-tell motel.

The cold case investigator was more interested in what Marsha had. She played it clean. Firebombing had always caught the interest of the Bureau when it came to racial, religious or political motivations she told him. Interestingly, the gas chromatography done at the scene matched the gasoline used to torch a stolen Ford pickup truck with a fancy bumper. They found it set ablaze a few hours later. The truck was clean of prints or DNA except for that of the original owner. A witness, who stuck around the scene, described the truck by its unique front bumper as pulling out of the parking lot; however, the driver of the truck was back-lit by the flames shooting out of the motel.

The one-page ho-hum auto-theft report was appended to the homicide file. Thankfully, it included a short narrative from the victim of his twenty-four hours prior to the loss. In recent years, responding officers making auto theft reports had been taught that many thefts were owner give-ups. That was especially true in 2008 and 2009 when the housing collapse sent America into its worst recession since the Great Depression. Ramit would get the insurance claim file, if it still existed.

* * *

"We chased our tails for two years on that case," retired homicide investigator Lester McNulty said in reply to Marsha's opening. "We never gave a hate crime motive a thought." He sopped up his eggs with a piece of rye toast. She had promised to buy him lunch.

"Why not?" Marsha was working on her hot pastrami on rye.

"Look around the area where it happened, you can't swing a cat without hitting an *A-rab*. They run most of the small businesses in that part of town. Hell, they just about run Dearborn Heights. Besides, we had enough motive from the husband of the woman who died and the wife of the man that died to give them a hard stare. Both lawyered up pretty quick, and it took some doing, but they both came in for polygraphs and passed them." He stabbed the tater tots with a nonchalant practice, before they disappeared into his mouth.

"Who else were in your sights? After all, the firebombing was meant to kill people," Marsha prodded, pointing a sweet potato fry at him.

"The motel had several long-term renters who had stopped paying. The courts said that because they had stayed long enough to be treated as tenants, they had to be legally evicted. The owners had taken turns cutting off the electricity or water, so there was no love there. Legal aid attorneys got injunctions against the motel, turning the water and electricity back on until the evictions took place. When that happened, the owners were angry with squatters sitting there stinking up the place. We suspected that they put nails in the squatters' car tires and tossed away anything sitting outside of their units. On the day of the evictions, our people had to stand by while the sheriffs literally dragged the squatters out. It made all the news outlets."

Marsha exchanged glances with Ramit. *You think the family coulda mentioned that to us when we talked with them?*

"That meant we had the squatters on our radar and also their supporters. They would have the payback motive, and if that wasn't enough, we had the truck fire connected to the murders by forensics. That was the getaway car witnesses saw leaving the scene. That took us down another rabbit hole of who had the means, motive and opportunity to steal the truck. You see what I mean? It was a cluster-fuck." He shrugged. "Now you want to bring in a hate crime motive? Good luck with that."

He folded his arms over his paunch in the booth at the diner he met them at. His gazes went up to the flat screen with the cable news and down to her pickle. "Are you going to eat that?"

Marsha turned her plate, and he flinched the kosher dill clean. "So, what happened? Who did you like for it?"

Lester munched and then sighed. "We ran down all the leads. I alibied each squatter. One was in lock-up, another was in the hospital. The third was staying with his sister on the other side of town, and their downstairs neighbors confirmed he was home all night. We worked with the intelligence unit to identify their most-vocal supporters and protesters. We ruled most of them out."

Ramit, working on his rice pudding, was first on the uptake. "Most?"

McNulty produced a weathered notebook. "These two squirrels lawyered up and we couldn't pin them down for the night in question. We were waiting for them to get jammed up for something else, then we'd see if a cellmate might hear something."

Ramit put his spoon down and set about copying the names down.

"Now that I think about it, you might have something, Agent O'Shea. You're coming at this from left field, but it might explain why my well went dry."

Marsha smiled. "My dad was a cop in Philly, he used the exact notebook." She reached over to touch it, and for the first time in a long time, it brought her back to pleasant memories of her father.

McNulty puffed his chest and smiled back. "I've got a four-drawer filing cabinet of them at home, all filed chronologically. My notebooks were proof of what I did, if I was ever questioned. My pension, those notebooks and a bunch of newspaper clippings is all I got left from the job."

"My dad said that a detective's notebook was sometimes more important than his gun."

"Tru' dat." McNulty nodded back.

"Lester, if I get lucky on this, I want you to be at the presser when credit is handed out. It sounds like you worked your ass off on this one."

"I'd like that, Agent O'Shea. I hated that this one got away. It had too many moving parts. Word came down from on high I had to get back on rotation and start taking fresh bodies. I played with it when I had time over the years. Before I pulled the pin, I made damn sure that the file was tight."

"Call me Marsha, Lester."

* * *

They drove in silence over to the truck theft victim's last known address, both mulling over the facts. This was the only time that Robert Orr made it obvious. Photos of the truck in the homicide file were taken from two oblique angles and of the interior.

The neighborhood was definitely working-class, but the lawns were kept up and there were no unregistered heaps resting on cinder blocks in the street. The American flag attached to the front portico post next to the ringer and mailbox looked like it was either new or brought in every night. The expanded cape was worn, but clean on the outside. The yard was freshly cut.

"Hello, Mr. Burns, I am Ramit Ravikant, I called earlier. This is my assistant, Special Agent Marsha O'Shea. May we come in?" They were taking turns now on who would take the lead.

The older man with the tubes in his nostrils and a caddy for his oxygen bottle nodded and they followed him in. The living room was a shrine to his days in the Marine Corps.

"Sorry, the place is not as tidy as when my wife was alive. The girl that comes in every other week can only do so much." He directed them to the couch, and he moved slowly over to his favorite recliner. He muted the TV but kept it on.

Ramit took out his iPad and brought up the photos of the truck tucked away in the homicide file. When Mr. Orr torched it, he made sure to saturate the interior before tossing the match. The seats were burnt down to the springs.

"Someone didn't want to get caught. The cops never showed me these pictures." He took his time swiping the screen. "They thought I had something to do with it. I loved that truck. It made me good money. Pissed to see it go like that. Lost money on it from insurance pay out too." He swiped back and forth and enlarged the interior shots.

"The fucking insurance company wouldn't pay me what it was worth and then they said the honey badger attachment was an add-on and was not covered. With them bastards for forty years and they dropped me like a hot potato after I fought them on it." Burns shook his head and handed the iPad back to Ramit. "You coulda roasted a few marshmallows with that fire, I reckon."

Ramit was quick to ask, "How much did you lose on it?"

"Had to be close to ten grand."

"Have any ideas who might have taken it," Ramit asked.

"My wife was a light sleeper before she passed. She

would have heard it start up. I had it parked right where your ride is sitting."

Ramit waited.

"Whoever they were, they had to be pretty strong. After they opened it up and got it in gear, they pushed it out into the street and started it down the hill."

Ramit waited, pen poised over his notebook.

"The cops figured that whoever moved it had a key. That's why they thought it was me."

Ramit wrote that down and looked up, nodding for Burns to continue.

"The insurance company had their investigators go over the truck and they worked me over pretty good too, as I recall."

Ramit cocked his head. "Why?"

"They said that whoever took it didn't jimmy the ignition. That whoever took it just jammed a big screwdriver in the key cylinder to make it look like somebody hot-wired it."

"Oh?"

"They found the ignition on the floor. Whoever clobbered it, made it unusable, and therefore me, as the only key holder, was their number one suspect."

"Oh, no!" Marsha chimed in for the first time verbally.

"I ran a couple of landscaping crews back then, mostly for banks and realty companies on short sales and repo properties. In the summer, I used the winch to pull stumps and bushes with deep roots, and in the winter, we would plow all night long. Like I said, I made money with that truck. I had all my maintenance records at the office, and I showed the cops and the insurance investigators that the week before I had got an oil change. Who the fuck would get an oil change for a truck that they would set on fire? Gimme a break."

"Show me what you mean," Ramit said as he handed back the iPad.

"This here is the winch and that there is the snowplow attachment. On the back I had a bumper hitch to tow the trailer with the mowers on it. See it here?"

Marsha and Ramit looked the front assembly closely.

Ramit nodded at what Marsha was thinking and she took the lead at that point.

"Mr. Burns, that is an expensive-looking front bumper assembly," she said.

He nodded.

"Looks strong too. Bet you could hit somebody with your front end, and it wouldn't slow you down a bit."

He smirked. "There were times when some asshole cut in front of me and I thought about how easy it would have been to shove them out of my way."

"Just like Aisha's mini-van," Ramit was surprised he said it aloud.

The old Marine looked confused. "What was that?"

"We think that somebody had a different purpose for stealing your truck, and when that plan didn't work, they used it for the motel firebombing and then covered their tracks by torching it," she said.

"No shit."

"No shit," she replied in turn.

* * *

During their travels earlier that summer, they discovered Masri Sweets in Dearborn, near to their rented house. With a late lunch straining their belts after talking to Lester McNulty, they opted instead to get their sugar fix before heading back to the ranch. The coffee was strong, and the sweets were addictive.

They huddled in the corner, lest anyone overhear their macabre conversation. To the casual observer, their conversation was obviously not of spring and autumn lovers, but more of co-workers with the notebooks and a laptop out on the table next to the goodies.

"A key was needed to steal the truck that Orr would use to bump off Aisha, literally. When her brother took her mini-van, he had to come up with another plan. He was desperate and settled on using high-octane fuel to kill Amber. He made it look like the truck's ignition was defeated, but only after he parked the truck in its final resting place," Marsha said, after swallowing down the gaibeh with nuts and before sampling the macaroon coconut.

Ramit was alternating between his petit fours and mini baraziks lined up on either side of his Chromebook. "How did Orr get the key?" Glancing at his notes. "He would be too careful to leave a vehicle where the truck was burnt in the factory courtyard. He would have had his car stashed somewhere nearby in walking distance."

"That's what we have to work on tomorrow. First thing, we will walk the area around the old factory and knock on doors. How is he getting house keys and car keys so easily? We have more than enough proof that our boy has a way of finding targets and copies of their keys."

"The keys are the key," Ramit agreed.

She told him about the DNA testing. The test results on the DNA on Nabila's house key came back. It matched the DNA on the back of the headrest on Nura's car. She had sent the results off to Stanfield and was waiting to see if Mr. Orr's DNA was ever taken in by a law enforcement agency.

"I'm getting a full tray of baklava for the kids back in the garage. Want anything to go?"

Ramit shook his head.

Marsha reached for her purse and walked up to the counter. The *A-rab* community, grinning over Lester's slant on the word, had found a suitable replacement for booze. The dopamine hit from the sugar flooding her system would tide her over until bedtime.

Three fingers of Jack Daniels would help with forgetting all the autopsy and funeral photos.

CHAPTER 24

SOME PEOPLE ARE HERE. Hurry back!

Ramit was on a doorstep talking to one neighbor of the old factory where the truck had been torched when he got the text.

"I've texted back twice now with no response. I can't bring up the camera feeds either. Something is going on," he said, while Marsha added more horsepower on the yellow light.

"Strange," Marsha said.

Traffic was light this morning in Dearborn and they pulled down their quiet residential street. Rounding the slight bend to their house, they came upon several tinted-out Chevy Suburbans parked wherever they felt like. There was a half-dozen black-clad ICE agents with crew-cuts and dark sunglasses going back and forth from the front door to the vans.

"Way too much testosterone for me this hour of the morning," she said as she jumped out of the Mustang like she was shot out a cannon.

"Wait a minute, lady, you can't go in there," one of the no-necks said.

"FBI, get out of my way." She flashed him her credentials.

Ramit, trailing Marsha by a good twenty feet, had his credentials out and waved them about like he was warding off Michigan mosquitos. The other ICE agents migrated towards them.

A different no-neck made the mistake of purposely blocking her as she went to move to the step leading to the front door. He extended his hands to both of her shoulders. "You—"

The speed and ferocity of the next move even surprised Marsha. Before she knew it, she had him down on the ground with his left arm twisted painfully behind his back. Ramit grabbed her credentials and stepped around the embarrassed DHS heavy-weight pinned to the ground.

"What part of FBI didn't you understand?" She pushed off of him and back pedaled through the open front door. A few shocked ICE agents who had been taking photos of their situation room stared as Marsha flew through the breezeway connecting the quaint Cape Cod to the garage.

"Hey, lady." A no-neck at the fire door leading to the garage was smart enough to sidestep the charging mama bear.

Leaping into the garage, which had been converted into a cramped workspace for the college students, she observed them all sitting on the concrete floor cross-legged with fearful expressions on their faces. A large white man in a tailored charcoal-gray suit was hovering over the student who had texted Ramit.

"And who the fuck are you?" Marsha was not taking prisoners.

When he stood to his full height, she guessed that he probably would have to duck under archways. He had to be twice her weight. He turned slowly to look at her. Ramit was behind her at the doorway with his arms braced against both sides, holding back the no-neck who wanted to have a rematch.

"Agent O'Shea, what kind of off-the-books operation are you running here?" The hardened eyes narrow into dots of anthracite coal.

She reached around his block of granite frame and reached gently for Said's elbow. "Come over here." To the others on the floor. "Get up and go sit in the living room. Don't say another word to these people."

They quickly scrambled to their feet and hustled from the room.

"Tell your jack-booted storm-troopers to get out of my house." She was now a step from his chest and just needed the tiniest provocation to send his testicles into his throat.

His jaw stiffened in the way bullies do when somebody stands up to them. He nosed up a whiff of his adversary and waved ever so imperceptibly to the raging bull and other no-necks to retreat.

"You don't know who you're addressing. I'm George Osterman, Department of Homeland Security Regional Director. I have jurisdiction here and you need to explain yourself, Agent O'Shea."

"You've got a warrant to be in here?"

"That young man, Said, was nice enough to invite us in," he smiled.

"Invite, my ass. Party's over. Get out!"

"Be careful, Agent O'Shea. Your local field office has not approved your little sideshow here."

Marsha had not moved an inch during this exchange

and she now slid to put herself between the table holding Said's laptop and Osterman. "I am not telling you again, pal. You need to leave. NOW."

He stood hovering over her and clenched his hands.

"In the next three seconds, one of us is going to jail and the other to the hospital. Do you want to walk with a limp for the rest of your life?" Marsha stared unblinking, hardened eyes through the back of his skull.

He slowly backed off. "You are crazy. Your brief experiment here, Agent O'Shea, will be over by the end of the day and I will have your badge."

"Think again, Georgie Boy."

He slowly turned, and then, for a second, turned back. In the battle of wits, he came unarmed. He couldn't come up with a witty retort and smiled the way bullies do when they knew that there would be a round two.

Marsha breathed and gave him his space. Ramit granted him a wide berth.

Ramit exhaled. "I don't think anyone has called him 'Georgie Boy' in quite some time."

"Somebody needs to bitch-slap that motherfucker," she replied with adrenaline coursing through her body. She looked about the garage. *Was this going to be our last day on this case?*

"I'll go check on the security system," Ramit said.

Said came back into the converted garage. "They said they were ICE, and that they were checking out IDs to make sure we weren't illegals or on some watch list."

Marsha could hear the rumble of the big-block Chevy engines come to life.

"They made us sit on the floor and began interrogating

us. It was awful, they treated us like we were criminals."

The last of the Suburbans faded off down the street.

"Did they hurt any of you?"

"No, I was lucky to text Ramit before the one goon grabbed my phone."

"Goon's an excellent word. I've got no love for them after today. Did you get your phone back?"

He nodded.

"Why don't you wait with the others?" Marsha lifted the garage door to the bright sunshine of a warm July morning. She breathed deep. She would lose them all if she didn't do something fast.

Ramit squinted at her frame, back lit by the dazzling daylight. "The system is up and running again. They just turned it off."

"We need to get a fresh one, I am sure it is feeding into that fusion center even now as we speak."

He nodded. They were at a crossroads. "What's next? Can he really shut us down?"

"No," she said, "Maybe a month ago, when we didn't know our ass from our elbow, but not now. There is no denying two decades of victims who just happen to be women of Muslim faith dying on the same date every year under suspicious circumstances in all the zip codes around here. If he would shut us down, it wouldn't have gone down like this. My boss would just call me in for a meeting and that would be that. This bozo isn't telling me what to do. He did this Gestapo crap to intimidate us and to get a free lookie-lookie at our operation."

They both stood in the driveway now and waved to neighbors who wondered what all the commotion was about.

"He can make it more difficult for us to get help from

the locals now. Between us calling Nabila's cartwheel from the overpass onto the interstate a murder and our visit to the Fusion center yesterday using the words 'hate crime,' it got him really nervous. A call to our best friend Callahan at the field office probably is what set him off. He had to see for himself what we were up to. Damn, I wish he didn't see the big board though."

They made their way back into the living room where the eight students sat expectantly on couches and dinette chairs. The coach had to give the team a great half-time pep talk, or she would lose them and all the momentum they had built up.

"When you guys woke up this morning, did you have any idea how exciting today would be?" Marsha chuckled and it broke some tension. "If any of you had any questions about the importance of our work before today, do you still feel that way now?" She looked around. They all shook their heads no. "Their visit today told me that we are onto something. We have to double down now."

She regretted not telling Ramit before this moment, but she hoped that he would forgive her. The way they ran the case had been a collaboration from their first day driving out from Philadelphia, two months earlier. Now she had to take the lead, or she would lose her entire team. She had talked about the novel idea with Charlie and Shira back in Clearwater and hadn't run it by Ramit yet.

"You have worked hard, with minimal direction, bringing all the data into *CaseSoft*. We will grow the investigation as we fill in more of the blanks." Looking at the big board, she said, "You can see the blanks yourself. We have to keep attacking each individual case hoping it will lead us to the killer.

"The software will uncover additional leads that

aren't obvious to us. It will help us see the forest from the trees. But we have reached the point that we are caught up and it doesn't seem like you will have enough work as we enter each of the remaining cases, a little at a time. So, this is an excellent time to ask." She looked at them and continued, "Before I tell you what we will tackle next, is there anybody that wants to say adios, goodbye, au revoir?"

Farah, perhaps the quietest and most introverted of the group, said, "Are those guys going to go after us?"

"No, we will close the garage operation down. It will make it look like we disbanded your group."

Ramit started to say something, but held off when Marsha gave him the *follow my lead* look.

"You will be able to work remotely on this phase of the project while Ramit and I pound out the street work," she said.

Hakim, who could have been Ramit's younger brother, spoke next. "What are you proposing, Agent O'Shea?"

"Call me Marsha, Hakim." Looking at them all she asked, "What if we burn the candle from both ends between now and when you all have to go back to school a month from now?" She had their attention. "We are grinding away on twenty-something unsolved murders by one serial killer. One killer that plans meticulously every year. We will work each case until we exhaust every lead. We have his DNA now."

She got their attention with that one. Marsha took a calculated risk of letting it slip about a sensitive piece of evidence. "We have seen him develop after Aisha was spared the fate of her brother and Amber paid for it later that night. He has access to car keys and house keys and knows the victim's routines better than we know each other's." She looked around at them. She had their rapt attention.

"What is driving this guy to brutally murder your female neighbors, friends and members of area mosques? It's too easy to say that he is just a sicko." She nodded to herself and wound up for the final arguments. "There are cold, snowy days in December and January when he is selecting his targets. He has to test out his ideas somewhere before he executes them. He's not gonna wait until the fall to see if something will work. How do you pull down a house with nobody knowing what you're up to? How do you know how to rig a gas stove so that it blows up an apartment building? Every day this guy wakes up with one overriding goal: how does he arrange a death in the second week of September to make it look like an accident or a suicide? He lives for this. He's a murderer for sure, but our expert, Myles Hanski, says he is highly organized and has a job where he is probably good at what he does. He has probably never been in the criminal justice system."

She continued, "Myles said that like most sociopaths, he can compartmentalize and be laser-focused when he needs to be. We doubt that he was doing any of this before 9/11. We don't think he pulled the wings off of flies or abused puppies as a kid. Something happened that day that sent him over the edge. It was that something that got him started murdering the victims and innocent bystanders every year. Mike Hollins, the visiting detective from Philly, said that if we found the motive, we would find our killer. We have to question who would have the most motive to seek revenge. What made him want to take it out on people here in Detroit as payback?"

Looking at Ramit. "I haven't run this by you yet, but I didn't expect the Gestapo show today either. This had changed our plans. I hope you will agree with me here why we need to take on another approach."

To the others, she said, "I think that we have to look at this problem from two angles. We will continue to pound on the unsolved murders and hope that he made a mistake or that a pattern emerges, but we need to speed up our search for the suspect by other means.

"Who is in our pool of suspects? Our DNA match says he is Caucasian and from either Western Europe or the UK. We know he calls himself Robert Orr. We went back to the convenience store owner where he bought the burner phone to use when he placed the calls to the Realtor. The store owner said that he only sold a couple of phones to white guys. Nothing stood out about the white guys that came in for the phones."

Ramit, who conducted the follow-up interview, interjected, "It was ten years ago and how was he supposed to remember a regular customer?" He left the question hang.

Marsha pressed on. "This all brings me back to the motive. I want you all to consider a question. What if the killer lost a loved one in 9/11 and now is committing a revenge killing every year?" She looked at Ramit and then the others. "I know what you are asking me. There were nearly 3,000 deaths that day. We will need to identify their closest living relatives *and* narrow our pool of suspects. The list is in the public domain. So are their obituaries. First, we will run the victims to see who had ties to Detroit and then we run their survivors through social media and decide which average-looking Caucasian males we want to consider."

"Three thousand." Said shook his head.

"Three thousand," Marsha said.

The daunting task seemed like climbing Mt. Everest at

first, but the more they talked amongst themselves, the more they realized it could be done. This was an industrious bunch, and this case motivated them, Marsha realized as she stood back and let them volley the mechanics of how to do with Ramit.

Farah interrupted the brainstorming. "If you don't mind, I would rather continue inputting your findings from your fieldwork. I don't think I can handle reading obituaries every day of people who died that day."

Ramit looked at Marsha and shrugged. "We've got plenty of daylight to work the field leads and could use her help with *feeding the beast*."

"Okay, Farah, that works," Marsha said. Key stroking data into their case management system had earned that moniker, *feeding the beast,* from the entire group.

"Grab your laptops and split up the names. Everybody can work remotely. Farah, you can work here still, if you want." Marsha clapped her hands. "We are back in business."

Back in the car, Marsha told Ramit, "We need to put in a panic button for her, just in case."

"Tru' dat," he replied.

They rode in silence until they were off their street. She felt the ICE raid only made their collective work more important. A community tired of being harassed for something terrible that they had absolutely zero to do with was taking action righting the wrongs that no one seemed interested in correcting until she and Ramit moseyed into town.

CHAPTER 25

"THANK you for following my lead back there, Ramit," she said.

"I wasn't sure what you would say to them, but I trusted you," he replied.

"You've always had my back. That means a lot to me, pardner." Marsha kept her shaded eyes on the road but conveyed the sentiment with a fist bump. "Me and you against ICE and DHS, we would have kicked some butt, I'm telling you."

"Do you really think the killer is a relative of somebody that died that day?"

Ramit was back to business and wasn't holding a grudge, Marsha noted. She was driving them to where they were canvassing when they got the text from Said.

"Hanski is leaning that way, but I wasn't too sure until we got all the death certificates from State Vitals. Two decades of killings in the same manner the victims died on 9/11 got my attention. I reasoned that he was thinking to himself: *You killed someone I cared for — fill in the blank — I am going to kill one of yours*. He couldn't travel to the

Middle East, so he did the next best thing. It started out as revenge, now we know different."

"What are you saying?"

"Myles gave me a couple reasons he thought that is the case. Our boy is committing the crimes only one day a year and tries deliberately to mimic how people died that terrible day. It takes careful planning in the selection of the targets and knowing their schedules for the day of the week that 9/11 falls on. Then, he has to make the deaths look accidental or suicidal within reason, taking into account the victims' daily routine. This is a ton of work. Surveillance, stealing cars and trucks, getting house keys somehow, doing dry runs on how he makes it look like a suicide or an accidental death like the original victims. Myles thinks he has morphed from a revenge killer to someone who is enjoying it."

"Holy shit."

"Those were my exact words when he told me that," Marsha said.

"Why is he killing women only, all the hijackers and planners were men?"

"An eye for an eye, a tooth for a tooth. You kill mine; I kill yours, or maybe it's a control thing or a domination thing," she said. "We thought that he was killing only women to make it look like a serial killer at work, but then he was selecting only Muslim women, that changed the profile. If this was happening in Saudi Arabia or one of the neighboring countries, that wouldn't stick out, but in the good old U S of A, it sticks out like a sore thumb." She sighed. "Killing women is the stuff that they make serial killer movies of, but adding in the religious component changed the whole profile, made it more of a hate crime. We won't know until we find him, Ramit."

"Any thought of filtering the search to just female victims?"

"No, I figured we'd have the kids for about a month, better to get all the victims entered. We can always sort by gender later."

Ramit said, "I'll text Said about creating a gender column. Anything else?"

"No. Let's see what the first pass looks like. They may come up with ideas themselves as the spreadsheet grows."

Add a gender column for the victims and if you guys think about any additional columns besides their last name, first name, full addresses, zip codes and their family's names, let us know. Ramit texted.

They were back in the area of the abandoned factory where the pickup was torched on the same night that Amber died in the motel fire. They were reminded that forensics showed the same gasoline was used in both fires. Both Marsha and Ramit had photos of the F-150 with the special front attachment. They then split up and returned to canvassing the neighbors.

"Do you remember seeing this truck in the neighborhood about ten years ago? It's kind of unique," she asked.

"Ten years ago? I can't remember what I had for breakfast, honey," the retiree said.

"I didn't live here ten years ago, I am just renting," a nervous, youthful woman with a baby on her hip told Ramit.

No one answered at many of the houses. It irritated Marsha those times when someone was home, but didn't answer the door. *Do I look like a bill collector or a process server for Christ's sake?*

This was a poor neighborhood. There was a smattering of abandoned houses, probably homes of the factory workers who disappeared when the factory shut down. Marsha would tickle the databases that night to locate residents who had lived on the street and weren't home at the time of their visits or had moved elsewhere.

She would text them a jpeg of the truck, after she established rapport.

They worked the first set of streets immediately surrounding the factory with negative results. There would be as many phone calls that night as persons who answered the door that day.

An interesting anomaly to these hungry door knockers from the City of Brotherly Love were the presence of Coney Island luncheonettes scattered around the area. They didn't have to drive far to find one. No server explained how Coney Island restaurants found their way out to Michigan. Each one was individually owned and bore only the name and signage. Marsha was tired from the morning's excitement with "Georgie Boy" whose nickname now stuck.

The BLT and soup with a sweet tea for Marsha, who slumped in the tattered booth across from Ramit, was her standby comfort food. He was working on a ham and Swiss on a roll with chips. Sipping from an energy drink he smuggled in, they weren't worried about getting called on the transgression, given the seediness of the joint.

"We know the truck was only stolen for about a week before he would use it to ram Aisha off the road. He had to keep it somewhere."

"He would have torched it either way," Ramit said.

"Not necessarily," Marsha said. "If he didn't have to bump her off, no pun intended, it would never have been connected to the 'accident.' With that tow package and winch, he could have planned to save the truck for another day."

"That became moot when he went to Plan B with Amber. It got burnt, no pun intended, when he used it at the motel," Ramit said.

The lunch did nothing for Marsha's energy. The adrenaline dump that morning was catching up to her. They had an afternoon of canvassing with a quick circle back to the "no answer houses" after dinner, but before it got dark. This edge of the eastern time zone gave them dusk and twilight on cloudless sunny days until after nine. She was staring at another six more hours of door-knocking unless they got lucky. *GOYAKOD, Marsha. You make your own luck by doing the work.* Charlie used to tell her. They would enjoy a delightful meal at Sheeba's, she promised Ramit.

The afternoon dragged on for Marsha like the morning. Confused looks, fear why someone from the FBI would knock on their door or persons peeking through raggedy curtains and refusing to answer the door continued unabated. Somewhere in the world it was four twenty, and with the Michigan marijuana laws firmly in place, many a door opened with a whoosh as powerful as a bong hit.

As the sun began its descent, people were now home and out and about on their driveways and porches. She would amble up to the residents, flash the badge and show them the pictures.

"This truck was used in a firebombing that killed a woman ten years ago, did you see it around the neighborhood back then? Look close and take a minute."

She had gotten the patter down to a science. She wrote the names of the people she talked with, noted the addresses, wrote down landlord names, wrote down names and telephone numbers of people that lived there but weren't home at that moment.

In the evening's gloaming, the dope smell and sounds of lovemaking now emanated at the same time from a few open windows. Did she linger a little longer until carnal delights reached their peak? God knows she didn't want to interrupt regular people doing what regular people do. She promised herself that she would get back in the game after this case was over. Her Tinder finger was getting itchy. She was being polite and not perverted she reminded herself while she waited for their climatic scene to end.

She left cards on mailboxes, screen doors and anywhere she could affix a card where the occupant would be sure to see it. Some cards left earlier in the day were getting responses and she talked to the callers while she traipsed across front yards, careful not to step in dog shit.

* * *

"Hello, sir, my name is Ramit Ravikant, I am with the FBI. A truck was set on fire in the factory over there ten years ago." Ramit pointed to the factory. "That truck had been used in murder the very same night."

"What did you say your name was," the elderly man asked through the screen door.

"Ramit Ravikant."

"What kind of name is that," the man tried to focus on his Ramit's face in the fading daylight.

"Indian, sir. Can I show you a photograph?"

"Hold on a sec." Turning his back to Ramit, the man yelled, "Edna." He yelled louder, "EDNA!" Then, "Turn down the TV." A pause. "Bring me my reading glasses."

Another pause. "BRING ME MY READING GLASSES!"

Turning back to Ramit, "Edna's a little hard of hearing, forgive me for shouting."

"Thank you, dear," the old man said to the owner of a frail arm that reached out to hand him his reading glasses, "She's hard of hearing and I can't see a damn thing without these. She's deaf and I'm blind. What a pair we make. Show me that photo, what did you say your name was?"

"Ramit."

"It's kinda dark, can you put a little light on it *RAY MEET*?"

Using his cell phone light app, he complied.

"Where you from?"

"FBI, sir."

"I'll be damned," the man who was nearly three times older than Ramit said.

Ramit reached for his magic pen and pressed record. "What's that?"

"Easiest money I ever made," he said.

"How's that?"

"A young fella said he needed a place to store some stuff. Offered to rent my garage for a year, gave me cash. Upfront. Edna and I had to give up driving automobiles years ago. I put an ad in the paper to rent my garage and he answered my ad."

"Okay, what else?"

"He only used it for about a month. I had to go in the garage one day. I used the back-door key to get Edna's pots for her herbs from the garden. She wanted to get them in our sunroom before the frost. She always did that after Labor Day. She was religious about that. Rosemary, Thyme,

Sage, Parsley, Chives. 'Get the pots out of the garage, Al,' she would tell me."

"And?"

"I went in there to get the pots and I saw this here enormous truck in there with that there front end." He stabbed a finger on the photo. "I snagged my sweater on it and almost fell down. Never forgot it. Then one day, I remember him taking it out. It had a rumble like a bigger truck, not a diesel though. I was edging the walkway and waved to him. He was a nice fella. Funny."

Ramit waited as the man collected his thoughts. He turned and looked across the street again. There was an empty lot backing up against the rear of the factory. The brick smokestack was bright in the setting sun while the green tree tops bordering the shuttered buildings settled into a fading magenta.

Mike had taught them not to jump in with a bunch of questions at times like these. Ten years of dust and cobwebs on the man's memory were slowly being whisked away.

The man continued, "Funny, he came back that afternoon and pulled his car out and then put the truck back in. He slammed the garage door down. I was pruning the bushes, and he didn't return my wave and drove off in a huff. Didn't think much about it until later that night."

"Please go on." Ramit and Marsha had watched Mike do that kind of open-ended questioning for three days and nights. Hollins explained why it was necessary to keep the witnesses in their memory banks and not answering silly-ass cop questions as he called them.

"Sometimes I get up in the middle of the night. Wide awake, can't go back to sleep and I heat up a cup of milk to help me get sleepy. That night I heard him hot footing up the driveway, and he was huffing and puffing. Pleasant night, cool breeze blowing in. He opened the garage door real quick and set it down. About then, I heard the sirens and looked out at the factory and could see the fire licking up into the sky and I smelled the smoke of burning rubber. Once you smell that kinda smoke you never forget it. You know what I mean, *Ray Meet?*"

"Never forget it," Ramit repeated.

"So, I can't see the fire trucks over there, but I can hear their radios squawking and I see their lights shining up on the smokestack. By the time they got it out and drove away, I was getting sleepy and went to bed. Heh, heh. I didn't put it together until now."

"What's that Mister...?"

"Kilvinski. Aloysius Kilvinski, call me Al."

"What's that, Al?"

"He was hiding his truck here so that he could burn it over there. The next day he was gone, and so was his other car. Never saw him again. He never asked me for any money back either. Like I said, easiest money I ever made."

Ramit took a breath and asked a direct question, "What was the young fella's name?"

"Theodore Williams, like the ballplayer, I'll never forget that. I might still have the receipt."

CHAPTER 26

"THIS IS A FALSE FLAG," Ramit said, "I'm sorry."

"Shit," Marsha agreed with the faster reader.

"Double shit," Ramit added.

They had gone right to 2002 to work on the death certificates Ramit secured from State Vitals. With twice as many cases to look at than they already had, it was now starting to feel like a sprint and not a marathon.

"Hoping that our boy made his rookie mistakes on this one. Were there any other ones that looked promising for that year," she asked.

"I might have jumped to conclusions on this one. I will go back and check again tomorrow more closely."

Staring the FBI team in the face were the facts of how Selma died in the fire. He was correct to pull the death certificate. It certainly met their criteria, but the Dearborn Fire Department reports spelled out the rest of the grisly details. They stood flipping pages on the trunk lid of her Mustang.

Selma's elderly father had fallen asleep with a cigarette while watching TV downstairs. Her mother and Selma had also perished in the fire that consumed their bungalow. The toxicology report ruled out the possibility of Mr. Orr drugging them all and then lighting up the old man. The arson report was impressive. The photos of the bodies *in situ* were not for the squeamish. The V pattern from the couch onto the drapes and up the stairs, combined with the absence of secondary burn locations or accelerants made a ghoulish and compelling conclusion that the old man's clothes and skin were part of the fire load.

Marsha again wondered when all these death scenes would come to haunt her in her dreams. *Here is another couple, just in case you haven't had enough for a lifetime, Marsha honey.* They didn't even have to pull the insurance claim file for this one. "This one is a duck." She concluded from the way it quacked and walked. They hopped in the car and headed off to the next death scene.

She glanced at her disappointed sidekick. Marsha was glad that he didn't grow an ego about having to defend himself for the actions that he took. Ramit hadn't caught the virus amongst coppers where they could never, ever, not even under the penalty of death, admit to making a mistake. It only took getting burnt on the witness stand once by a criminal defense attorney to mistake-proof one's testimony. It was a small leap to doing that on reports and then conversations with your supervisor and finally your co-workers or spouse.

Making up shit rather than just say that you could have been mistaken doesn't get taught at the academy but gets learned on the street very quickly. She was guilty herself at times of doing it, but not with Ramit and not on this case. She would not teach him that dirty habit. Marsha finally spoke, "Take Said with you and tell them that he is interning with us, in case we have to go back more than once."

He nodded. "Good idea."

They already had the mosque's attorney's paralegal doing tax assessor work and title abstracting. They could use all the help on essential lead running.

"Selma's death is not going on the big board," she lamented, "Damn, I wanted this one for 2002 bad. How he killed that year will be the key to this case, I just know it."

"I don't disagree with you," he said.

Cueing on the double negative, she asked, "Whatcha thinkin', mi amigo?"

"Maybe he didn't get his shit together in time for 2002 or lashed out on another day and then dialed in his first 9/11 for 2003?"

"All three are possible." She weighed the odds. "What triggered these two decades of death might not have surfaced right away."

"If you are right, he is avenging a loved one's death, then grief might have been his primary reaction."

Marsha said, "Yeah, but from the flight manifests, America learned pretty quickly who was responsible for all four planes going down. He could make the jump from the terrorists to his targets pretty quickly."

"Do we go back to Vitals and look from September of 2001 into September 12 or 13 of '02," he asked, already knowing the answer.

"Better pack a lunch for both of you," was her reply.

* * *

After the discussion with Aisha and the meeting with the FBI, Tamara and Omar talked more about his plan to help with the excavations, but she was still feeling unsettled.

"I am worried that the killer will find out that you were helping the FBI," she said.

He reached over to her in the dark of their bedroom and gave her a reassuring hug. "I dig out foundations for new homes all the time."

She rolled him on his back and with her long black hair framing both of their faces. She argued, "Omar, if the killer was smart enough to collapse the house with no one the wiser, then he would pay attention to someone working on the property where he did it."

Omar made a compromise. "When the time comes, I will use none of my trucks or my equipment and I will rent everything, okay?" He kissed her and let his kiss linger.

He would keep his promise when the time came, and it made her feel safer. She responded to his kiss and began rubbing against her muscular man.

Then another thought came to mind. She broke the kiss, smiled at him and raised up her nightie and with practiced hands shimmied him out of his boxer briefs. He responded to her surprise immediately, and that was how Tamara and Omar ended the spoken portion of their evening.

CHAPTER 27

THE SIGNED Riddell Lions football helmet drew the interest of many of the sports-savvy customers who sat in his office while he drew up the sales contracts for their new car or trucks. Next to it was a picture of Sean with a Muslim pro football player who signed it. He thought it was ironic that he used that exact helmet the year previous of the Lions drafting the rookie. It was a memento of his favorite 9/11 mission. That is what he called them now: his missions.

He had visited the Quickie-Mart on Telegraph Road many times where Khadija worked. They chatted while she filled the coffee pots. He even helped her carry the bulky cardboard boxes to the dumpster. Her husband worked the day shift and took care of inventory. He talked about the business and how well the car Sean sold them was performing.

Kadija handled the books and worked nights. Sean feigned a lotto habit. He studied how the dilapidated two-bay gas station had been converted into a convenience store. While she punched his favorite number in or boxed that number and processed his meager winnings, he studied the construction. He would take a handful of scratch-offs out to his car and pretend to work on them, watching where she sat when there were no customers in the store. This was a different mission for him, for sure. He would sit in his car for thirty minutes pretending to be on the phone while sipping their coffee left on the burners too long. She gave it to him for free sometimes, knowing that it would be poured down the slop sink.

On those warm summer nights, with his windows down and his Red Sox on the satellite radio, he enjoyed hiding in plain sight. There were no security cameras anywhere in the immediate area.

He watched as she sold cigarettes, lotto tickets and milk as loss leaders to get customers in to buy the other marked-up items. This was a store that had the old fashion pumps without the credit card machines selling non-brand gas at the lowest price in the Southfield. It forced the grumbling customers to come inside to pay cash before or retrieve their credit card to finish their purchases. Best of all for Sean on those evenings, there were no cops pulling into the store.

There was no test drive for this plan. That's when he decided to don a full football uniform with all the padding and rib protectors. Instead of cleats, he broke in a pair of steel-shank and steeled-toed boots.

As summer faded, he located an old customer's truck. *Due for replacement anyway*, he reasoned. He reached under the fender where the customer kept a spare set of keys in a magnetic box. Sean chuckled to himself for he had given the customer the key box and a spare key on one of his oil changes and showed him where to hide it a decade ago. He drove the truck from the cul-de-sac where the customer lived and secreted it on the back lot of the Ford dealership with a "borrowed" plate. The lot inventory that he volunteered to do that month didn't include this special vehicle. It would be the last place anyone would look for a stolen Ford truck.

On the morning of the eleventh, he drove his rental to a location a couple of daytime businesses south of the Mart which was situated on the western side of southbound Telegraph Road. He waited for the bus that arrived a few minutes later. Two transfers and a quarter-mile walk, he found himself back at the dealership working a full day. He waited till the other daytime employees went home and he grabbed the truck and drove past the Mart, confirming that she was working alone, as usual. Retail Loss Prevention bulletins warned against this practice as it made the lone shopkeepers prone to stick-ups or worse. Having two workers on premises from opening to closing greatly reduced this threat.

He enjoyed a nice sit-down meal at a nearby restaurant and watched as the local police took their evening meal. He knew them by name since he had struck up conversations with them at the register on previous occasions. He even took in a James Bond movie, which pumped him up for what he had planned. All that daredevil driving, crashes and explosions by stuntmen under controlled conditions was exciting, but not as exciting as what he planned. He had wondered what it would be like to do it live with no extra takes.

He used his burner phone and a high-pitched voice to call in a hoax home invasion, even supplying the make, model and marker plate of a teenager's car parked on the street of a wealthy family on the other side of town.

Then he saw Khadija turn off the exterior lights illuminating the pumps and parking lot. He knew that he had to time it so that southbound traffic got the red light a quarter mile before the store. It would give him thirty seconds of time to do the deed and make his escape. He had timed the lights before, and when it was time, he put on his shoulder pads and uniform jersey.

Sean donned his helmet and cruised down Telegraph Road. There were a few variables that would cause him to abort the mission. If he saw any northbound traffic, especially cops or fire trucks, he'd keep on cruising by and make another loop.

He hit the darkened, empty lot at thirty miles per hour. It was a go. He turned the truck's lights off. He had the angle planned out from many three in the morning test runs.

At ten forty-five, he didn't swerve away that night, instead he pressed his foot on the accelerator to the floor and aimed directly at Khadija counting money at the register. The glass doors and aluminum frame exploded in a shower of glass. The truck and counter made of Formica and pressboard propelled her backwards where she crumpled against the steel reinforced brick side wall.

Sean had disconnected the airbag, so that it wouldn't go off in his face. The truck's windshield cracked, but didn't shatter. He had planned for with the helmet's visor blocking any glass shards. The pickup's front end buckled and both doors hinges were turned inwards by the fenders crumpling back. Soda bottles hissed, dollar bills and lotto tickets settled to the ground around the truck.

Once the seat belt relaxed, he released it and threw the keys on the floor where he had deposited a couple empty six-packs to make it look like it was a drunk's pickup that rammed the store. None of his DNA or fingerprints were on the cans. He crawled out the back window into the truck bed. The store's roof hadn't collapsed, and he jumped to the debris on the floor of the shop. The lotto machine was beeping a distress call, lights flickered. Broken-open cigarette packs and busted Mountain Dew bottles combined for a sickly-sweet smell.

One look at Khadija's slumped body confirmed she felt the full impact. His plan worked. He didn't need to swim into the debris and use the tire iron he carried to finish the mission. The pleasant conversations, the polite banter and his cheerful attitude all served him well. The time spent in the store verified its construction weaknesses and her work patterns. He had not spent as much time with any target before or since.

Dropping the tire iron with someone else's fingerprints and DNA, he turned and rushed out of the enclosure only to snag the side of his pants against the sharp edge of an aluminum girder protruding from the plaster wall. He backed up and pulled hard on the pant leg, leaving behind a bloody swatch. He remembered running like a halfback the several hundred yards behind the closed buildings to his rental. With labored breathing, he pulled off his boots and uniform. He threw them into a garbage bag and tossed on cargo shorts and a T-shirt. He had thrown away the bag in Detroit, but kept the helmet. The gash in his leg required just butterfly bandages and left with a nice scar to remember the night he was a stuntman.

CHAPTER 28

"WHADDYAMEAN I NEED A SUBPOENA?" Marsha acted incredulous with a palms up shrug.

"As I told you, it's an open investigation." The doughty records clerk at the Southfield Police Department dug in.

"But I am a Special Agent with the FBI."

"The Chief flagged this file a week ago. He said you might come in for it."

Marsha's jaw dropped. This was a new one for her. She glanced at Ramit and realized immediately that her buddy Georgie Osterman was behind this. *Damn it. Damn it to hell. I wished he never saw the big board.* She cleared her throat. "Is the detective working this *open* investigation available to speak with us?"

The clerk said curtly, "You need a subpoena."

Marsha and Ramit stood there like scolded schoolchildren. It was one thing to be told they couldn't see it because it was an open case, but it was another to be singled out a week before her request was even made. She looked around the records room and not one clerk lifted up their heads to make eye contact.

She said in a warm and pleasant voice, "I'm sure you are just following orders. I get that. When you go and blow the dust and cobwebs off this *open* case to put a note in it that the Federal Bureau of Investigation has fresh leads—" raising her voice for the room to hear, "—on the unsolved death of a woman brutally killed so long ago that, maybe, just maybe, you will think about the victim's kids who grew up without their mother."

"Anything else, Agent O'Shea?" the clerk said, reading off Marsha's business card from the other side of the protective glass.

Her mood was dark and cold like the soaking rains of the last two days. Marsha admitted to Ramit of being self-diagnosed with SADS. When the sun didn't shine, she was short and grumpy with him.

Luckily, they had stopped at the nearby library and had pulled the micro-fiche copy of the local newspaper articles of the hit and run at the Quickie-Mart on Telegraph Road. The photograph, grainy with time, showed the rear end and truck bed of the pickup sticking out the store. It was a weekly paper and a quick scan of the following month's publications didn't yield any further leads.

"Let's see if our good buddy pulled the same shit with the Fire Department," she said.

Five minutes later, she had her answer.

The Fire Chief's secretary buzzed with apprehension when she located the report number for the ambulance assist for September 11, 2005 at the store's address. "One second, please." She got up quickly and tapped on the Chief's door then silently slipped in.

Marsha shook her head at Ramit and blew exasperated breaths while they shifted their stances towards each other.

The Chief opened the door for his secretary to exit and

snuck a peek at the FBI team standing at her desk before shutting it quickly.

She sat down and quickly wrote on a writing pad. "This is the town's attorney's name and address. You can forward your request on letterhead to him." She pushed the paper across her desk without looking up.

"That's strange," Marsha said, "we usually have no problem accessing closed files."

"I-I don't know what to tell you," the Chief's secretary stammered.

Lowering her voice to a whisper and leaning in close, Marsha said, "I know what you can tell me. What did the note say in the computer about this case?"

The woman looked back into the FBI agent's eyes and said just as quietly, "Do not release, per chief's orders."

"Was that note generated about a week ago?"

After a quick calculation. "Five days ago."

Marsha nodded and mouthed a silent thank you.

They scampered to Ramit's van and got in. Ramit was about to say something, but Marsha held up a finger to her mouth. She then wrote a note on her pad and showed it to him. *Bet you a donut that they've bugged us and put a tracker on our vehicles.*

He arched his eyebrows in surprise and penned back, *I'm on it.*

They knew what to do without hesitating. Marsha punched in the country-western station on the radio and they began crowing and crooning along in purposely shitty harmony.

* * *

Back at the ranch, Ramit sat in front of the enormous screen and he brought up the Skype feed. Farah sat off to the side and stayed to eavesdrop with his permission. Khadija's widower Nabeel agreed to meet with them after midnight his time. His image filled the screen.

Ramit had learned from the present owner of the store that shortly after Khadija's death, he moved the family back to Bahrain and he was working in the government there. Farah had been responsible for digging his name out of the Ministry of Tourism blog and confirmed that with them in halting Arabic and English for the team.

Ramit pushed the record button and introduced himself.

"Hello, sir, thank you for meeting with me. My name is Ramit Ravikant. I am with the FBI and we are investigating the death of Khadija. First, I want to say how sorry I am for your loss. We tend to focus on the facts of the cases too much and forget how the families are affected by the loss of their loved ones."

"I left Detroit many years ago. I am remarried and have a growing family here. My children with Khadija and I miss their mother very much and we remember her not just on the day she died, but every day in our prayers."

Ramit added, "We know with talking to other families that lost their wives, mothers or daughter, we are opening old wounds and are changing forever the way they think how the victim's died."

"How is that?"

"It is because of what I am about to tell you, sir. We believe that Muslim women are targeted to be killed on the same day every year and that the killer is planning another one this coming September."

"The police didn't believe me when I told them that I

thought it was not an accident," Nabeel said, "They said it was a drunk driver in a stolen vehicle who did this."

"The killer is very careful to make it look like—" Ramit quickly changed his words not to say *like the people that died on 9/11* to "like it was an accident or a suicide."

"That is why Khadija was killed?"

"I'm afraid so," Ramit said.

"My wife was picked at random to die for what purpose?" The emotions and thoughts from so many years in the past were rushing out of his lips with no time to think about them.

"Not at random, Nabeel, but by extensive planning and surveillance."

"Who would drive like that? Why Khadija?"

"We think the killer crashed the truck on purpose to make it look like a hit and run.

"That's what I told the police when I watched the video," Nabeel said.

"What video?"

"We kept a hidden video camera pointed from the back of the store along the back wall to capture the counter. Sometimes my wife and I couldn't work the store, so we had my nephew watch the store. We noticed the days after he worked that the inventory was off and the register was short. One night we went in at closing and busted him. We kept it running 24-7 after that. We watched the entire thing happen. It was awful. The guy got out of his truck with a tire iron and dropped it before running off."

Ramit's adrenaline surged, finally a picture of Mr. Orr. "Can you describe him?"

"Don't you know what he looks like from the tape? The police took it."

"We have to go through the courts to get it," Ramit said truthfully, "Help us out here."

"He was wearing football uniform and helmet and he was wearing gloves."

"A football uniform makes sense. He was wearing it for protection from the collision," Ramit surmised.

"I told that to the cops," Nabeel cried in agreement.

"And?"

"They just said it was just a crazy drunk. It was a big beer day for my store. The Lions lost to the Packers that day at home. They always dressed up crazy for home games. You should have seen some costumes. They convinced me of that. It made sense at the time."

"You remembered all that?"

"Mr. Ravikant, can you tell me what you were doing four years earlier on the same date?"

Ramit wound the clock back to September 11, 2001. He could. "Yes, I see what you mean."

"Did you keep a copy of the tape?"

"It was the old VHS tapes, they promised to make me a copy, but they never made me one. Is that the way I want to remember my wife from a video of her being killed? I have other photos and memories, thank you very much."

Sometimes grief overcame the memory recall such that it shut down further recall. Ramit sensed that was about to happen and changed the subject. "Did they tell you what they found out about the truck and identity of the killer?"

"A while later, a detective told me the pickup was stolen, and the plate came from another truck. They were checking out fingerprints and DNA, but didn't have any leads. I couldn't bear to work at the store anymore and sold it to my brother. That same nephew works there now. He can steal all he wants for all I care."

Ramit followed up on his question marks noted on Nabeel's direct recall and then asked his checklist of questions. When he was done, he looked at Farah and Marsha, who had returned from working another lead and they both shook their heads that they couldn't think of other questions. "Is there anything that I forgot to ask you?"

Nabeel slumped as they usually did after reliving the horror of their loved one's demise. He shook his head no, but then stiffened up. "If you catch the bastard, can I have him alone for about ten minutes?"

"We will let you know when we catch him, Nabeel."

Ramit ended the recording and closed the Skype call on the attendee, who was sobbing.

"I'm glad we are taking turns being the bearer of dreadful news now," Marsha said. "Look at this."

Ramit stood up and stretched, then reached for Marsha's cell phone. The text read: *Call retired detective Chance Dakkinen at 313-555-1212. He cared about the case as much as you do.*

"The kid at the Quickie-Mart said a lady with the wide brim hat and sunglasses paid him ten bucks to send the text.

"Our Quickie-Mart?"

"Our Quickie-Mart."

* * *

She hesitated when he said he wanted to meet at Millers on Michigan Avenue. It triggered her to that first day in town when she thought about having one or two or ten. She promised Ramit she was the designated driver, and she even took her car.

It was a cop's bar in every sense of the word. A shuffleboard with sawdust, a dart board a few feet from a concave toe line on worn linoleum floors, photos of coppers long past end of watch, and framed sayings about onerous Supreme Court rulings that couldn't be repeated in polite society. The paneling was dark, the beer on tap, cheap and wall mounted screens played replays of English Premier League Soccer on mute.

"Nobody gave a shit about this case after I took my Sergeant stripes and finished my career out in patrol. Then out of the fucking blue, I get a call wanting me to come in last week and tell them where I left off on it," Chance said.

He still wore a crew cut from his days in the military before joining the department. He let the sideburns grow down on his ruddy cheeks though. He had worked his share of construction road details in his day and the skin cancer removal scars were as many as the wrinkles on his forehead.

"They warned me that some crazy FBI bitch would hunt me down — their words, not mine. I told them I was glad somebody wanted to work the case. It had stumped my sorry ass."

He worked his beer mug from hand to hand like a shuffleboard weight on the slick wooden table where they had hunkered down away from the jukebox.

"The detective who inherited the case last week was a snot-nosed rookie when I pulled the pin and I could tell he still didn't know his ass from a hole in the ground." Former Detective Dakkinen took a good throaty swallow. Ramit tipped the pitcher perfectly with a steady hand to produce the right amount of foam almost cresting over the top of the thirsty ex-cop's mug.

"So, I asked him if he knew how to work a VHS player and he gave me a strange look and asked me why. I repeated back to numb-nuts, 'Why? Because that's how you have to play the VHS tape of the truck playing demolition derby with the store.' And do you know what that sorry sack of shit said to me?"

"What VHS tape?" Marsha was feeling the former detective's anger as well. A double shot of cheap whiskey neat would have stoked her fire a little bit, but she settled on swirling her ginger ale with a straw and crunching ice like a pile driver instead.

"Fuckin' A. What VHS tape. He had the evidence box on the table and my initials were on the tag as the last person in it before that dickhead." Chance was foaming, figuratively, as his three-times-refilled mug.

"I grabbed the box from him, and he told me that I couldn't do that, and I asked him if he would put me in retired cops' jail. That's when I looked for the DNA and blood sample taken from the scene. 'Crazy Legs' Hirsch, that's what I called the pretend football player who escaped from the truck and jitterbugged from the store. He fled the scene, but not before leaving a souvenir that a sharp-eyed ambulance attendant working the gurney pointed out to me. Crazy Legs ripped his pants on some sharp metal and left it there for us. We bagged it and photographed it."

Now Dakkinen was frothing. "So, I asked the little twit who was about to shit, what the fuck happened to the DNA and blood sample, and do you know what the simpleton said?"

"What sample?" Marsha was seething along with Chance now. "You gotta be fucking kidding me."

"I kid you not, O'Shea. I wanted to pull the evidence room tapes and bitch-slap the evidence custodian. This crap doesn't happen on my watch, and then I remembered." He set his mug down, and like a light switch turning off, became eerily calm, almost serene.

"It was not on my watch. I retired. The good folks I

served and protected for twenty-seven years, four months and three days are paying me a pension for the rest of my goddamned life and I wasn't about to bust a blood vessel and go 10-42 and save them all that money that I slaved for. Even the photo is missing, but they didn't take the photo log. The photo was still listed on the photo log. I didn't tell shit for brains that I spotted that."

"If somebody walked into the Chief's office and told him it was a matter of national security, and that same someone held most of the purse strings for federal grants to all the law enforcement agencies around here, what would your old boss do?"

Marsha stared at Ramit, who just asked what she was thinking, and he said it with just as much cynicism as she would have phrased it. *Way to go, Ramit.*

Chance looked at them over his mug, drained it in a long swallow, belched and sadly shook his head. "What do you think?"

CHAPTER 29

IT WAS A SUNDAY MORNING. It was days like this Omar usually reserved for his family. Working with two masonry crews during the week and on a nearly finished house in Livonia, evenings and Saturdays was wearing on him. Barton Street in Detroit had all the trapping of a ghost town. Abandoned homes, weed-strewn roads and empty lots stretched in either direction as far as he could see on this foggy morning.

Firing up the rented Komatsu excavator, he slowly rolled it off the trailer and began digging through the debris of the burned-down single-family home. A team of private Origin & Cause experts standing by to inspect each bucketful of charred wood and putrid water. As the sun rose, the fog disappeared, and a sticky-hot end of the weekend was shaping up for those getting outside and doing things before the college kids went back to school the following week.

The summer was flying by, but he had promised the FBI agent and her associate that he would help them. They were paying him a premium. In his mind, he already had the money spent on upgrades for his new house that he would be able to enjoy for a lifetime. Besides, he figured that he would never get the chance to rent this monster toy again and today he would have fun with it.

He made debris piles around the caved in basement for the teams to sift through. They photographed each pile and pulled them apart with rakes and hoes, stopping only to look for things that seemed out of place for the type of construction of this particular model. By noon, when he took a break for lunch, he had dug out most of the basement. They had laddered down into it to scrape through the lowest level of debris in place.

Their dogs hit on several spots where the possibility of accelerants were found. It was amazing that after all these years, the telltale signs of gasoline or other flammable liquids would still be present. The locations were diagrammed and photographed. He munched on chips and his Subway foot-long with double meat and watched as they carefully filled containers, marked them and handed them out.

His lunch break was over about the time they hustled out of the basement and he then moved all the debris into a waiting hauler who carted it all to the dump. It would return later to capture all of what had been the house on Majestic where the Realtor had died.

He drove the excavator from the one property to the other. It was too soon to determine what evidence was gleaned from the first house as they repeated the process with the second. The scorching sun and humidity was making it difficult for everybody. He hoped that they would find what the killer had left behind when the house collapsed.

When Omar had removed the top layers of debris, the metallurgists scampered down the ladders while he and the arson experts and dogs sat under a shade tree. At 5 p.m., the lead expert called out and everyone ran to back edge of the basement.

Two intact I-beams were lifted out. Neither showed a single bolt sheared off. They had been cleanly removed from supporting the structure, just as Omar had predicted. Next, they produced two sets of 4x8s bolted together. Lastly, two tire jacks were unearthed. They found remnants of heavy rope knotted around the handles. They found the jacks closer to the rear basement Bilco door entrance.

They photographed this evidence in situ, diagrammed, and tagged it. They would dust them all for prints and scrapings would be taken for DNA. The arson team was particularly interested in the rope as a section of rope was found in the house's basement on Majestic. The rope could figuratively and literally tie the crimes scenes together, he was told.

The hauler who had come back to the scene looked at the jacks. "You don't buy these jacks at any auto parts store. They are sold to service stations. I can't tell you how many tires I rotated at my old man's garage back in the day. They are heavy-duty suckers."

"Jenga," said Ramit.

"Jenga?" Omar furrowed his brow at the word.

"Jenga," Marsha repeated.

* * *

"Agent O'Shea?"

She looked at her caller ID. *Dennis Horton, campus cop, Aaliyah.* "Hi, Dennis, what's up?"

"Today is your lucky day. I just finished talking to the 9-1-1 caller on our case."

Our case? Our case. Okay, I can use a little help here, she thought. "How'd you find him? We ran dry on that."

"After he graduated from college, he took a Peace Corp job in Kenya and liked it so much he stayed."

"You're in Kenya?"

"No. No, I kinda sorta put him in the system as a *BOLO* after we talked. I got a call at home about two in the morning from an arresting officer in Inkster. Our 9-1-1 caller got popped for a DWI last night. Seems he came home for his sister's wedding and drank too much at the reception."

Wonders never cease, help from the locals. "Wow, that's great, Dennis." Marsha's day was getting better and better. They were wrapping up the scene on Majestic and she said to him, "Hold on a second."

She walked over to Ramit and told him. "I've got Dennis from Aaliyah's case here. Dennis, I have you on speakerphone with Ramit." It was about that time that Omar fired up the excavator. "Hold on a second."

She signaled to Omar to cut the engine. "Go ahead, Dennis, you were saying."

"Yeah, because he doesn't have an American address, he's being held over till tomorrow for court. I went and talked to him at the jail after he sobered up. He vaguely remembered the incident. He said he had to hang up from leaving a message for his mother to make the 9-1-1 call. You are never gone believe this."

"What?"

"Listen to this." Then a scratchy call started from an original source. "*Somebody fell down the stairs. Call 9-1-1. I am going for help. Second Floor, hurry.*"

"Holy shit."

"Holy shit is right. I am standing with his mother now.

She is a friendly lady who doesn't understand how her answering machine on her home phone worked and never erased her son's messages, ever. Don't worry. I will send it to you in a minute."

Marsha's mind was racing. Finally, she was catching some breaks on this maddening case. "Did he remember what our guy looked like?"

Dennis said, "Not really, the usual Average White Guy description, but I think a sketch artist would be able to put something together. We've got a private artist we use sometimes. You want me to call her and see if she can meet us at the arraignment?"

"Yes, Dennis. We can pay her double her normal rate. Send me all the details. Let me know if we need a Plan B with someone with an Identi-Kit."

"No need, I do that for the Sheriff here. That's how I know this artist when we need to bring in a memory retrieval expert who can draw portrait quality in charcoal."

"You don't know how happy I am that you called, Dennis, and I am sorry for thinking that Ramit and I were alone in this. You had a murder case swept out from under you and you never forgot it. If you didn't keep your file and talk to us, we would never have his voice and a possible description. Bring your appetite to lunch tomorrow, Mr. Horton."

"Roger that."

Marsha walked over to Omar.

"Can I leave now?" he asked.

She surprised everyone in eyeshot and threw an enormous hug on him. "Thank you so much for all you did today, Omar. This is wonderful. It's just like you said it happened. He pulled the building down like a house of cards."

Embarrassed and blushing, he said, "You haven't seen my bill yet."

"Give my best to Tamara." She reached into her pocket and peeled off a fifty-dollar bill, stuffed it into his hand. "And take her out to dinner." It was the happiest Marsha had been in months.

Arson at one house, proof of the collapse at the death scene, Mr. Orr's voice and a possible physical description all added up to one thing. Sometimes you get lucky, but many times you make your own luck by working the cases hard.

After dinner and too much ice cream, she'd call Mike and Charlie. There was a time when she'd share these victories with her brother and father, but she talked to them now only in her dreams and nightmares.

CHAPTER 30

"TELL us what you've done, Said."

"Here's what we have, Ramit."

They were all on a first name basis now. Half the college kids would go away, while the others would attend local schools next week. Ramit could never agree with colleges starting before Labor Day, the unofficial end of summer. Said nodded to Farah, who lit up the gigantic screen.

"I put an infographic together to explain our method." He used the laser-pointer to move through them. "We took the list of all the 9/11 victims and sorted them by their familial connection to Michigan. We populated the list from their obituaries and created family trees. Then we sorted it by surviving male family members and ran them through the databases to create these 144 names. From that list we removed people who were too young and too old and those that died between then and last September 10, bring us down to seventy-two.

"Most of the Michiganders worked either in the

Pentagon or for Cantor Fitzgerald. They lost 685 employees working in the top five floors of one tower."

It dawned on the kids that a company got obliterated that day, as they read countless obits of the employees.

"By familial connection, what do you mean?" Ramit asked.

Farah shifted to the folder of obituaries and she displayed one. "The OCR scanner highlighted in yellow all towns mentioned."

Said explained, "They were either born or lived in Michigan."

"Did you attribute a state to every victim?"

"Yes, by birth or residency at the time, but not everyone had an obituary, so we had to cobble that data together with Open Source Intelligence — OSINT, for short. Farah handled those so we could keep moving on the bulk. We knew that we didn't want to have to data mine the list twice, so we took the time to filter and sort by many ways. Farah, sort by birthplace, then by sort by residence at the time, please."

She scrolled through them alphabetically by state from Alabama through Wyoming. The largest group was New York, of course, followed by Massachusetts where two of the planes departed from that fateful day. Seeing nearly three thousand names scrolled through twice was sobering for all in attendance. Ramit realized it was not the same as looking at autopsy photos, but for these kids, it made the events of 9/11, when some of them were babies or not even born yet, very real, very palpable.

The front door opened with a whoosh and Marsha strode in. "Good, I'm in time. Here is a composite of our killer." She pulled a copy from a Staples bag and tacked it on the wooden border of the big board. "He is late thirties-early forties now. He's of average height, a white guy with an average weight five years ago. He didn't dress like a college student, but more like a working adult taking night classes. It's too soon to call him a professional or white-collar worker."

She plugged the Bose radio into her phone and cranked the volume. "This is what he sounds like." The room was jolted by the decibel level, but she played it through, anyway.

Somebody fell down the stairs. Call 9-1-1. I am going for help. Second Floor, hurry.

She then lowered the volume to less than rock concert levels: *Somebody fell down the stairs. Call 9-1-1. I am going for help. Second Floor, hurry.*

And then she played it again at a normal level. Then, there was an ear-ringing silence, a long, electrified silence.

"Split up your list of names and give me a new list. Average White Guys in this age cohort."

They scrambled to their old seats at the folding tables in the garage and fired up their laptops.

Marsha said to Ramit and Farah, "We have the bastard's DNA, we know his voice, we have a composite of him, his profile is starting to take shape. We have three names for him, Orr, Russell and Williams and—"

She stood looking at all the work on the board and screens. Said was overheard giving out assignments in the garage.

"And?" Ramit didn't like the look on Marsha's face.

"Stanfield is not responding to my emails. He's gone dark on me. I am flying solo on a big decision."

"No, you're not." He startled her by raising his voice at her, probably for the first time of working together. "You are not the Lone Ranger. We are in this together, Kemosabe."

Farah remained a silence witness to their bond.

"Let's talk about why you want to go public with this to prevent another murder by scaring him off," he said as if reading her mind.

Marsha looked taken aback by his unwavering commitment to the mission and their partnership, not to mention the stern stare that Ramit was giving her. "With the composite, the voice and the DNA we might get fresh leads from the public. We might be able to solve this sucker and stop him in time. If you haven't noticed, we are running out of that precious commodity."

"You'd be bringing in the FBI field office, the State Police and the locals, you'd be off the hook," he retorted.

"Don't you give me the stink eye, Ramit," Marsha said, "I realize full well that it looks like the escape hatch, but if we don't go public, we might have the blood of another dead Muslim woman on our hands. Tell me that you want to sit down with another set of grieving family members. BUT this time YOU will have to explain to them how we didn't warn the public or scare him off."

Farah flinched with that volley.

"Or drive him underground until next year, or maybe the year after," Ramit fired back.

"I thought of that too," she said, jutting her chin in defiant agreement. "This isn't easy."

Ramit wasn't finished and kept hammering. "Maybe Stanfield is playing us like pawns on a chessboard. Did you think of that, Marsha?" and to Farah, "Stanfield is the number two guy in the FBI who is paying for all this." He waved his hands in a large overhead circle, but kept his eyes riveted on his senior teammate.

"Whaddyamean?" Marsha gave him a furrowed brow look.

"There is a reason we hadn't gone public before and involve anybody here," he answered.

"Which is?"

"Something above both our pay grades. Listen, Marsha, I don't pretend to know the answer. But if he didn't want something done about this, he could have just kept quiet on the illegal bugging. What's one death a year in the big picture, right?"

"Wow, that's harsh, Ramit," Farah spoke first.

"Yeah, I wasn't expecting that either." Marsha looked at him quizzically.

"Exactly, that's why he wanted us to solve the case and prevent it from happening again, while keeping his other options in play. Did you ever wonder why he didn't go public after the imam gave you the first three victims? It took the bugging off the board. You have a complainant, you have multiple victims, and you have a jacketed case."

"The easy answer is that a mass murderer with political motivations operating under the radar for two decades would be an embarrassment to everybody and would—" Marsha said.

He saw the light bulb going on. "That's right, Marsha, you look at America like your family stepped off the Mayflower. Some of us," glancing at Farah, "look at living here differently. If it came out that some nut case was offing Muslims, how long before the other nut cases declared it open season?"

Both women appeared stunned at the possibility of a parade of copycats.

"Yeah, that's just one reason we play the cards we are being dealt, right up until the last call," he said, "Besides, I think if we catch him, we might find out the real reason for the hush-hush."

"What's the other?"

"The other reason is a little more personal. You go rogue on this and your career will go down in flames. I don't want any part of it." He was getting through to her, he saw. "For now, I will work like a crazy man to catch this madman." Pointing at the composite.

Their eyes were on Marsha now. She looked at the big board, the spreadsheet of seventy-two names shimmering on the flat-screen display, the flurry of activity in the garage and Farah's unsettled countenance.

"We have three weeks to make the last call on that, Ramit. I promise you will have plenty of time to put on your parachute if it comes to that."

CHAPTER 31

HOW DOES he get their house keys and car keys so easily?

The print out in her hand pointed to that simple fact. Sixteen deaths had him using one or the other or both as part of his plan. They had been banging their heads on that question for weeks.

Marsha stared at the reports of Zaineb and Ghida killed in 2003 and 2004, respectively. The somber mood in the back room of Sheeba's took on that of a funeral home. This was becoming the place where Marsha and Ramit broke the news. The wait staff and owners moved about with all the hushed respect reserved inside funeral homes. Tonight, she was flying solo as Ramit and the team whittled down the list.

According to her family, Ghida had no business being in the tallest hotel in Troy, Michigan that day. Her car was left running in the parking lot with a handwritten suicide note. All it said was *I'm sorry*. It was her handwriting, they said.

They talked about her working full time, going to community college at nights and saving to go away to a four-year school the following semester. Her family had a spare set of keys and they were accounted for. Ghida had not complained about any skeevy, middle-aged white guys following her. She wore a hijab and extended scarf over modest clothing and attended a mosque in Detroit on the border with Dearborn. She didn't have time for any serious boyfriends and was content to work hard, study and save. It came as a shock to them, as it did to all the families, that their loved ones may have been stalked and killed.

Which was worse: thinking that they committed suicide or were murdered; thinking for years they committed suicide only to find out that it may be another manner of death; or something more sinister and horrific? Marsha mused as the families relived their grief all over again.

Per the police report, the hotel staff had no video of her arriving in the building or making her way onto the roof before plunging to her death. The cameras on the rear stairwell and doorway to the roof were not aimed properly. The responding officer noted. No one in maintenance gave it a second thought when they readjusted the cameras to properly cover the stairs and the unlocked roof entrance.

The autopsy report was easy to get as the blanket thrown over Detroit and Wayne County by DHS did not extend to Sheriff's Deputy Dennis Horton. Ghida's blood showed the presence of barbiturates, but not enough to kill her. He told the Medical Examiner's office that he had a suicide of another family member and wanted to put the two cases side-by side to see any similarities. They shrugged their shoulders at the man in uniform from the county and told him to knock himself out.

Treated as a straight up suicide, no mention was made of defensive wounds. With zero video of her coming into the building, it was assumed that she had not been checked in that day, but was a visitor of a guest who checked in over the weekend.

The police report obtained by Dennis included the initial autopsy summary, the toxicology supplement and photos of the car sitting in the parking lot all by its lonesome. The police officer was used to seeing cheater's cars in the back lots of hotels as the women and the men would make separate entrances and exits. The officer told the family that most likely she was having a secret affair with a married man, and when he jilted her, she took a plunge that Saturday night. They didn't believe it then and was now getting validation of their suspicions.

If it had not been for an "anonymous" guest saying that the car was still running in the parking lot, it could have been days before it was discovered, she gleaned from the last notes in the cop's report. That is where they found the suicide note.

If she was already in the hotel, why go back and leave the note in the car?

Marsha kicked around several ideas with Ramit and Dennis and decided that the earliest known victim was unconscious in the trunk of her own car. It was parked where there were no cameras. They hypothesized that a proper guest with an oversized rolling suitcase walked in, took an elevator to one of the top floors and make his way to the roof, opened the suitcase where her inert petite frame spilled out. He then hoisted her over the concrete half wall. They lost the records of guests from nearly two decades ago in digital antiquity, the hotel had told Dennis.

By the time first responders arrived, the killer could have been sitting in the hotel's hot tub with his favorite beverage. They batted the idea of him checking out Sunday morning with an empty oversized roller suitcase.

It wasn't as sophisticated as later killings, but it showed planning. Get into her apartment where she lived alone, surprise her, get her to write the note, drug her, drive her car to the hotel and make it look like a suicide with the leap and the note. It didn't have to be fancy. There was no crime scene investigation of the apartment or the car which was no longer on the road. Her body had been interred without a casket, and an autopsy would now be cruel and useless.

All the information would be entered by Farah into *CaseSoft*. The copies of the reports would be scanned and filed accordingly. It was becoming so routine now.

These were women, not just cases or statistics. Marsha only needed to look at the autopsy photos to remind herself of her mission.

* * *

Zaineb's husband had died several years previously and his obituary listed a daughter in Santa Clara, CA who worked in an acupuncture practice. She was clueless as to missing keys or stalkers. The team was denied the Medical Examiner's report and the Police Reconstruction report, but luckily, both were in the insurance claim file they obtained. The carrier was not digitizing old claim files, and it took a week to get the file out of archives, but when they did, it was a treasure trove of information. Not only did they have both the ME and PD reports, but they also had their own accident re-constructionist report complete with hard copy 8x10 glossies and hand-drawn measurements.

Marsha had gone to the scene with the expert, now since retired, and walked it with him.

Zaineb was belted in the driver's seat when other travelers came upon the smoking wreck. It was assumed that she apparently fell asleep after working the four to midnight shift at a 24-hour pharmacy. Instead of turning with the left curve in the road, she ran straight into a closed hardware store made of sturdy brick. The impact of the crash killed her it was determined.

The insurance company went along with the police that she may have mistakenly taken a night-time cold medicine and gotten drowsy and fell asleep at the wheel. A photograph of the half-empty bottle in the car was the proof they leaned on.

This woman was a Pharmacist for Christ's sake, Marsha screamed silently to herself. *How many people with colds or the flu did she counsel not to drive after taking that medicine?*

Asked to look at the findings again, but with the possibility that she may have been dead from a different blunt force trauma before she hit the brick wall at forty miles per hour, the retiree looked at the photos, walked the scene, re-measured his measurements. He said yes, that could be explained by the evidence. When her Ford jumped the curb at an angle, instead of veering left or right, it went straight into the store. Someone must have corrected the steering from the back seat with her dead body resting on the steering wheel.

"Start here. Lean a brick on the gas pedal, nudge the transmission into drive and hold her hands on the steering wheel and hunkered down in the back seat before impact." He had said also for the benefit of Marsha's pen recorder.

"But you know what that means?" he said. Before Marsha could reply, he answered his own question, "The insurance company would be off the hook. She was murdered, and she didn't die from the accident."

None of Charlie's accident recon experts could give her

a crash model for how a body reacts to an impact when its curled on the backseat floor in a car accident. They could put a crash dummy in the fetal position behind the driver's seat in an identical make and model and try to recreate it, but the consensus was that any idiot who tried that once, wouldn't do it again. Cutting brake lines and playing bumper cars would be smarter the next time you wanted to try that stunt. Everyone agreed.

The daughter, Rihanna, was told all this, thought for a long moment before speaking, "Who would do such a thing?"

Marsha pulled out the composite sketch for her. "This man."

"I was young at the time, but for some reason, I recognize him."

Marsha kept a poker face and said, "Take your time," while her heart leaped into her throat and her temples pounded.

With a racing heartbeat, she reached for her triple-iced ristretto with coconut milk that the friendly folks at Sheeba's overlooked. She pulled a long draw on the straw until she emptied the cup. Setting it down, she nonchalantly reached for a sweet as the out-of-town daughter searched her memory.

"Can I keep this?" She clutched it to her chest. "I want to mediate on it more when my mind isn't racing."

Marsha nodded, and her heart quickly sank to the pit of her stomach with a thud.

CHAPTER 32

WITHIN A FEW DAYS, Marsha was feeling the fury of DHS. Each of the local college students who assisted her were yanked out of classrooms by black-clad ICE agents and roughly questioned at the Rosa Parks Federal Building which sits across the Detroit River from Belle Isle Park. Around the country, similar stories were repeated with the rest of students who helped out.

Each one of Ramit's posse provided the name of the mosque's attorney and refused to say anything, reminding the crew-cuts with bulging biceps of the constitutional right to remain silent.

Once they were cut loose, Marsha and Ramit heard from each terrified student of the taunts and vague threats made during transport when the agents were out of earshot of any witnesses. She assured them that when Mr. Orr was captured, they would be able to tell their classmates about the case and what they did on their summer vacation.

The cable box outside of their rental was vandalized and the cable company promised repair times and dates and then failed to keep the appointments. They had to rely on their phones as hot spots to have an internet connection for their laptops. Finally, out of desperation, they paid for a year's service in advance and had a satellite dish installed on the next-door neighbor's house. They boosted the feed. By the time the neighbors returned from vacation, they would have a wonderful surprise with all the deluxe premium channels.

The emails to Grayson Stanfield piled up with no reply, Marsha began calling his office daily and leaving generic messages. Her last resort would be to send FedEx overnight letters. She was also bothered by the fact that after submitting the DNA results to Stanfield, she had received no word if the sample had matched the one taken at the scene of the convenience store crash. She would leave a trail of breadcrumbs, but as much as she was tempted to go public, she kept her promise to Ramit.

As long as she could use the American Express credit card Stanfield had given to her, she knew that she was still in business.

If the Bureau cut that off, they decided they would slink out of town and activate Plan B.

* * *

The mosque was a busy place on the Friday night of the Labor Day weekend. Given the flurry of calls to the mosque's attorney by the scared college kids, Marsha and Ramit felt the need to come in and provide an update. Since pointing Marsha in the right direction, the imam had remained mostly in the background, but the attorney who had been actively assisting the investigation was regretting his decision.

"Agent O'Shea, what do you make of the Homeland

Security interference in this matter?" The formality of the question from the imam reminded Marsha of the first time they sat at this conference table in the mosque.

"To be honest with you, I first thought that they didn't appreciate me operating outside of channels, but when evidence disappeared from an evidence room of a nearby police department, and the word went out not to cooperate with us, I suspected they had other motives," she said.

"Please continue," he replied.

"Now with the harassment of the students who assisted us, coupled with the bugging of our vehicles and residence, I considered more sinister reasons."

"Such as?"

"Such as, they didn't want us to find a mass murderer operating under the radar for two decades who targeted Muslim women. I still don't know which three-letter agencies was illegally bugging here after 9/11, but I am getting a clue. I now fully realize Ramit and I being in Detroit is bad for their status quo."

Marsha looked at the imam and the mosque's attorney with no guile or pretense. "It's easy to understand how we are working at cross purposes, when you think about it."

"You said it yourself, Marsha," the attorney spoke in more acquainted and friendlier terms across the table. He had been pitching in his support and guidance with her from their initial meetings right through to the present. "They didn't know exactly what you were doing, but when they raided your operation, knowing full well that you and Ramit were elsewhere, they could figure it out. Imagine them seeing the big board, as you call it, with all those names on it? They must have thought that they stumbled into a hornet's nest."

"They didn't like it for sure," Marsha said, "Here we

were running an operation without their knowledge or the blessing of our field office. It was too much for them to stomach. They couldn't control us overtly, so they played games with us and used the kids as pawns."

The imam listened quietly while the attorney spoke his mind. "By working this case without their authority, you were rubbing their nose in it. The DHS has grown exponentially since its creation and now they don't want to give any of it up. It is a bureaucracy, filled with bureaucrats, looking to maintain the propaganda campaign, stoking fear that terrorism of 9/11 magnitude would occur on our soil again."

Marsha took a deep breath and looked at the three men at the table and let it out slowly before speaking. "What it boils down to is a simple question. How can these two FBI representatives, acting outside of their normal chain of command, coddle a cultural group DHS so insidiously want to portray as the breeding ground for domestic terror?" Marsha raised her hands in a sign of surrender. "It's not like the FBI's hands were always clean here, either, given some highly questionable sting operations of the recent past."

Ramit then added, "I was clearly an outsider to this area, and after spending all this time interviewing grieving family members and others living here, I am shocked how easy it can be to marginalize a group. You have a hard-working, upwardly mobile community who fiercely exhibit all the values that America was built on, but they are portrayed as bad guys. Today it's Arab Americans, tomorrow who knows who is it going to be — Latinos, Pakistanis, Indians?"

"But they hold the power and have subverted your mission," the imam concluded. "Where do you stand with the investigation now with a little more than a week to go?"

He left it unspoken, but it was the 800-pound gorilla in the room.

"We have approached this investigation by uncovering every lead we can from each of the cases. We feel confident that we have identified every one except for 2002. We cannot find a suitable death certificate for that year that fits the profile. Speaking of profile, I have a call out to our profiler to get his last report.

"The original investigating detective on the convenience store hit and run tried to track down the submission of blood and DNA found at the scene to the state labs done back in 2005, as the results had been removed from the case file in the police evidence room. The state lab did not have the evidence or the report either. Someone got to them too," she said.

"That's outrageous." The mosque's attorney was visibly angry. "Hiding evidence in a homicide, why the cover up?"

"I suppose they did it to keep us from proving that the killer operated with impunity on their watch for two decades," she answered with a shrug. "We got lucky with a witness who saw the killer and we even have his voice and handwriting."

Ramit played the answering machine message back, while handing out two composite sketches, along with copies of his handwriting. He also provided them both with a thumb drive with everything on them.

"He has used three aliases. He had rented a garage from an elderly man who also verified the composite sketch as the likeness of the renter who used his garage to store the truck used in the firebombing of the motel. That is where we got his scrawled handwriting on a receipt. We are still pursuing leads but have also taken on a second prong to our inquiry." She nodded to Ramit to continue.

"After the students added all our findings from the killings into a better case management system, we had them run each victim from 9/11 to see what family ties they had to Michigan. We are looking at the profiler's suggestion that the killer was avenging the loss of a loved one. We whittled the list down to twelve males in the age cohort for the killer. In the past week, we could eliminate all but one," he said.

Marsha took over. "What makes the last one both a good and bad candidate is that his twin brother died in the Pentagon that day. After his brother's death, by all accounts, he unraveled, slowly developing depression and spun out of control into homelessness and the revolving door of the criminal justice system. He was never incarcerated during any Septembers. That fact kept him on our radar. We gave all the information we had about him to our profiler and we are looking to see if he's matches the profile. Age, weight, height and hair color all line up." Marsha then glumly added, "He is in the wind, however. No one has seen or heard from him for over a year. He fell off the radar completely. One second." Marsha recognized the caller and took the call.

"Hey, Marsha it's me, Dennis, I just wanted to give you the bad news. Some Department of Transportation workers were clearing out a drain culvert under an overpass in my county and came across a body. The on-scene ME said the body has been there for a long time, probably over a year or more from the decomposition. His backpack had his state-issued ID card, and they called me on the BOLO. It's the twin. Looks like we are back to square one."

"Shit," slipped out before she realized that she cursed in a holy place.

* * *

Back in the car, Marsha checked voice messages and returned the most important call first. "Yes, Mrs. Hanski, this is Agent Marsha O'Shea returning your call....Yes, I see....I am so sorry....No, I completely understand....Please, don't be sorry, you had so much on your plate...Yes, that will do....Priority mail is fine. Thank you for thinking of us.... Again, let me say I am so sorry for your loss."

Marsha stared out the window at the postcard sunset and then began banging her fist on the dashboard of the van. "When it rains, it fucking pours."

Ramit had learned to wait her out in situations like these.

"Myles Hanski is dead and his widow is sending us his hand-written notes. He went into the hospital two weeks ago with a massive stroke and didn't come out. He wasn't ignoring us Ramit, he was dying."

CHAPTER 33

THE DRIVE to Philadelphia was unusually quiet. Marsha and Ramit both notified the Philly office that they were taking a week's vacation after the holiday and that would bring them up to September 12. In their exhaustion, they talked about everything else in their lives that they didn't mind sharing with the unfriendly folks who bugged Marsha's mustang. The GPS tracker would show them retracing the same route they took three months earlier.

It was also important that they stopped thinking about the case. It had consumed their every waking moment for four months. Ramit had some respite on alternating weekends in May and June when he had gone home to see his girlfriend. When the case ballooned with all the death certificates uncovered at Vital Statistics, he had curtailed his visits to just the July Fourth weekend and again once in August.

Marsha had a little downtime during the marathon leading up to their drive back home. The urge to drink, which had been dampened by her workload and sugar, were coming back and she was tempted to call Charlie, but instead alternated between energy bars and sweet tea on the ride.

They had been going non-stop and just had to turn their brains off for twenty-four to forty-eight hours. Yes, the deadline was looming, but at this point, they just needed to press the reset button. Also, in agreeing to Plan B, Ramit would not be in Detroit when the shit hit the fan. He would work the case remotely from afar.

They had been standing too close to the leads, and the case stopped talking to them. The same questions kept whirling in their brains, and they just needed to stop that incessant chatter.

Traffic was light that evening, and they made it as far back as Clearfield, PA on Route 80 before pulling into a Hampton Inn after midnight where a couple of "heavenly beds" in adjoining rooms awaited them.

The following morning after a hearty breakfast, they made their way the final five hours to West Philly where Ramit kept his apartment. Marsha watched as he fell into the waiting arms of his girlfriend, Manju. Marsha could see why her comrade-in-arms wanted to be a comrade in his girlfriend's arms.

She was envious, not of Ramit's girlfriend, but of seeing a couple holding each other. Thoughts returned to DiNatale in Clearwater. The minor league season would be over soon with some kids in the higher levels of the farm system getting a nod to play on the big-league team. What fate awaited her friend after his first year of coaching at the instructional league level, she wondered.

She decided when the case was over, she'd fly down to Florida and check in on Charlie and Shira. She'd let her friend know that she was back in town, in case he was interested in a quiet dinner by the water. She was sure that her former neighbors, Jess and Briana would be working the Saturday night shift at their favorite restaurant and they could have a mini-reunion.

Even though she was a mile from her condo she felt closer to Clearwater and the people there than anywhere else in the world. Philly was a familiar in locale but barren for genuine connection, save Hollins and Ramit.

That Saturday, arrangements were made for movers to clean out the rental and donate the furniture. Dennis Horton agreed to take the big board and store it in his basement for the week. None of them could bear erasing it just yet.

Before going to the mosque, Marsha had followed Ramit to the van rental place, and he returned the van. He thanked the affable people there, but kinda sorta forgot to tell them of the bugs or tracking unit. It should make for some crazy hijinks when the buggers and trackers picked up on the chatter and watched the van move about Detroit in real time.

For all intents and purposes, they made it to look like they shut down the investigation prematurely. Farah and Said were told to stand by for the final push the following week; same went for Dennis, Chance Dakkinen and Lester McNulty. Marsha knew that the deputy sheriff and the retired detectives wanted to get one more crack at the guy that had eluded them for years. Good police never forgot their unsolved cases, she reasoned. She was right about these guys. Mr. Orr was unfinished business for them.

It felt strange driving to her condo. She parked in her usual garage and told the attendant that she would start up the monthly rent again. It felt stranger to place her key in the double locks. *This is no longer home.* Her place greeted her with a musty smell of a medieval cloister and she immediately threw open her windows to let in the pollution and street noises of the Fairmount section of the city. It was a just stone's throw, or really, a righteous tee shot from the Art Museum, where tourists did the *Rocky* dance every day on the top step.

In a couple of hours, she would meet Hollins at their favorite stand up cheesesteak place at Tenth and Oregon, then walk several long blocks to Citizens Bank Park for a beautiful night of baseball. She had not once attended a ballgame in Detroit's Comerica Park that summer and regretted it now. She wrangled her suitcases of clean and dirty clothes into the utility room and immediately reached into the fridge. She remembered that she had diligently tossed out beer and liquor after returning from Clearwater and that brief stopover at Quantico before motoring to the Motor City.

* * *

They sat behind the mesh screen, Mike on one side of home plate and Marsha on the other about fifteen rows up. Both were avid fans and could enjoy the pitchers' duel that held both teams scoreless until the eighth. The vendors had stopped hawking beer, peanuts and hot dogs by that point. The Phillies power-hitter bunted away from the shift and then took a lazy lead off of first base. He surprised everybody by stealing second. They sacrificed him to third and he tagged up on a long fly ball ending the Reds starting pitcher's night and his shut out. The Phillies closer came in and they giddily watched his sinker fall off the table in the strike zone. With the win, the Phillies stayed in the hunt for the division and had a comfortable lead for a Wild Card.

Could they hang on for the home stretch? she wondered.

Can I hang on for my home stretch? Her mind returned to the case that bedeviled them.

* * *

"I'll have whipped cream on top too," Mike said to Dot, their waitress at the Penrose Diner.

"You can never have enough whipped cream," Marsha added.

Dot nodded as she collected their menus.

Both were having sundaes to celebrate the win and for not drinking alcohol at the ballpark. Marsha appreciated Mike's gesture to follow her lead on ordering sodas, but now they were ready to talk shop.

"I had to get out of Dodge. I was suffocating under the weight of the case and all the fuck-fuck by Homeland Security."

"Not the first time to that rodeo, Marsha," he said, "I have to tell you, you look like you need a vacation, you look fried."

Mike had made some progress with his arm since she saw him last. The physical therapy was progressing. He was also working out and, except for this cheat day, had been dropping weight with a new diet.

Under the glare of 24-hour diner lighting and sitting across from him face to face, she replied, "You're not kidding. The clock is ticking louder and louder in my head every day as we get closer, but you look better. How are you handling it?"

"I think I will teach at the academy for the next class of recruits. I can use my noodle until this thing works again." He shook his left arm so that it flopped unresponsively.

"That's great," she said.

"Besides, it gets me back in the game and off the sidelines. I can talk to the guys doing the bribery probe again as brothers and not as a victim."

"I'm afraid to ask," Marsha said.

"Best I can tell, it's bigger than anyone imagined, but they seem to be tightening the probe around a handful of serious players in the department who won't give up the ringleader. Guys that would rather eat their gun or do hard time than drop a dime. It's almost like the Sicilians. It's like they made an oath."

"It's hard to believe that it was only last winter, for Christ's sake. So much has happened since then." Marsha looked up to the visage of two sundaes with hot fudge sauce, whipped cream and cherries on top arriving to their table.

"Here you go, more coffee, hon?" Dot said to Mike.

He nodded as he looked down at his impending carbicide.

Before he picked up his spoon to start his oral love affair, he said, "I've been backstopping you almost from the beginning and you have beat this case to death, no pun intended. How many murders over two decades were uncovered?"

"Every one except 2002."

"Right, and you put together some solid cold-case files on everyone with just you and Ramit doing all the heavy lifting."

"We had some help from you and caught a couple breaks with Dennis Horton throwing in with us."

"Don't kick yourself, Marsh, look what you have done in less than four months," he said between mouthfuls of gooey deliciousness.

"Just the same, we've pretty much hit a dead end. I keep having this nagging feeling that something is staring us right in the face and we are not seeing it. I hoped that this break might give us some separation so that we can see what's been staring right back at us all this time."

"I know what you mean. When I caught a break on some of my cases and did a review of what we had early on, it was always something minor that got overlooked that held the key to the case, but I just didn't see it at the time. That is the benefit of 20/20 hindsight."

Marsha agreed before swallowing her spoonfuls of decadent delight. "Clock is ticking though, tick tock. I hope when I go back tomorrow night, we can look at everything with fresh eyes."

"You think by closing up shop the way you did is going to throw them off?"

"I hope so," she said, "It's bad enough that I can't use any of the bureau's resources or go public with the sketch, DNA, voice or handwriting. I don't need them throwing up more obstacles as we make our last turn on the final stretch."

"Still no word from the head honcho?" He had to grab his left hand with this right to grasp the sundae by its glass base while he twirled the spoon for every last drop.

"Nada."

"You think he's hanging you out to dry?"

"Don't know. Ramit seems to think that there is a bigger game going on than trying to stop a mass murderer from committing his yearly murder."

"Fucking brass. Can't trust them," Mike said as he poured a Niagara Falls of sugar into his coffee.

"Look at the bright side. I could have been working in some backwater burg or dying a slow death by paper cuts in D.C.," Marsha said. She realized then and there, that this case that was driving her to drink, metaphorically, was her salvation. She was getting her mojo back. Strutting with a swagger again, she was playing in the big leagues and still had nine days and some change to catch the bastard.

They talked in the parking lot a bit before calling for their car services to take them in their separate directions. It was a cool starry night with a steady parade of jets landing at Philly International.

"If you need me out there for the final push, just give me a holler, pardner."

"Will do, Mike, you've been a big help, I wouldn't let you miss out on the fun."

The hug was powerful, but brief, and she settled into the back seat of a spotless clean hybrid sedan.

* * *

She hadn't taken her clothes off yet. She stared into the empty fridge and looked in cabinets again where she kept her booze. She didn't have to report to the office in the morning. The case was on hold in her brain until she jumped on the plane back to Detroit the next evening, with reservations that she had made on her own credit card. No more transactions on the AMEX Card from here on out. This was her cloaking device. She would operate under the radar, just in case Stanfield was playing both sides against the middle.

I could walk out to a nearby taproom and nobody would be the wiser. Hey, I deserve it. No sex, no booze, working six to seven days a week from breakfast till bedtime. What would it hurt? I proved that I could live without it, right? I never drank out there, not a drop. Ramit never saw me lift a cold one or two or ten.

It wasn't quite the zombie walk, but her feet led her out of the building and around the corner. *An hour till closing.*

Good, I can't get shit faced unless I drink shots. She reached for the door handle and stopped. *I promised I would call Charlie.* She turned away as two boisterous college students barreled out the door talking some graduate level thesis nonsense.

"Hey, Charlie, I hope I didn't wake you."

"Almost there, but I had a sense you'd call me."

"Really, Yoda? How d'you figure I'd be calling?"

"You're alone with your thoughts in Philly where it all started. You've got nothing but time on your hands. Dangerous combo."

She had given him a head's up on Plan B and ran some scenarios by him. He knew that she would hear this Labor Day weekend. "Yep."

"It's a trigger. You have some time to deal with your emotions and you might have had some thought about drowning them. Am I right?"

"Yep."

"But you did the right thing by calling Old Charlie Akers first."

"Yep. How's Shira doing?"

"Wouldn't know, she's going back to her place this weekend. She says she can't stand me doting on her all the time. It's driving her crazy. I'm up in Brockton for a grand-niece's baptism tomorrow. I come up every summer for a spell to get away from the heat and humidity, anyway. This was my excuse to get away and give that hard-headed friend of yours a break from me, too, I guess."

Marsha turned back towards her condo and realized that she dodged a bullet. *What if I started drinking like a fish back in Detroit? I could have really screwed the pooch.*

"Anyway, Mike and I took in a ballgame tonight and didn't really talk about the case until later. He told me about the bribery scandal and it brought me right back to when all the shit started. It brought back all the memories that I pushed away the whole time I was in Motown."

"Makes sense. Doesn't it? You are back at the scene of the crime and are exhausted from running around like a crazy woman all summer."

"Guess I didn't see it coming." She started laughing almost to herself. "You know this case is driving me bonkers. Mr. Orr, or Williams or Russell or whatever his actual name is all I think about. 24-7 all the time, morning, noon and—"

"What did you say, grasshopper?"

"The guy, the UNSUB, the prep, he goes by three aliases. Robert Orr, William Russell and Theodore Williams. He's all I think about. I've been trying to get into his head for months."

"Marsha, what is another name for Robert?"

"Whaddyamean?"

"If you had a brother named Robert, what might you call him?"

"Bob."

"Little brother, Marsha."

"Christ, I don't know, Bobby, I guess." Marsha had been down this road with Charlie in the past. He would never come out and tell her the answer. She had to figure it out herself.

"Good. What about William?"

"Bill."

"Theodore?"

"Ted."

Charlie took a couple of beats and slowly said, "Say the last names again now with your answers."

"Ted Williams, Bill Russell— Oh my God!" Marsha

was near hysteric with the realization. "Bobby Fucking Orr. Holy shit. Holy shit."

The grad students waiting for their ride gaped at the blonde-haired women bouncing up and down yelling into her phone.

"Oh my God! Oh my God! Ted Williams, Bill Russell and Bobby Orr. Boston's greatest sports icons. I betcha he has used the alias of Thomas Brady somewhere, somehow too. I will bet you good money on that, Charlie Akers. You are the best. I gotta make calls."

The graduate students watched her skipping away and high-fiving an imaginary person as she yelled, "Ramit! Ramit! Answer the phone!"

CHAPTER 34

HE HAD TESTED the plan for Tamara. On Tuesday, he would do one more "day in a life" surveillance of the stay at home wife while her kids were at school and her tradesman husband left to work until dusk. But for now, on this brisk Labor Day Sunday mid-morning, he was happy to go to work and walk the lot.

Sean greeted tire kickers who weren't expecting to see the salesman in his dapper Brooks Brothers "346" sports coat with the brass buttons over a striped blue and white pressed collared shirt. Khakis and docksiders completed the friendly no-pressure ensemble.

Sundays on the lot were not about sales, after all they didn't come on that day to talk to a salesman and, truth be told, they visited the lot to avoid the salesmen and that's when Sean did his best work. He would chat them up and never, ever try to sell. He would listen and learn. People think they make their decisions to buy a car with their logical brain, the great salesman knew that people made their decisions with their hearts. It was how they felt about the decision mattered.

With the Lions playing the later afternoon time slot, there were fewer things to do after church. He slid from one family to another, from one couple to another and then to this young couple. Word had gotten around the Arab community that this dealership gave great deals; little did they know that Sean was offering below market pricing as loss leaders to get their personal information on a credit application and them into a car where their key fobs and house keys were easy to replicate.

They were both recently graduated computer engineers and were looking at the all-electric cars and hybrids. The husband worked for the City in finance. Rashida worked at home for a company building an on-line scheduling app that integrated with all the e-commerce platforms. It was getting ready to go public with an IPO and she had stock options she told him excitedly. They showed him pictures of the home on the Westside they were fixing up.

As they walked across the lot, he asked about all the improvements. No home security system was installed yet. Balancing student loans with mortgage debt made buying their first new car a tough decision. Sean didn't tell them that he had a hybrid that just came off lease and that it would cut a new car payment in half. He knew it would buy them time as their salaries grew.

On Wednesday, he'd tell them about his "find" and ask them to come back in for a test-drive of the low mileage gas sipper. He'd help them see it a bridge to their new car. It was never too soon to prospect for his actual purpose and life's mission.

* * *

The curse of fresh information in a case of this magnitude meant testing all the leads against all the facts already gathered. Where exactly did this piece fit in the jigsaw puzzle? That night's sleep in what felt like a strange bed was fitful at best as she played out more scenarios.

Marsha called Hollins, Ramit and Charlie first thing in the morning from the sidewalk outside of her favorite Starbucks.

Black clouds turned into thunderstorms and lighting later that Sunday morning. She waited for Ramit on the main concourse of 30th Street Station. The Acela from Washington to Boston stopped here, and she had her ticket for the 1:15.

She wanted to talk to Ramit for an hour alone before she talked with Mike. With this fresh information they may need to alter Plan B. She wanted his input before heading off to meet Charlie.

"Each name alone meant nothing to us, and certainly nothing to anyone out in Detroit. Each name individually would not cause a stir. Common names, right? But for someone from Eastern Massachusetts of a certain age, they collectively became a clue," she continued, "If he used Dennis McLain, Robert Lanier or Albert Kaline in Detroit, it would have been the same thing," she said.

"Who are they?"

"Think, Steven Carlton, Bernard Parent and Charles Bednarik in Philly."

"Ugh, okay, I guess," Ramit shrugged humoring her.

"Anyway, when he had to give out made-up names in Detroit, it was a painless way to bring them right off the top of his head. Don't you see it?"

"So, if he's from Boston, what do you hope to find?"

"I'll bet you a donut that is where we will find the 2002

case. After that, he moved to Detroit and we both know why."

"If you want to hunt wildebeest, you go to the wildebeest watering hole." Ramit repeated what they had said that often about this case and the ease of selecting suitable victims in Dearborn and surrounding towns.

"Exactly," she said. She was jazzed. It was something the killer unwittingly gave them, but they had worked hard to find each name. A library card, a name scribbled on a rent receipt and a phony name given to set up a realty appointment were used for three separate killings. It gave the case new legs.

Ramit said, "You missed the presentation by Said and Farah. They sorted all the 9/11 victims by where they were born or lived and we can create a search for their family members in his age range. We can repeat the steps of pulling obits and then creating the family trees to see who we can shake out. I looked at the subsets and there are between 120 to 149 victims in those groups."

"Do you think they can get started on that right away?"

He said, "I already talked to them and they started this morning. With luck, we will be able to finish by Monday night. We can all work remotely on that."

"That's the beauty of the case management system that Mike suggested for us," she said.

"I've asked Mike to meet us here for lunch. I told him that we may need him out there while I'm running around Boston. What do you think? I wanted to run it by you first." She truly wanted to show deference to him but had an ulterior motive.

"He's been out there before and knows the case. He's got more experience than both of put together," Ramit said.

"If we were to team him up with Dennis, Chance or Lester, who would you choose?"

"Are you looking to bring them into this?"

"Mike knows the case and Dennis has been working enough clues that we could bring him up to snuff. Maybe have Dennis and Chance and Mike and Lester? You've met the old dogs; do you think they'd want to get off their rocking chairs and rock it out on the street one more time."

"I think that would work. The retired cops might open a few doors that have been shut to us."

"Yeah no shit. I think this lead is going to break things open for us and we will need boots on the ground."

"Can't you bring the field office in, if we figure out who it is?"

"We've never considered that for a moment while we worked it for four months. Why the change of heart, Ramit?"

"Because next week another woman dies if we don't stop him," he replied without blinking an eye.

"It's not the same thing as us going public, is it?"

"No, it's not. We get his name and then bring the entire weight of the FBI down on him." Ramit was seeing Marsha's end game.

"And what if they thank us very nicely and pat us on the head and tell us they'll handle it?"

The light bulb went on and Ramit said, "You're right. Nothing happens, and it stays quiet and—"

"Another woman dies on their watch and we still incur the wrath of the number two guy in the FBI for going to the field office."

"Yeah, I guess I didn't think about that possibility. I just expected them to go after the guy once we identified him."

"Don't beat yourself up on that, Ramit," she said, "They might jump all over it."

"But we don't know, and once we do tell them, there are no do-overs," he said.

People walked by them, oblivious to the concerns of this duo who were stuck between a rock and a hard place. Families were saying goodbye or greeting loved ones. Lovers were snatching a good, long, last kiss. Journeys were beginning or ending, just like theirs.

"You didn't say what you would do after Boston," he broke the silence.

"I'd take the overnight train to Detroit as soon as we beat all the Boston leads to death. I can't ask Charlie to go out there. I'd be flying solo. You wouldn't happen to know a good wing man, would you?" She peeked over her third iced ristretto of the morning.

There it was. Ramit had to shit or get off the pot. The difference this morning amongst the hustle and bustle of the comings and goings in this cavernous neo-classic sandstone and marble building, is that when they had returned to Philly, they didn't have any promising clues to break the case. Marsha would activate Plan B. He would still have a job to go back to after his vacation.

Instead, they could double down to try to catch the killer.

"I'm using cash from here on out. I'm paranoid about them seeing what I am up to," she added, seeing that he was still weighing the options.

He looked at her. She honestly didn't know what he would say, and she held her breath while he let his out. "I guess I should hit the ATM and get a train ticket later for myself."

She slid the Amtrak tickets across the table to him. "You've got time for a quickie before you and Mike have to depart on the 4:16 to Chicago. You're burning daylight, pilgrim."

CHAPTER 35

HE WELCOMED her with a hug and reached for her overnighter. South Station on Sunday evening was busy with travelers and tourists making their connections. The thunderstorms in Philly followed Marsha up the eastern seaboard to Boston and they dodged puddles running to Charlie's rental.

"It's good to see you," she said, "How was the baptism?"

"The baby wailed during the entire service. It was great. What could the parents and godparents do? The more they tried shushing her, the more she cried." He butted into traffic on Atlantic Avenue much to the ire of the idiot laying on the horn.

Boston traffic hasn't changed much since the last time I was here, Marsha mused.

Ignoring the ignoramus, her former boss continued. "These days I've been going to more funerals and not as many weddings, so when Uncle Charlie gets invited to a baptism, he goes."

"How was the party afterward?"

"They had tents set up outside, but the lighting put a

kibosh on that, so they moved everything into the house and we grilled from the breezeway to the garage. We sat around in lawn chairs and ate too much."

"Where we headed? Seems like you've got a plan." Marsha looked over her former boss and unofficial sponsor and it felt good to have him pushing some pieces on the board. She trusted him and knew they were on the hunt.

"With it being the middle of the Labor Day weekend and all, it presented some challenges. My sister is the family historian, and I asked her in general terms how I could look up this stuff from two decades ago. She told me that the best place to start was the Boston Library on Boylston Street."

That surprised Marsha. "They are open on a Sunday night of a holiday weekend?"

"No, grasshopper, but old Charlie Akers figured out a way to get his favorite FBI agent into the building."

She grinned. "Okay, I get it. I'm gonna pick the lock while you're on the look-out and act as my getaway driver?"

He shook his head and laughed with her. "I called in a favor from a former Assistant United States Attorney, who now has her own law practice here. She sits on the BPL's Board of Directors. We are meeting with her and the library director across the street at a coffee shop. They will decide if we get a 'special tour' or not."

Marsha and Charlie walked into the independent coffee shop catering to college kids and locals from the nearby neighborhood. It was Boston bohemian at its best. The poster board by the entrance was overflowing with flyers touting upcoming coffee house events, open mic nights, storytelling and research studies that paid cash for participants. Starving artist art adorned the walls and most of the guests were head down wearing headphones and staring at their laptops as coffee beans grinded. The aroma reminded Marsha of her favorite shop on Chestnut street in Philly. In the moment's din, they all stared at each other. The two seated women stood.

Charlie then made the introductions. "This is Marsha O'Shea. I worked with her when I was the Supervisor in Charge in Miami. She's working a very sensitive case in Detroit."

Marsha stuck her hand out to the older woman first. "Thank you for meeting us on such brief notice, especially on a holiday weekend."

"I'm Elizabeth Polan, call me Liz. It must be a hell of a case for you to be running down leads on a Sunday night."

"Yes, there is a time component and I can explain that to you both." She shifted her gaze to the younger woman.

"Hi, Marsha, my name is Diane Ainslie. I've never met an FBI agent before. What can we do for you?"

Charlie said, "What are y'all having? I'll grab them while you chat."

The women gave their drink orders, and Marsha got right to the point. "I was tasked about four months ago to work on a special assignment in Detroit. They gave me strict orders to work by myself outside of normal channels with the help of just one analyst." She moved her head closer into the center of the round table.

"The Bureau had picked up chatter about three or four suspicious deaths of Muslim women on the anniversary of 9/11 over the past several years. We started looking into it and the pattern emerged of deaths occurring in the same manner as those people who died on that fateful day all those years ago. The killer made their deaths look accidental or as suicides with only one case being ruled a homicide. He does this just once a year — on the anniversary of 9/11 with Muslim women.

"Why Detroit," the attorney asked.

"It has the highest concentration of Arab Americans in the United States. We think that is why he moved there."

"What brings you to Boston then?"

"I believe this is where the trail starts. We worked like hell to locate many of the deaths from State Vitals, newspaper accounts and family recollections. Every death that fit the pattern happened every year on September 11 and no other dates, except one woman who died from her injuries the following day," she paused. "Except for one year, 2002. We spent days working on that year, but it stumped us. Finally, last night, I was crying in my beer to Charlie and he figured out the clue."

Crying in my almost-beer is more like it. She wanted to correct herself, but for the sake of her listeners she continued. "The killer used aliases in Detroit to set up appointments, get a library card, buy cell phones, rent a garage and fill out a cash receipt. They were the full names of three Boston sports heroes, Theodore Williams, William Russell and Robert Orr. We think that if he had to supply a name off the top of his head, this is probably what he did. He went into his memory and pulled out a name that would mean nothing to Detroiters, but would be easy for him to retrieve."

The former US Attorney said, "That's a little thin, Agent O'Shea."

I wish I had a nickel for every time an AUSA told me that. She agreed. "It's thin, but I am almost certain the 2002 death didn't happen in Detroit. I'm running out of time. I have run all my obvious Detroit leads into the ground. The odds of him using those three specific names has me thinking that I've got nothing to lose by being here. I need to find the 2002 case. I hope that he may have made his rookie mistakes here."

She looked at the women seated across from her. "Do I have evidence of who the killer is or proof beyond a reasonable doubt of how he committed two decades of murders? No. Am I trying to figure this out in a week to prevent another woman's death? Yes."

The two women stared at the third who carried the badge and gun. Then at each other.

"I think what you might need could be sitting across the street," Diane said as she pulled out keys from her purse.

They all looked up at Charlie who said, "I got them all to go. Is that all right Diane?"

She smiled. "I won't tell the librarian if you don't."

They walked in the rain past the glistening onyx statue on the library's front steps. Diane used her keys to open the heavy black doors. She slid in first and turned off the alarm, motioning the others to follow as lights began illuminating their way. They proceeded up marble steps between stone-carved roaring lions and eventually wound their way to the genealogy room where *The Boston Globe* was on file. She located the September 2002 box of microfilm and deftly threaded it into the reader as the photocopier warmed up.

"We will check Wednesday the eleventh first, in case it happened just after midnight of the tenth and the *Globe* were able to get it in," Diane said as she flew through the paper with expert eyes scanning each page. The others had to step back. By trying to follow her lead, they were all getting dizzy.

On Thursday the twelfth, whirling through the Metro section, Marsha saw the photo and nudged Diane. "Go back, I want to read that one."

Working the controls in reverse, she stopped and

centered the page "Is this what you are looking for? 'Gas Explosion Kills One.'"

A picture of the leveled stick-frame house accompanied the two-column article. It identified the victim as Alia Mansoor, age thirty-four. Luckily, she was the only one home at the time. They reported it. Neighbors described her as a nurse who worked the midnight shift at Mass General. The explosion was under investigation by the Quincy Fire and Police Departments. She left a husband and two children.

Marsha nodded and reached for her laptop. She opened it and went to turn it on and stopped. *I can't take any chances that they have infected it with a program that shows them real time what I am key stroking or where I am.* "Can I access a computer here?"

Diane said, "I can get you set up while I keep searching for follow-up articles."

They walked to another room where the public use PCs were kept and Diane logged in with her ID and the timer started. "Here you go. Let me know when you have to print anything off."

Marsha and Charlie set about using his databases with his passwords to do lookups on Alia, her family, and the address. He did the key stroking and she made notes. They filled up the hour and put many documents into the printer's cache.

Diane and Liz walked back to them. "You have a death notice from a funeral home, a day later, but no obituary. A week after that, the Quincy Chief of Police gave a statement that the explosion was still under investigation. Here's everything," Liz said.

Marsha read it all aloud for the benefit of the pen recorder as Diane printed out the computer findings. She would scan each page of the microfilm and then of her database searches with her portable scanner and upload it all later that night to *CaseSoft* from her hotel's computer set up for guests.

She text from her burner phone to Ramit: *Bingo. 2002, Alia Mansoor, Gas Explosion, Cops investigated. Quincy, MA. Family still in the area.*

He replied from his burner: *Slow going with our searches, about a third done. Taking on passengers in Pittsburgh.*

It elated her to be making progress. She had been beating her head against the wall all summer and she had an agreeable feeling this is where it all began. She stuffed everything into her satchel. It relieved her that she was operating under the radar and didn't have to look over her shoulder for DHS. They didn't poison the well here. She stopped just before they had to go back out in the rain. Lightly touching Liz and Diane on the sleeves of their summer raincoats. "You did good. Where can we get good Italian or seafood? I'm starving and I'm buying."

CHAPTER 36

"IT'S your turn to buy the donuts."

She recognized Charlie's voice even though she was still half asleep. The *Mission: Impossible* ring tone didn't go off. *Fuck.* At that moment, she realized that she turned her phone off, once she departed Philly, using the burner for texting and calling. She was supposed to meet him in the hotel's lobby where they were staying. It was an old saw that anytime you were late, you better bring donuts to the meeting.

"Shit, Charlie, my alarm didn't go off. I need a half-hour to shower and pack."

"Cutting it tight, Marsh, but if the traffic's light, we should be alright. I'll get everything, but you owe me."

Trying to work the weird shower controls and brushing her teeth at the same time didn't work so well. *Is this an omen?* she asked herself as she alternated between freezing and scalding her left hand. *Big day, we might get the answers on this case.* Finally, she got it right and jumped in. She squeezed most of the hotel bottle of shampoo onto her head and suds up. *Can we stop this guy before it's too — shit got soap in my eyes. It burns. How can a solve this case when I can't even bathe myself properly?*

She remembered that just before bedtime, she had gotten a call from the desk guy at Quincy PD saying that they could come in at 9:30. She then woke up Alia's widower and explained their need to meet him at noon, but that meeting hinged on what they learned at the PD.

The findings at the library and a heavy meal in Boston's Little Italy had put her right to sleep. She hadn't slept that good in months. Getting the pieces of the puzzle to fall in place at this stage of the investigation was gratifying, after months of grinding, false starts, and stiff arms.

While blow-drying her long, chestnut blonde hair, she went with her charcoal blazer over white blouse and gray slacks. Business casual for the boys in blue today. *Dress the part, walk the part, talk the part. You are badass FBI Agent Marsha O'Shea and don't you forget it.*

She dressed quickly and threw her toiletries in the roller along with yesterday's clothes and slung her overnighter over her shoulder. Badge and holstered gun were snugged onto her waist band. *This is how we rock-and-roll.*

She told the desk clerk she was checking out, but might check back in later that night if her work carried over into Tuesday. He put a hold on her room until four p.m.

Charlie took the overnighter and handed her a Dunkin' Donuts regular, which in New England meant cream and sugar. They jumped into his car, double-parked at the valet station, and roared the brief distance on surface roads to I-95 north where Charlie stayed heavy on the pedal.

"How do you want to handle me being your sidekick," he asked.

"I was visiting you for the weekend and the case broke with leads in Boston. You know the area and we've worked together in the old days. It just seems natural that you would do the driving while I rode shotgun."

"That works," he said, "Did you get any read on who we are meeting?"

"Nope, typical bored desk cop working an evening shift on a holiday weekend told me to show up at 9:30 and announce myself. He knew nothing else."

The traffic gods were smiling on them. It was too early for city folk to be returning from the Cape on the Labor Day weekend. The weather was perfect for the beach. The storms blew out to sea overnight and left behind a beautiful warm sunny summer day. Marsha remarked to Charlie, "It was a fantastic summer in Detroit. Some rain, but mostly days like today. It was nice to have long daylight hours to knock on doors and talk to people on their front stoops. Ramit and I used every bit of that sunshine every day."

"I don't doubt it. Seeing how you didn't have the field office to draw manpower from as the case grew and grew, you really covered a lot of ground." Changing gears, Charlie added, "Why do you think Stanfield went silent running on you?"

"Think about it, Charlie. He never surfaced after he gave me the case. For all I know, my status emails are going to a porn site in Romania.

"As long as I could use the AMEX card, I knew I was in business. There are political reasons why he needs plausible deniability, right? Ramit and I have just resigned ourselves to the fact that he wanted eyes on this case and maybe a couple of sacrificial lambs."

"Don't kid yourself, kiddo." Charlie glanced over to his favorite FBI agent. "You have demonstrated on more than one occasion how to swim against the tide."

"Thanks. Charlie, but we both know that doesn't mean

a hill of beans, if we don't stop Mr. Orr from another killing in eight days."

They had their choice of *Police Only* parking spots on Sea Street in front of the three-story yellow brick Classical Revival structure. It looked every bit like it was built a hundred years ago. After announcing their purpose, a young, dark-haired and mustachioed plainclothes officer met them at the door.

"Come this way, Chief Durkin is waiting for you. I'm Detective Rusty Hart. He asked me to sit in for the meeting."

To Marsha, that signaled that their visit may breathe fresh life into a long-forgotten death. They wound their way through the building to a conference room with the Chief, in full uniform, seated with a folder on the table. Introductions were made, and Marsha could hardly take her eyes off the jacketed case. It was weathered and showed the wear of filing and refiling reminiscent of how they were stored in the pre-digital days.

As they settled in, Marsha was first to speak, "Thank you, Chief, for agreeing to meet with us on such brief notice, especially on a holiday weekend."

"I left my wife with the grandkids in Barnstable and I promised her I'd be back by lunchtime to grill the hamburgers and hot dogs. What's so important that it couldn't wait until tomorrow?" His cap sat upside down on the table next to the file. His hands were folded over his waistline, which was probably much trimmer when he was a patrolman.

Vacationing at the Cape, but he had time to go home and throw on the authority robes?

"My father is retired from Philly PD as a captain and he gave up on my brother and I having kids, so there won't be any grandkids." Marsha tried to connect on a personal level.

"Is that the brother that was killed last March in the shoot-out with the Russians?"

Marsha's heart sank. What she thought was a way to establish rapport just turned into a lingering fart. That is when she noticed the fresh manila folder in front of the young detective. She furrowed her brow at his smart phone laying on the table. "Normally I ask permission to record conversations," she said. *This isn't looking good.* Flying solo had its advantages, but she didn't want to crash and burn this close to the truth of how it all began. It sat three feet away from her.

"Is there anything, Agent O'Shea, that you are worried about saying in this room?" the Chief leaned forward, tenting his hands above the file.

"No, not really. You are correct. That was my brother and there is not a day that goes by that I don't miss him." Glancing to Charlie. "I stopped beating myself up over the wouldas, couldas and shouldas and I'm slowly working out my grief."

"Your Philadelphia office says that you are on 'special assignment.' What does that mean?" Durkin showed no kindness to the woman sitting across from him whose brother was murdered six months earlier and he was not to be deterred.

"Exactly what it means. I was tasked to look into a matter in Detroit involving a number of suspicious deaths, the trail has led me to your fine town and that file." She said pointing at it.

"Funny thing is the Detroit office Area Supervisor in Charge Callahan said you were a loose cannon. I just got off the phone with him." Durkin pushed the file to the side further away from Marsha.

"Give Callahan my warmest regards when you call him back and be sure to ask him why the Assistant Director of the FBI in charge of Field Operations passed over his entire office and chose me to work this case." Pleasantries were forgotten. Marsha wanted the contents of the file.

Durkin shook his head and nodded to the Detective who opened his file and, like he was quizzing a suspect, asked, "Is it true that you confronted an armed man in a women's shelter?"

"And saved the life of my neighbor Jess, her daughter Briana and a dozen or so other women from a nut-job with an assault rifle." Pointing to Marsha, Charlie said, "She could have waited outside for back-up and we know how that would have played out. What's with the twenty questions, Durkin?"

"Excuse me, Mr. Akers — and it is *Mister* Akers — you are no longer with the Bureau and your exact reason for being here is?"

Marsha said, "We are here because in 2002 a woman died in a gas explosion in Quincy. You know that. What you don't know is that the man that made that look like an accident, moved to Detroit and started killing other woman making it look like accidents on every 9/11 since." Marsha repeated, "Every year since." She continued, "And I think the information in your file may prevent him from doing it again next Tuesday. I have three questions for you Chief Durkin, the first is — Do you want her blood on your hands?"

"I will deal with your Boston field office, please make your request through them." He stood up. "This meeting is over. I have more important things to attend to."

The detective hastily turned off the smart phone recording the meeting, shuffled his papers and stood up to help his Chief glare at her.

Still seated and very calm, Marsha recrossed her legs and replied. "Maybe you can tell me who the detective was on the case back then? He or she may not want to find out that following protocol stood in the way of preventing another innocence woman's death."

"I was the detective on the case and *back then* the DA said there was not enough evidence to get an arrest warrant. He said it was an accident." Durkin glared down at her.

Bingo, he had a suspect. "The last thing — a name. All I want is the name buried in that file two decades ago," she said, "I can leave your jurisdiction and go find him in Detroit."

"I have a cordial relationship with your colleagues in Boston, I would be most happy to take under advisement a request made through proper channels."

Charlie was standing now as well. "We are meeting with Mr. Mansoor in a couple of hours, what would you like us to tell him?"

The Chief, who was not accustomed to being talked to so bluntly was now red-faced, whether from shame at not stopping this madman when he could have or from anger, which either way still translated to anger from this authority figure who would rather put his grandchildren on the barbecue grill than admit to making a mistake. He picked up the case jacket and clutched it to his chest with one hand and pointed a thick stubby finger to the door.

Marsha made a show of clicking her pen, which ended her recording. "We normally ask for permission before taping. Now that we are off the record, I will make a transcript of this tape and send a copy of *The Detroit Free Press* articles of the woman that dies next week to *The Boston Globe*. How's that sound, Chief? Call me if you change your mind." She threw her card on the table.

* * *

"I'm getting sick and fucking tired of punching with one arm tied behind my back. No official support, no subpoenas, no lab work, no CSI, limited access to BAU. I'm tiptoeing in the tulips while a tiger is on loose," she vented to Charlie in the car.

"Durkin is just an asshole. He thought that the girl from the FBI would show him up, make him look stupid. He would not give you anything," Charlie seethed.

"Wow, they know how to use Google, wasn't that just so amazing? Looking me up and acting like they caught me red-handed. Those twats. Loose cannon, my ass," she snapped.

"Proves that you were right, O'Shea. You need to email to Stanfield and tell him to pull a string and get you the name out of that file. Tell him Charlie Akers will kick his ass if he doesn't. I am not kidding. I don't give a rat's ass. What is he going to do, put me in retired agent jail? At some point, people are more important than politics. Damn it."

Stunned at the outburst, Marsha looked at him and said, "Gee, Charlie, tell me how you really feel." She typed the email to Stanfield: *Only time I will ask you for a favor. Chief Durkin at Quincy PD outside of Boston has a suspect for the 2002 gas explosion that killed Alia Mansoor. Was told that I had to go thru channels to get that name. I am going through channels.*

"I ain't your boss anymore, but how that man treated you in that room was just not right and for Stanfield to put you into the position where you couldn't walk in with the Boston ASIC and two other suits really pisses me off."

She knew that it was more than that. His heart was breaking for her. She saw from how he raged and grabbed the steering wheel in a death grip. Yes, it was the case that remained just outside of their grasp, but the way she was bullied in the PD and how he couldn't stop it, really must have fueled his anger.

She next texted Faiz Mansoor: *We are on schedule. We can be there in an hour for our appointment.* It was confirmed immediately.

Their anger ebbed and flowed until it was time to meet the widower. Charlie had not been exposed to this part of the case and Marsha related to him many of the reactions she had gotten from the families. "First, we are dredging up old feelings and then we are telling them that maybe it was not an accident or a suicide."

"That must be tough," he said.

"For them and for us, I gotta tell you, I don't want to look at another autopsy photo for a long time. We've talked to two decades of families, trying to put back the pieces of their lives only to shatter their worldview with the prospect that their wife, sister, mother or daughter was targeted and killed on purpose."

"Bad enough to talk to one family on a cold case, but almost twenty? Jesus." He whistled softly.

"Still some of them remember it like it was yesterday; what they were doing, where they were at, the timelines. Mostly they remember being told that it was an accident or a suicide and almost to a person they rejected those theories, but who were they? The experts told them what happened and tried to make the facts fit their conclusions, not the other way around."

They arrived at the Mediterranean restaurant in the shadow of the Harvard campus where Dr. Mansoor taught Economics. He waved from a back table and took a seat facing them and the other diners. "How was your drive from Quincy?"

"Easy. Traffic won't start clogging the roads until later," Charlie said.

"There was no construction in the tunnel? That's hard to believe," he said.

They chatted more until their order was taken. Marsha was first to address the reason for their meeting, "Dr. Mansoor, we are sorry for your loss. Sometimes as investigators we are so focused on the case that we lose sight of the fact that a loved one died and the people we are talking to are in different stages of dealing with their emotions. We want to remain mindful of that while we ask people to relive the days leading up to the deaths."

"Thank you. I had never given up hope that someone someday would again look into the explosion that killed my wife and destroyed our home."

"Please continue," she said as she placed her recording pen on the table and wrote notes in her notepad.

"There came the time to replace our hot-water heater. We heated the house with gas and we replaced it with another one, but it stopped working a couple days before the.... We had to take cold showers and wash the dishes in chilly water. The salesman was apologetic and said they would replace it at no charge. He came out with the installer. He said they would pay for the repairman's labor. I had a class to teach and my wife went upstairs to lie down. She worked the midnight shift at Mass General and was tired. Two hours later, my neighbor called me and told me what had happened. I rushed home. There was nothing left of my home and Alia was dead. Thank Allah, my children were in school. My daughter said that she wasn't feeling well that morning and I had to convince her to go to school that morning."

Marsha was head down writing notes. "What did you see?"

"The gas company was there and turned off the gas to the block. There were fire engines and police cars all around. I was able to see Alia getting pulled from the wreckage, but they would not let me go to her until they brought her to the ambulance. It was horrible. I barely recognized her. They began asking me questions, and I told them about the hot-water heater problem and where we bought it from."

"What happened next?" Charlie was on board with open-ended questioning.

"I collected my children from school and told them what happened. They begged me to go to our home, and I relented. I regretted doing that. They were inconsolable. We stayed with friends that night and planned for her to be transported to Sullivan's Funeral Home. We had many friends at the hospital and at the community college where I taught at the time. A few days later, there was a brief service for everyone and we buried her."

His eyes welled up with tears, just as the food arrived. "Forgive me."

Marsha reached her hand across the table after the plates were set down and patted his hand. "No, forgive us for having to bring this up again."

"Why after so many years?" His food was cooling off.

"We don't think it was an accident." She looked at him and ignored her food. He had to lift his fork first.

"Why would somebody do this on purpose?"

"My answer will not make you feel any better, Dr. Mansoor. Your world is going to turn upside down," she said, "We believe that a year earlier on that same date, someone died during 9/11 and this is how he avenged their death."

He appeared confused by that motive. "I am not sure I understand."

"Every year since 9/11, on the anniversary of that date, he makes it look like an accident similar to the way people died that day. His targets are Muslim women. I'm sorry, but we believe that Alia was his first victim."

No matter how many times she had to say something similar, it got no easier.

"Who would do such a thing?"

"This man." Marsha removed a photocopy of the composite from her satchel and handed to him.

Recognition replaced rage. "That was the last person to see my wife alive."

Marsha gave him a quizzical look.

"The repairman swore in his deposition that the hot-water unit was installed properly and was operating correctly when he left my house. He said that the salesman stayed back to go upstairs to tell my wife that everything was working fine."

"Yes?"

"That is the salesman," he said, stabbing the likeness. "Where did you get this?"

"From an eyewitness of an 'accident' in a stairwell in Dearborn, Michigan. You say that you talked to him?"

"Several times."

The waitress came back with an alarmed look on her face. "Is everything okay?" Other diners took notice of the sketch and of the food getting cold.

Dr. Mansoor looked at her and his tablemates. "Can I get mine to go? I'm sorry."

Marsha looked at Charlie, who nodded. "And ours too. I will take care of you on the tip for burning up your table during the lunch hour."

With the food cleared away, Marsha sent him a text message with the killer's voice on it.

He went to the men's room to listen to it.

"Deposition," Charlie said.

"Durkin can go F himself." Marsha leaned over to his good ear.

Mansoor returned and nodded. "I can't be 100 percent sure, but it sounded like he was trying to talk deeper than normal."

"You said the repairmen gave a deposition."

"Yes, we sued the manufacturer, the appliance store and the repairman. We let the Gas company out of the suit because they had no liability and there were no reported gas problems before the explosion.

"My insurance company tried going after them all, too, and joined in with us. Before trial, we settled. Each party accepted one-third liability. It was never about the money; it was about who was responsible."

Their packaged food arrived, and Marsha peeled off a fifty and handed it to the server. "Keep the change."

"Thank you, stay as long as you like. More tea?"

They all shook their heads.

Marsha turned to Mansoor and asked, "How do we get in touch with your attorney?"

"You can't. He died several years ago."

That's what happens on old cases. She didn't know the statute for how long the court had to kept settled cases in their archives, but on the Labor Day weekend, they wouldn't get the answer until the following morning.

Charlie looked at his cell phone and said, "The court for Norfolk county is in Dedham."

Mansoor nodded.

"Darn, I was hoping to look at the file today," Marsha said.

This case had been the ultimate in frustration; dead end leads, governmental obstruction, limited resources and the sheer passage of time. Every time she thought she was getting somewhere, reality knocked the wind out of her sails. They were running out of time, and the thought of chasing two-decade old civil files and insurance claim files on a short week, was not promising.

Mansoor pulled her out of her stinkin' thinkin'. "But you can. When he died, his office staff gave all their clients the opportunity to take their own closed files. They sent it to me. I have it in storage."

For the first time that day, Marsha smiled.

* * *

It was crude, but it worked. They pulled out Mansoor's dining room table in the storage unit. The storage building was in the next town up from Cambridge. It had once been a clothing factory mill and was now repurposed into dry storage. After the kids grew up, he downsized to an apartment near the campus and bicycled to work every day he told them.

Eating their cold take out while reading discovery motions, interrogatories and depositions, they were able to piece together the case.

The big box store had supplied the two sales invoices with a salesman's scrawled signature. Kelly was the last name. In the repairman's deposition he only knew the salesman by his first name as Sean. They tried deposing Sean Kelly, and the process server said that he moved with no forwarding address. When the attorney defending the store contacted their client, they told him that he had abruptly quit and did not return for his last paycheck or monthly commission pay-out.

Two decades ago, he disappeared into the wind.

Marsha scanned the pertinent documents while Mansoor and Charlie boxed them up when her burner rang. It was Ramit. She scurried to the hallway and out of earshot.

"Marsha, I think we have a hit. Mary McGrath Kelly lived in Charlestown, MA and she died on the American Airlines flight going to Los Angeles, her husband was—"

"Sean Kelly."

"How d'you guess?"

She could hear the incredulity in his voice.

"I am sitting in a storage loft in Somerville staring at the name of the salesman who was the last person alive in the house that blew up back in 2002. He fled Boston and landed in—?"

"Michael Sean Kelly. He has a Massachusetts Social Security number." Ramit could not contain his excitement. "He is in the age range for our guy. He's using a mail drop in Dearborn. Gave that same address for his driver's license. He's unaffiliated at voter's registration. We have Farah trying to sort through all the social media to get a line on him. Not an easy name, though. The guys are headed over to the mail drop to put it under surveillance."

"You did good, pardner." Marsha's neural pathways were on fire.

You too, pardner. Hurry back." He was equally pumped.

"Will do. We've got a killer to catch."

* * *

After profusely thanking the widower on their way back to Harvard where they dropped him off, Marsha needed to get back to the Motor City as soon as possible. That is where the action was.

There were no direct flights from Logan to Detroit, so Charlie drove her to T. F. Green Airport in Providence, RI. They were on speaker phone with Ramit, Farah and Said the entire trip. Said continued to focus on ruling out other New Englanders with ties to Detroit, but everyone knew the house money was Mr. Kelly.

According to Mary Kelly's obituary, she worked in human resources for a local tech company, came from an extended family, and left a husband, Sean. They had no children.

The databases placed him in Charlestown, MA in 2002 and then shortly thereafter in Dearborn, MI. No cars in his name, no real property, no liens, judgments or bankruptcies. They had hoped for public utilities which can sometimes flush out a street address, but that was negative as well.

They learned where he banked and how he kept a low balance in a checking account. With ATM access and online banking, he would never have to walk into his bank branch. His credit cards all came to the same address. There were dozens of people associated with him at his mailing address, which when googled turned out to be a UPS store. If one was a friend or roommate, a connection remained to be seen.

It was becoming obvious that Mr. Kelly wanted to leave only a small footprint in his new hometown. Without the profiler's notes, they were only guessing if he might be remarried or have children.

Charlie pulled into departures and hefted her roller out of the back seat, while she and Ramit went over last-minute task items on the phone.

Standing curbside, she flashed her badge to the airport security cop who wanted them to move along. Marsha and Charlie were alone with the roar of jet engines and the smell of jet fuel. She said, "Can you stay up here for the week?"

As if reading her mind, Charlie nodded. "As a last resort, if you need me to run around to Mary Kelly's family to see if they have an address for him, I can do that. I can use some ruse, like he's got money in the unclaimed property funds or something."

She smiled. "You've always been there for me, Charlie. You've always had my back."

"Don't get all sentimental on me, O'Shea. You've still got a lot of work to do to catch this guy," he replied.

"I wonder." She paused.

He cocked his head.

"I wonder if Sean Kelly took his wife to the airport that morning just like all these folks are doing—" she waved along the sidewalks bustling with people hugging goodbye "—and that was the last time he ever saw her again."

He nodded and then gave her a genuine hug. "When it's over, come down to see me and Shira and your boyfriend."

"He's not my boyfriend," Marsha said about Joe DiNatale.

"Yeah and I am not ancient. Offer still goes, call me anytime, no matter when," he said.

She waved and turned, but not before making a mental picture of him. *You never know when it's the last time you'll see someone you care about ever again.*

CHAPTER 37

WHEN SHE WALKED into the suite at the Country Inn & Suites, she felt that she had come full circle. On her initial trip to Dearborn, she didn't know if there would even be a case jacketed. Now, after midnight, they had just eight days to stop a mass murderer. They could all hear the clock ticking.

Standing before her now were over a hundred years of investigative experience, two college kids committed to the cause and her partner in crime-solving, Ramit.

He pointed with the erasable marker to the big board and said, "You have the honors, Agent O'Shea."

She took the marker away from him and stepped up on the stool to be able to reach the top of the board and next to 2002 wrote: *Alia* Mansoor, *Quincy, MA, Gas Explosion, Blunt Force Trauma* and on the copy of the sketch, *Michael Sean Kelly DOB 8/13/80 LKA Charlestown, MA.* She decided not to erase the aliases. They had handed clues to her and deserved to stay on the board. Marsha stepped down and back to take in the whiteboard. Two decades of death neatly laid out in columns and rows, and now they had a named suspect. They knew all the crimes, all the victims and could put a face, voice, DNA, handwriting and finally a name to the killer.

She turned to them and said, "What have you got? What's the plan? Bring me up to speed."

Dennis used masking tape to affix photos of the UPS store to the bare wall next to the board, while Chance spoke, "Closed today for Labor Day, but open eight to eight otherwise. Couple of suitable eyeball positions."

Dennis pointed to the map of the layout. "Here and here."

"Why one car across Michigan Ave?" Ramit asked.

"In case our boy makes a left across three lanes of traffic. We don't want to get stuck in the parking lot pissing ourselves," Chance replied.

Those that knew that surveillance set-ups nodded, and those who didn't just had a teachable moment.

Dennis said, "We will take turns getting vans and cans tomorrow while the other guy keeps the eye-ball."

"What about your other job?" she asked.

"I kinda figured you might need me this week, so I told them I am using up all my accrued Comp time."

"I owe you big, Dennis Horton," she said.

"Catching this bastard and solving twenty-some murders is good enough for me, Marsha."

Everyone nodded.

Lester was next. "Tell them what else, Dennis."

"Oh yeah, Mr. Kelly has trouble abiding by the highway laws of the Great Lakes State. Had himself a couple citations in the last couple of years. I found out from running him in Secretary of State's driver history."

Lester said, "We figure that Mike and I can chase down his License Photo and those tickets tomorrow as I will assist this visiting detective from the east coast."

Chance said, "I made up some letterhead for my PI license that I am putting in for tomorrow and here are my business cards." He passed them around. *Leave it to Chance. Chance Dakkinen, Private Detective.* The monopoly image for Chance was his logo. Below that appeared his mailing address, email and telephone number.

"Ugh, looks nice, Chance, but—" It confused Marsha.

"Said is going to blanket every municipal and state office that must comply with Freedom of Information requests made on my letterhead tomorrow by email. Police Departments, Town halls, Licensing units, everybody we can think of."

Said was next. "After that, I have a couple of classes, but can be back by one. We think it is still prudent that I keep searching for additional suspects, just in case."

No one disagreed, given that their best suspect before Michael Sean Kelly was homeless and died in a drainage culvert.

"Ramit is going to help me with social media searches during the day, I have a night class tomorrow," Farah said.

"We both will take turns doing case input as well. It's not doing just data entry at this stage, Farah has a real knack for analysis, we can work side by side," Ramit said giving her a nod of approval.

"We have to give some credit to my old boss Charlie Akers for connecting the dots on our boy's aliases to Boston sports heroes. He is going to stay close to Charlestown in case we need to bang on doors of Kelly's in-laws," Marsha said.

Hollins was next to speak, "Everybody keep in mind

that we are still trying to stay under the radar, we don't want to spook him. All he needs to do is get wind of us and he will rabbit again."

"He would probably change his name this time, if he gets away," Lester McNulty added.

"It's a tightrope, that's for sure," Marsha said. Mike, Ramit, and Marsha spent hours on this discussion before they decided to tread lightly. That Mr. Kelly kept such a low profile for two decades after the scare in Quincy made it clear that he would not stick around if he got wind of an investigation. They had beat the hell out of each murder and the leads were tough to come by.

Dennis opined, "We won't talk to the UPS store guy until he gets ready to close next Saturday. I would suggest Mr. Akers does the same on Sunday with his in-laws. It's too early now, but we might want to entice him to show up at the store Saturday morning."

"Which brings us to Plan B," she said, as she filled them in. No one disagreed. If he boogied, they would go public, Stanfield be damned.

When the last leads were poured over and assigned, the locals went home to their own beds and Ramit, Marsha and Mike were left staring at the board.

"Microchips and shoe leather," Mike muttered though the exhaustion catching up with him.

"What's that?" Marsha asked.

"It's gonna take a lot of internet searches combined with door-knocking to find Mr. Kelly."

"I'd put this team against any field office in the country, and do you know why?"

Both weary men looked at her.

"Because, it's not just another case. We all want this case solved and nobody wants to see another woman die."

CHAPTER 38

"I'M Lester McNulty and this here is Michael Hollins." Lester made the practiced move of flashing his credentials to the Driver and Vehicle Records Division clerk in Lansing.

Mike show her his active badge and ID card while Lester tucked his away his ID card with *Retired* stamped on it that he had covered with his thumb. "Hoping to get his DL photo and most current address." He slid a piece of paper with Kelly's full name, mail drop address and date of birth on it.

"One moment." Typing it in, she said, "It's current, no restrictions, same address, his photo is coming out in a moment." She then handed the blown-up photo to Mike.

"Thank you—" looking at her name tag, "—Patricia."

Lester added, "Have they told you that you are wonderful yet today?"

"It's still early, but no. Is there anything else I can help you with today, gentleman?" Patricia asked.

They smiled and shook their heads.

Once outside, Mike pulled up the composite and laid

the photo next to it on the hood of Lester's car. "Damn," they said simultaneously.

Poking the composite with his index finger, Lester said, "Put a little color on those cheeks, add a smile and a little twinkle in his eye and you have a dead ringer."

"Can't say I've ever seen a better match myself. Gotta tell Dennis that his sketch artist is a keeper," Mike added. Next he angled his smart phone to avoid a shadow from the morning sun and took a photo. He sent it to Marsha and Ramit with the caption: *When Irish eyes are smiling*. Next they drove to the nearest copy center and made a couple dozen prints of just the photo.

They talked the way cops talk when they are getting to know each other all the way to Inkster Police Department.

Yes, the PD had a copy of the paid ticket, they were told. Mike fibbed saying that the driver cited for following too closely back in May was wanted in Philly for questioning in a mob case. That answer earned them an escort into a conference room. Where the day-shift detective met them. They exchanged handshakes. Lester told them that Mike, and he were old friends and that he volunteered to caddy him around the area for the day. Mike put the DL photo on the table. The detective produced an accident report that went along with the ticket.

"Looks like a rear-ender," the bored detective said, "We get them all the time there."

Mike asked, "Is this our copy?"

The detective nodded. "The officer that wrote this up is on day shift. He's coming in." He would hand them off after they made introductions. This is how courtesies between departments were handled. Someday, they might need something in the City of Brotherly Love and would remind Mike of his visit.

Lester scanned it for vehicle information. "Damn," he said, "it's a rental." They were hoping for it being a company car or at least a leased vehicle.

Mike made up some bullshit about why he flew out to Detroit to find Michael Sean Kelly. Lester was listening in case he had to explain why his "old friend" was visiting him again later that week. They would keep their stories straight as partners were wont to do.

The responding officer appeared to be in his early twenties, never met visiting detectives from out of state before. "Yes, sir, that was my case. I ran both operators, and neither had wants nor warrants."

"No worries, patrolman," Mike assured him. "Just wanted to know what you remember about the accident."

He shrugged at the DL photo. "I see a lot of people every day, can't say that I remembered him. Said he would see his own doctor, didn't need me to call EMTs." He turned the citation around and studied it. "I would have put something here if he gave me any shit." Pointing to the comments section. "Just another accident. I did everything by the book."

"Anything special about the guy?"

"Seemed like he was a little out of it," the uniformed officer said, "I just chalked it up to get punched in the face and chest with an airbag."

They all nodded. "Thank you for your time, gentlemen," Mike said as he and Lester stood up and stretched. "Next stops are the other driver and the rental place."

Lester acted indignant. "You promised you'd feed me after this stop, Mike," then added to everyone's amusement, "After all, a good patrolman never gets tired, wet or hungry."

They worked well as a team in the interactions so far

and that carried over to the older gent who had a lot more to say about the accident. The damage to his truck hadn't been repaired. It was still drivable.

"I had a bunch of scratch offs that I wanted to turn in at the store. All of a sudden, the guy slams into me from behind. Hit me hard enough to set off his airbags. I expected him to walk up to my truck and ask me how I was doing. He just sat there. Never got out of his car, never called the cops, just sat there. I called 9-1-1 and sat on the curb until the cop came. It's like the guy was in some kind of daze. The cop had to bang on his window to get his attention. I figured something was up with the guy. Cop told me that he gave him a ticket and would write it up that that he was at fault. Guy never told me his was sorry. Never got his phone number either."

Lester slipped a copy of the DL photo across the table. "That the guy?"

"Yep, except that he wasn't smiling that day."

"You injured?" Mike asked.

"Yep." He dug into his wallet with greasy fingers and dirty fingernails and pried out a dog-eared business card. "They totaled my truck, but I kept it anyway. I figure it's my good luck charm now. My lawyer's working on getting me some money for my pain and suffering and inconvenience." He pushed the card across the table.

Mike jotted the name on the card into his notebook and avoided touching it. "Anything else?"

"Just that Smiley never said he was sorry."

The rental company was able to bring up Mr. Kelly's account. He rented mostly SUVs and usually for a day. His account went back several years. The phone number he gave them was not working. He used the same credit card each time. The clerk couldn't remember if he was dropped off or picked up. She had worked the counter for several years and knew the repeat customers. She never saw him with anybody else. She printed off the list of Kelly's transactions for the past three years. The dates and times would be placed on the timeline in *CaseSoft*.

Lester slipped the young lady a twenty-dollar bill and his business card and asked her to help them out; that they would appreciate a call the next time Mr. Kelly came in.

Mike had sent Ramit the information for the rental car company's insurance company and the claim number. They hoped that they took a recorded statement of Mr. Kelly, although it was not always practical for the carriers to do so on these straightforward liability cases.

The afternoon moved quickly as they learned that once the previous moving violation tickets were paid, they were disposed of. Records of issue date, violator, violation and payment is all that was left. The car Mr. Kelly was driving was not part of the kept data. Mike and Lester both bemoaned that these violations happened in the in-between time of trashing hard copies in favor of data input and now of scanning of source documents before destroying them.

Chance and Dennis stayed on surveillance at the UPS store with no activity until eight.

Ramit, Said and Farah kept clicking away. Farah plotted the dates of rentals and she saw a trend of days of the week repeating for the upcoming day of the week of 9/11 and then disturbingly, the following year.

"Kelly isn't using a rental for next week." Lester told them. If they had more time, they could have set up on the rental agency on Tuesdays this summer.

. . .

Marsha turned every page of the hand-written notes of Myles Hanski and decided that she couldn't crack the code to decipher them. She scanned them into the system and shipped them off to a former administrative assistant at the BAU who had been at his funeral and told Marsha that she could interpret the handwriting of her former boss.

* * *

Sean returned the SUV demo to the Ford dealership used car lot, switched plates back to the original cars and drove home dog-tired, but was excited that Tuesday evening. He was out before dawn that morning and had taken up his eyeball on Tamara and Omar's house. He watched Omar leave shortly after arriving. Omar was leaving the house after seven lately, as the morning sun rose later now at the end of this sun-splashed summer.

Like clockwork, Tamara hustled the kids, whom Sean watched grow like weeds all summer, out the door and into her vehicle at 7:15. She then went straight home and didn't leave to retrieve them until 2:15. After following her to the school one last time, his drove by their house until darkness set in. He was confident that he could take his time between nine and noon next week.

He had to pee and was juggling his Chinese takeout with his surveillance notebook while trying to fish out his keys out of his pocket. He rushed down the thread bare hallway rugs under the lighting of two light bulbs at the front and back entrances of the house converted to apartments, when his landlady appeared in the hall at his door as he keyed his double locks.

"Here is your mail, Mr. Kelly, I thought you would like to have it before it got too late."

Sean opened his apartment door and set his things inside to accept the letters and junk mail. "Mrs. Spicoli, thank you as always. It is always so nice of you to fetch it for me."

He walked the postal matter to the kitchen table and returned quickly with a thick envelope. "Here's my rent and what I owe you for grabbing my mail. I am so busy these days at the store and you really save me a lot of time."

"It gets me out of my apartment and it's not far to walk, Mr. Kelly. I am glad to do it for you," she said, smiling as she took the money from him and returned to her apartment across the hall.

This four-unit building with off-street parking and a landlady who didn't ask any questions about his life was a perfect set-up for him to work on his mission. There was no trace of him at this address. There was never a single piece of mail addressed to him to be found in his mailbox on the porch, just the usual addressed to *occupant* or *resident* flyers and circulars.

CHAPTER 39

AS THREE WEEKDAYS FLEW BY, the leads dried up. The excitement of Monday night when Marsha returned with fresh hope and extra energy now turned into rancorous debates every night how to draw the predator out.

"Have him have to come in to sign for a package at the UPS store. The owner must have a way to contact him to tell him that he's gotta sign something," Dennis argued.

"What if we spook him?" Mike countered.

"He's gotten away with this shit for as long as he's lived out here, he will not be looking for a tail," Chance said.

"He's a meticulous planner, we don't know what his counter-surveillance moves are," Ramit chimed in.

Lester was next. "If he stays true to form, we will not find out where he beds down at night or where he works unless we shake things up a little."

"Marsha, Lester is right," Said added, "Mr. Kelly has given nothing we don't already know in any of our FOI requests that we have gotten returns on."

Mike played the out of town Organized Crime cop and Lester, his recent retiree sidekick at every location from the state capital to Detroit, hoping to scratch out additional identifiers from the FOI responses.

Marsha worked with Ramit as a team on all the social media leads generated by the Michael Kelly here and even across the border in Windsor, Canada. She wasn't about to ask "Georgie Boy" Osterman for passport stampings, but it was possible that Kelly commuted and used the mail drop only for essentials. She and Ramit showed the DMV photo to the victim's survivors. Aisha came closest with a vague recognition, but her memory, saturated with grief, left her frustrated and tearful.

They also worked the last leads from all the cases that needed one last phone call or a visit to button things up.

"Here's a perfect example. Mike Kelly shot a hole in one at the Oakland Hills Country Club at a Rotary function seven years ago in July. Is there a picture of him with his ball? No. Is he a member there? No. It was the Rotaries yearly charity event. How many Kellys in this area could have done that? Farah?"

Without missing a beat, she said, "Twenty-eight, Marsha."

Marsha steamrolled along. "Let's say, we approach a few well-connected Rotarians on a pretext and ask about Mike or Sean Kelly, right? They will take my number and have Kelly call me."

"Set up a phony name on a Google Voice number. When he calls, tell him that your husband died, and you were calling all the people on business cards in his wallet to tell them about the funeral. Then you get him talking," Chance said, "We are getting close here, Marsha." The surveillance team had plenty of time to ponder ways to shake things loose at the mail drop.

"I know we are, but it's Thursday night and if we gotta

start taking chances, they have to be the right chances, guys. We have to keep nibbling around the edges until Monday noon. What's the best plan for each day? Don't forget we have Charlie in Charlestown. Let's brainstorm this and come up with a plan."

"Keys," Farah said.

"Keys?" Marsha asked.

"You always said that the keys are the key to this case," the introverted analyst spoke up. "He had to have access to house keys and car keys. None of the families, friends or neighbors talked about break-ins. None of the victims reported theft of purses or keys. He has to have some way of getting access to the keys without raising suspicion. If you will allow me, let me massage the data and see what I can find. Since I did most of the social media searches, I know many of the Michael Kellys pretty well. I might make the connection."

"It's a better use of my time as well now that we have eliminated all the others," Said said.

Marsha and the brothers in blue looked at the data nerds and agreed.

"We rarely see the devil in the details until after the fact," Chance said, "It'd be nice to catch the guy before...."

* * *

"Yeah, he's got juvenile cancer and I want to send him a care package and a get-well card," Lester said to the clerk in The Lions Pro Shop at Ford Field, "Maybe a Barry Sanders jersey and an autographed football?"

"No problem, sir. We even have get-well cards against the far wall. If you need any help, let me know."

"Do you ship?"

"Of course."

"Next day?" he asked.

"Yes, it's extra but...."

"Mikey. Little Mikey," Lester ad-libbed.

"Mikey will get it tomorrow by ten thirty in the morning."

* * *

Charlie Akers looked up the steps to the front door as it opened. "Mr. Kelly, my name is Carver Daniels, I am a missing heir researcher from Tampa, Florida. I am looking to speak with the grandchildren of Edna Damon." He handed the man a brand-new business card he had printed at Staples when the store opened that morning. The phone listed was a Google Voice that rang on Marsha's phone and the email went to her as well. Overnight, Ramit created the Carver Daniels Forensic Genealogy website with that email and Google Voice number attached.

"She was my dead wife's mother."

"Yes, sir, her parents were Benjamin Damon and Wilma O'Malley who came over from County Cork in 1919. She was their only child. Had her when she was thirty-nine."

"How do you know all that?"

"That's my job, sir. I find estates worth a significant amount of money and I connect the money to the nearest living relatives. I get a percentage of the inheritance." he patiently explained. "I supply the heirs with an attorney, and I pay all the expenses. If they don't get paid, I don't get a dime and they owe me nothing."

Sean's father considered the well-rehearsed speech and

the smiling man on his doorstep that Saturday morning. "Well, you know that family tree pretty well."

"Yes, but I am sorry to say, the branch stops here with your three kids. I take it your girls married after your wife died and took their husband's names and I can't find your son anywhere in Boston either." He waited.

"Yeah, both my girls got married and are still around, but my son moved out of town a while back." He still hadn't invited Charlie in, but it was a nice morning on the crowded neighborhood street in Charlestown, so he didn't push the issue.

"Oh, where to?" Charlie asked nonchalantly.

"Detroit. Took a sales job out there. Doing good for himself."

"Oh really, what kind of sales?"

"Something to do with the internet, I am not sure, really," the father answered nervously.

"Does he get back often?" Charlie made it sound conversational.

"Christmas, usually. Sean always tries to catch a home game in Foxborough."

Charlie nodded, waited a couple of beats and said, "So, how can I get in touch with them? I need to send them paperwork. In there, I tell them to take it to an attorney or somebody at church who they respect and for them to look it over very closely before they decide to work with me."

"Do you have something explaining this all, Mr. Daniels? I will have them call you."

"Maybe I can call the oldest and he or she can talk to the siblings with more information?" Charlie smiled. He knew who the oldest was before he asked.

A moment of indecision in Mr. Kelly's face gave Charlie hope that a phone number would be forthcoming.

"That would be Sean and I will take your stuff and he can call you if he wants to."

"Sure, no problem. Here you go, and here is a pamphlet that I usually send out, so you can explain this all better to him. I do this all the time, Mr. Kelly. I am perfectly satisfied to do this one step at a time. Is your telephone number still 617-555-1234, in case I have to call you to follow up?"

He nodded while taking Charlie's newly minted, ink barely dried pamphlet touting Carver Daniels as a Missing Heir Researcher with testimonials from non-existent clients and recently deceased probate lawyers.

* * *

"Hi, Dad. What's up?"

"Man stopped by the house a little bit ago and said that you and your sisters are entitled to money from Grandma Damon's family."

"What did you say?" Sean's spider senses were tingling.

"Told him that he had done his homework. He said they came over in 1919 and that your mother was born late in Grandma Damon's life. He had the family tree in his hands."

"Sounds fishy to me," Sean said.

"He left some paperwork saying that nobody had to pay him until they got paid and he would take care of all the expenses."

"Did he say was his take was?" Sean asked. He didn't like the sound of it.

"No, he said he would discuss it with you and that you could explain it to your sisters."

"What did you tell him?" Sean asked. It worried him that his father may have told the guy how to find him.

"Nothing. Took his business card and brochure. Do you want to call him?"

"No, it's just a scam. If he bothers you again, just tell him that you will report him to the Better Business Bureau."

"Okay, son. I'm gonna stop by the cemetery and put flowers on Mary's grave tomorrow after church."

"I know, Dad. I think about her all the time, especially this time of year."

"So do I, Sean. Take care."

"You, too, Dad."

Sean thought it strange that someone would look for him in Charlestown after so many years. He was purposeful to be vague with his family about where he jettisoned to after that detective roughed him up. Slowly, as the years went by, he reconnected with them for a brief visit at Thanksgiving or Christmas and always around the Patriots schedule. He missed home, but his life's work became more important and sentimentality was to be avoided. A knock on his door interrupted his musings.

"Who is it?" he asked through the thin door.

"It's me, Mr. Kelly, I have your mail."

He opened the door to Mrs. Spicoli. "Edmund told me that you had to come in to sign for a package. Here is the slip. He said your number on file no longer works, otherwise he would have called you."

Sean could not recall another time when that had occurred. "Did he say what it was?"

"He showed me. It looks like you got something important from the Detroit Lions. He couldn't give it to me."

"Thank you, Mrs. Spicoli. Would you like me to stop by the bakery on the way back?"

"Only if you are getting something, Mr. Kelly."

He closed the door and called the UPS store immediately from a burner phone. He had to wait for Edmund to finish with a bulky shipment.

"UPS Store. This is Edmund, how can I help you?"

"Hi, Edmund, It's Michael Kelly. You have a present for me."

"Yes, siree, it looks like a gift package from The Lions Pro Shop at the football stadium."

With all the tickets he bought over the years, he wondered if it was a complimentary gift. "Can you open it for me and tell me what is inside?"

"No. Sorry, it's against company policy. You need to come in and sign for it. They need proof of delivery. I see this on expensive and insured packages all the time."

"Can I let Mrs. Spicoli sign for it with my permission?"

"I'm sorry, we can't do that, Mr. Kelly."

Sean looked at his watch and his curiosity overcame his concerns about making a personal appearance. "I can be there in twenty minutes." He ended the call.

He walked to the bakery first and bought the five-dollar sampler of four items and separated her cannoli from his bear claws and was tempted to start into his bag.

As he exited the bakery and walked towards the intersection, directly in front of him sat a man in his car, listening to talk radio with the windows down. He sat facing out of the parking spot and not into it. Sean retreated away from him and crossed the street a half of a block in the opposite direction. That is when he spotted another man sitting alone in an SUV facing the store.

From years of doing this himself and being diligent about spotting a tail, he backtracked to his apartment, got his vehicle and put them under counter-surveillance. It was probably nothing but a coincidence, but he had to be sure.

Sean changed his appearance for each pass when he

drove either east on the same side of the UPS store or west on the bakery side. He always made sure that he was in a stream of vehicles passing by.

As the hours dragged by, cars came and went from the parking lots on either side of Michigan Avenue, but those two cars didn't change their positions.

Both offered an eyeball of the front door, and finally, when the UPS store closed at eight, he watched both cars depart. It tempted him to follow one and get a tag, but he didn't want to get caught following them.

I was told to come in and there were two cars waiting for me. It was that simple.

He replayed the conversation with Edmund repeatedly and recalled nothing in his voice that hinted at fear or nervousness. But, then again, he rarely had ever spoken to him, so he couldn't be sure.

How about waiting for Edmund to leave the store and follow him home and make him talk? But Sean nixed that idea. They didn't know where he lived and having a mail drop for two decades was pricey. Now it became priceless. He had to be more careful now.

It was not until later that night that he thought about the coincidence of a man looking for him in Boston. He wrestled with the worry that they were finally catching up with him. *Will my luck hold out?* Should he beat feet now while he still could? He had plenty of stashed cash. He could get access to many vehicles for an interstate trip with the key fobs he collected over the years.

As Sunday morning dawned to a beautiful sunrise of red and purple, he had already been set up for an hour to watch for the watchers.

At 7:45 both cars returned and took up eye-balls positions further away from the store. He was sure they'd move in closer as the parking lots filled, affording them a closer view and more cover.

This is text book surveillance. He was safe, but for how long? He had to find out.

* * *

"Hello. This is International Missing Heir Finders," Marsha said to the caller through the microphone of her headset. Her phone was automatically recording the call, and everyone in the suite took a collective breath.

"You dropped some paperwork on my family and I want to know what this is about," the male caller said.

"Yes, and whom am I speaking with?"

"Why do you need my name?"

"So, I know which heir search this is pertaining to."

"A Mr. Carver Daniels left a card and some paperwork in Charlestown, MA, yesterday."

"One second, please." It would be nice to trace the caller but they didn't have an equipment set up that the bureau reserves for kidnapping and ransom calls. "I see it here. This has to do with the family tree of Edna Damon."

"That's right."

Marsha said, "I'm looking at the family tree and see that she had one daughter who has passed, but was survived by Michael, Megan and Martha

"Yes, that's right."

"I see from the notes Mr. Daniels left a card with a Mr. Kelly yesterday morning."

"Correct, so what's this about?"

Marsha had practiced this response so that it didn't

sound canned or rehearsed. "We find estates all over the country where people have died without a will. We do the genealogy research and then connect the heirs to the estates."

"What's in it for you?"

"When the heirs receive their inheritance, we receive a portion, we pay for all the court expenses including an attorney. There are no out-of-pocket expenses to the heirs. If they don't receive any money, we don't either and the heirs don't have to pay for any of the expenses." Marsha glanced up from her cheat sheet and waited.

"Yeah, I get that. Tell you what. Just mail the paperwork to the house where Mr. Daniels went yesterday."

"We can do that. Please tell Mr. Kelly to expect a Priority Mail package through the US Mail in the next couple of days. Who can I say that I spoke with for my notes?"

"Brady. Thomas Brady."

"Thank you, Mr. Brady, have a pleasant day," she got in before the line went dead.

To the others staring at her wordlessly, "He didn't even ask how much money was at stake. He was fishing."

She looked at Ramit who said, "The website was pinged ten minutes ago from the Apple store in Downtown."

Mike and Lester got up from their chairs. "Let's find us some video of this character," Lester said.

"Bet you a donut, he called us from a burner phone," she said.

Mike said, "We'll let Dennis and Chance know that Kelly's acting hinky."

"It is a burner. We can find out where it was purchased tomorrow when their corporate offices open," Ramit said.

The air in the suite this sun-splashed Sunday afternoon

was cool, but she was suffocating. Marsha got up from her table and walked out of the room, down the back stairs and out into the rear parking lot. She dialed Charlie, thinking how nice a Bloody Mary or three would go down right now.

"Talk to me, Marsha," he said.

"I got the call, Carver," she said using his fake name.

"And?"

"He used a burner phone and checked out our phony website from an Apple store downtown. He gave us a fake name too." The adrenaline dump of talking to the killer and not being able to reel him in was pounding blood into her temples and causing a tightness in her chest and shortness of breath.

"What name did he use?"

"Thomas Brady."

"It figures. I will cold call on the sisters now and brother in-laws — see what I can shake. Maybe they will let something slip. It's better that I go now. The Patriots are on at 4 p.m. I won't be able to talk to anybody during the game."

"We need a miracle, Charlie. Otherwise, I go nuclear in less than twenty-four hours."

"Roger that, O'Shea."

CHAPTER 40

THE VIDEO of Michael Sean Kelly was not available. Store personnel told Lester and Mike that they couldn't give them the tape without a subpoena. Apple was notorious for protecting the privacy of their customers. They walked in both directions from the store and noted cameras on buildings that were closed. They would approach those businesses on Monday morning.

Marsha wasn't happy with the news. With the way this case was taking on the gyrations of a Dorney Park rollercoaster, after three months of chugging up the tracks, she knew she was in for a thrill ride. Charlie was buzzing in on her phone. She pushed herself away from her laptop.

Without a greeting, he said, "Both his sisters told me in so many words to go shit in my hat. I played dumb saying that I didn't know how to find their brother and they repeated what he told you. I wonder if I should have hit the youngest first instead of Dad."

"We both figured that you'd have a better chance with his father," Marsha replied, "He's being careful. He left town in a hurry and only comes back once or twice a year."

"This was a good pretext, Marsha. We had a fake website, business cards and an excellent reason for him wanting us to find him; one that put some real jingle in his pocket. I would not have changed it at all, but damn, I'd like you to catch a break on this case. Any luck at the UPS store?"

"Dennis and Chance will brace the franchisee after he locks up. That won't be until around 8:15," she said.

"I'll stay here through Tuesday night, just in case," he said, "Something's gotta go right for you, Marsh."

"When I had him on the phone, Charlie, I was so tempted to say, 'Hey, Sean, can you do me a favor and try not kill any Muslim women this week,' but, of course, I had to stay in role."

"We were hoping he'd get greedy and call you from a traceable phone or give you his home address. That was the entire purpose for the setup. We had to try to smoke him out."

"You're right as usual, Yoda, gotta stay positive and keep punching. Gotta take this other call coming in." She disconnected with Charlie and said, "Hi, Rihanna, how are you?"

"I hope you don't mind me calling on a Sunday."

"Not at all, we're still working the case." *I have to keep reminding myself that for me it's a case, for them it's a murdered loved one.* "What's up?"

"I sat with the drawing you supplied me."

Shit, we forgot to send her the DMV photo. "Yes, you said you would meditate on it," Marsha replied calmly.

"I was young at the time, but the memory I have is that my father and I were sitting in the back seat of the car and my mother was driving and that man was a passenger. It was strange, though."

"How so?" Marsha prodded.

"I don't remember anyone else ever riding in the car with my mother and father. We were a close family and didn't have many friends outside of family. It was the only time my father sat in the back seat with me."

"Anything else?"

"No. I just wanted to tell you that is the picture that forms in my mind when I look at the drawing."

"Thank you, Rihanna, if there is anything else you can think of call me."

After she hung up, she added that info to the big board and gave her notes to Farah.

At 8:20, Dennis called, "Marsha, we may have something. We braced the owner of the store at closing. Told him we were looking for Michael Kelly. He about shit his pants. He said that Kelly called him yesterday and said he would come in to pick up the package. Said he would be there in about twenty minutes, but he never showed. The package is still waiting for him. Get this. Kelly has an old lady pick up his mail for him. She's a veritable chatterbox, says she's his landlady."

"What's her name?"

"Agnes Spicoli."

"S-P-I-C-O-L-I?

"Yep. Chance is copying the guy's calls from yesterday afternoon now and will email you as soon as he gets them all."

"The guy knows to keep his mouth shut?"

"He ain't going to blab to Kelly. Chance is putting the fear of God in him right now."

"When you are done with him, cut him loose, but sit tight. We will want to pay a visit to Agnes."

***

"Who is it?" the tiny voice spoke through the door.

"It's Marsha Drummond. Ma'am, I am trying to get a hold of Mike, Mike Kelly," Marsha said using her maiden name.

"Did you knock on his door?" came the voice again.

"Yes, ma'am. It doesn't sound like anybody's home. Can I talk to you please? I don't want other people to hear my business?"

By process of elimination, they had already figured out that Kelly lived across the hall. They had knocked on his door with no answer. The guys with the guns backed off, and the nicely dressed woman was alone in the hallway.

They had placed the multi-unit dwelling under surveillance at nine p.m. Now it was nine a.m. All the cars in the lot were connected to the other tenants. Some had already departed that morning for work. Twelve hours of pulse-pounding surveillance with no activity in order to catch a killer had taken their toll. Their nerves were frayed. Marsha was more polite at 3 a.m. but had to tell everyone to shut the fuck up when dawn broke. The tension was killing her, too, but she was the leader of this motley crew and needed to hold herself and them together.

They can bitch at me at the bar when I am buying, when it's all over, she groused.

The door opened, and a frail face peeked out below the chain. "Yes?"

"We had a business meeting to go to this morning, and he told me to pick him up. He's not home."

"He left very early yesterday morning. Now that I think about it, I don't think I heard him come home all day. That is strange. He usually tells me when he's going away."

"That's weird. He told me he was having car trouble, and that's why he wanted me to pick him up?"

"Are you a car salesman too?" Agnes asked.

"Why yes I am, but I am from an out-of-town dealership. Maybe he is already at work, I can try him there." *Marsha Drummond. Out-of-town car salesman.*

"I don't know where he works. I'm sorry," Agnes said and began closing the door.

"One last question, ma'am, do you know what kind of car he drives?" Marsha debated putting her foot between the door and the door jamb.

"Blue. He likes blue cars." She closed the door in Marsha's face.

Marsha was tempted to kick down Kelly's door across the hall but knew that an illegal entry would give a defense attorney grounds to suppress any of the evidence found in the apartment. Identifiers of who the next victim was could be sitting on his calendar next to the grocery list. She decided to bounce.

Chance, Lester and Dennis placed the house in the middle of their surveillance triangle. Marsha, Ramit and Mike sped to their hotel. They had a couple of hours to find the car dealership. Kelly's father had said he was in sales, Rihanna was probably out on a test drive with Sean and her family. Marsha called Farah to give her the latest on Kelly.

They walked into the room and saw Farah standing next to the big board. She had written in large letters: Fanner Ford.

"It's been staring at us all the time, Marsha." Farah's Chromebook was cabled to the suite's flat screen monitor. "When you look at all the photos of the cars of the victims, the truck that was burned and the pickup that crashed into the convenience store, they all had two things in common. They were all Fords, and look at the license plate holder.

Fanner Ford above the plate and below it, 'Since 1923.'" She scrolled through the photos and magnified the images.

"I'll be damned," Marsha said, "I knew you would figure it out."

"It was in the data," Farah said.

"That's how he is getting house keys and car fobs," Ramit added.

"That's how he is choosing his victims," Mike said. "Do you think if we send the DMV photo to the victim's family again and ask them if a car was ever bought from this guy, whaddya think they will say?"

Marsha was first to say it. "This is his prospecting pool. Tomorrow's victim is a customer of his. We might be able to alert them in time, if we can get to his customer list. Farah, I need you to go with us. Call Said and tell him to meet us there at ten thirty. First, I have to make a phone call on Plan B."

CHAPTER 41

THEY ARGUED BACK AND FORTH, but they struck a compromise. They pushed the press conference scheduled for noon back to four thirty p.m. Marsha guaranteed them that she had to be 100 percent sure that all the potential victims were identified and safely guarded before they would think about canceling the evening presser. She would then have armed security for all the potential victims starting at midnight. Chance and Lester would set up the security details. That American Express card in her pocket would sizzle with use.

* * *

Tamara reconciled the Tabrizi Masonry company's accounts receivables. That large payment from the FBI agent came in before the rental charges hit their business credit card. *Good for cash flow.*

After they moved into their new house later in the fall, Omar promised to take them to Disney World during winter break. They would pay for everything from their frequent flyer miles on the business credit cards. Yes, the boys would play on elite indoor soccer teams, but going there before their oldest became a teenager was important.

She had goodies for the school open house in both ovens and would bring them tomorrow night. Her sweets were always a hit at school functions.

Tamara had to admit, they had it good. They had their health, Omar enjoyed his work, and the business was flourishing. The boys were in an excellent school and studied hard. Their path into professional careers were paved with supportive parents, a faith community at the mosque and teachers who cared.

As she sat at the kitchen table balancing the books, the smell from her ovens reminded her that life was very good. It wasn't lost on her that tomorrow was the day that they were all dreading. She did not worry her children. Many members from their congregation would be having sad remembrances. Another poor woman could die. They had not heard about any arrests and Omar told her that the attorney would be on the news about the case later in the afternoon.

* * *

The pin-hole cameras that Sean installed around his apartment had captured the events in his hallway and parking lot. Those cops didn't break into his apartment and trip his silent alarm.

He patted himself on the back for leaving behind unnecessary belongings. One suitcase carried his traveling clothes and cash, the other his fake IDs, answering machine with Mary's messages and their VHS tapes and player.

He left the Apple store on foot and took a couple buses

until he was sure he wasn't followed and now he sat on a lawn chair in a garage rented to a John Pesky. He would not work today as he felt it would only be a matter of time before they showed up there. He weighed his decision to finish his mission in Detroit.

He could have left town after he made the surveillance team setting up again on the UPS store yesterday morning. Sean thought about Albuquerque, New Mexico often, thanks to reruns of *Better Call Saul*. He had even visited once. They would never find him there. As soon as he finished this last mission, he'd head off into the sunset.

He altered his last plan to allow for a fast getaway after a blazing finale. Because of circumstances, he had to bend his rule, not break it.

As he finished his last preparations, he wondered where he had seen that woman in his hallway before.

***

"I don't care that the general manager is not in at the moment. I want those records now," Marsha roared. She was flanked by two scowling men and trailed by two stern-faced college-age kids.

"Don't you need a search warrant or something?" the sales manager weakly sputtered.

"Do you need every major Cable News and TV station truck camped out in your parking lot for the next week? How would you like that kind of advertising, Buster?"

"It's gonna take me time to do what you want. You have to come back. I can't just press a button and make them appear."

Marsha took a step closer, and he flinched back. She whispered now, "You guys track sales stats for each salesman the way a baseball team does for batting averages. Now start moving before I get really mad."

"Excuse me, ma'am," a sheepish voice from behind her spoke up.

She whirled to look at a youthful woman with a stack of paper in her arms. "Don't call me ma'am. It's Agent O'Shea." Her eyes narrowed on the frightened girl.

"This is Sean's customer list from the first day he started working here." Pointing to the sales manager. "He knew that. Every day, I have to address birthday cards and each of these people get a Thanksgiving card as well. Sean signs each one, and I mail them out. He knew that too."

"Call me Marsha. Can you put this all on a thumb drive?" she asked, accepting the printouts.

The girl nodded.

The sales manager leaned around Marsha said to the receptionist, "You're fired. Take your things and get out."

"Mike, please escort this gentleman back to his office," Marsha turned to the sales manager. "Do you really want to continue obstructing an official FBI investigation? Knowing where his customer list was is count one. Firing her would be count two. Don't play with me, big boy." She nodded to the grinning receptionist to get the thumb drives.

Mike hadn't flexed his muscles in a while after a week of being the nicety-nice out of town visiting detective. "After you, sir."

The sales manager, not used to being bullied in his own store, appeared to be thinking of how he could retort or respond and got a not so pleasant poke in his chest.

"You are very close to count three, pal," the unsmiling Philly organized crime detective on medical leave said, none to politely.

"Said, when you get the first drive, go to Parts and look

for all keys and fobs made for every Arab American. Tell them to see me if they have a problem. Ramit—"

"Service department. Same thing. I'm on it," he said.

"Farah, go to the conference room and sort our people by DOB and work with the printout. Damn, I hope they have fresh coffee here."

* * *

He filled four five-gallon plastic jerry cans with super premium at the gas station. It was his favorite station, as it had no cameras on the pumps. *Not as good as aviation fuel, but it will have to do.*

Traveling the route, as he had so many times on his surveillances, calmed his nerves. He chose the kill zone carefully to maximize both stealth and getaway potential. The moped he carried in the bed of the stolen pickup would be positioned just right. The moped would carry him through the wooded trail to the Lions-Blue Mustang 5.0 waiting with his getaway stash on the other side of the wooded park. He'd have to buy some cowboy boots for Robert Parrish when he got to New Mexico.

* * *

Mike told Marsha that the sales manager would not cause any further problems. He was smiling devilishly. She knew better from her father and brother not to ask a Philly cop about some things. "Mr. Kelly had marked tomorrow off on his desk calendar as a vacation day. I suggested to our friend that we bag up all Kelly's belongings." Mike set two oversized garbage bags in the conference room. "We'll keep them here for safekeeping after I go through it."

Said was already seated next to Farah. They were uploading their findings as quickly as they received them. "He was busy in our community. I even recognize some of my friend's parent's names."

Ramit entered the room. "Finance manager pulled me aside and told me that Kelly made far more sales than the rest of them combined. You are taking down their meal ticket. Might explain why you got so much resistance."

"Fuck 'em if they can't take a joke," Marsha muttered. Every single victim except the motel clerk, Amber, was listed. *Maybe her husband bought the car in his name alone,* Marsha mused.

Kelly hadn't bothered to remove their names from his card list. She thought it was sick that he would keep sending cards on their birthdays knowing that he had extinguished their lives. She wondered what he did on his wife's birthday. She made a note that she would send him a card for his birthday every year until they executed him.

"Another thing," Ramit said. "The service manager clued me in how he got the keys. He said that Mike, as they referred to him, would take the customer's cars out for a car wash on the days when the car was in for service and he would make a big deal about it by handing his customers their keys. Other customers waiting for their cars to be finished bitched about how their car wasn't getting that special treatment. They said they would buy their car from Mike next time."

"Smart. Our boy makes the copies of the house keys while he was out getting the cars cleaned up. We always said the keys were the key," she said.

More important now, they started harvesting potential victims. It surprised Marsha to see Omar and Tamara. She would make sure to call them first. Tamara's car had been in for service and they had ordered an extra fob.

Ramit was tabulating the list, Said tickled the databases and Farah worked on open source intelligence known as OSINT.

Marsha and Ramit started making the calls. Marsha was not sure they had the complete prospect pool and realized they now only had three hours before they would trigger Plan B.

She decided she would work for Charlie and with Shira in Clearwater, rather than have a dead Muslim woman on her growing tab of people who died or got hurt because of her mistakes. Her ego drove her to solve her last big case. Staring at Mike's limp arm reminded her of that.

Four months of grinding had come to this. They found all the victims and probably most of the potential victims. They figured out how he did it, and how he was able to choose his targets. They knew his name, where he lived, where he worked, where he banked, where he kept a mail drop, but the most important thing missing, was where he was at the moment, and for that reason, she was okay with her contingency plan.

The calls to the potential victims all had a similar feel. It shocked the women to hear that the delightful man who sold them their car and took such excellent care of them did such terrible things to the other woman of their faith. Marsha and Ramit instructed each to go to their local police department or precinct and wait there until escorted home by armed security teams. They would be baby sat for all of September 11. They were given Chance's telephone number and he would coordinate the coverage.

* * *

Maybe the business could buy her a new cell phone. Hers was not keeping a charge for more than an hour lately. She kept it on the charger at home or in the car constantly. Tamara needed to get groceries and baking supplies before picking the boys up and worked on those lists after closing out the accounting software.

She moved the goodies to the drying rack and would have to remember to threaten the boys not to touch a single one until she separated the nice ones into containers and then the ugly ones could be set aside for growing boys.

She had a list swirling in her mind along with what to make for dinner and was preoccupied with shutting down her laptop. When she multi-tasked, she occasionally forgot things as she rushed out the door, locking it behind her.

* * *

Where the hell is she? She's not at home and hasn't driven by me yet. Sean was sweating in the firefighter's flame-retardant suit, even though he had the AC cranked to the max. The black helmet with the hard plastic shield sitting in the passenger seat would double nicely as a crash helmet when he screamed through the woods on his moped. *Wouldn't want to have an accident and get hurt.* He chuckled to himself.

He never tested this plan, but he visualized it a hundred times. He was sure it would work. All the rest of his plans had worked, except for that day he wanted to play bumper cars, but in the end that was a flaming success too. His puns amused him. *Flaming success.*

* * *

"I can't get a hold of her." Omar was panicking. "I am loading bags of concrete on my truck, I'm at least fifty minutes away."

Marsha stood up at the table and motioned to Ramit to get up too. "Where could she be?"

"Damn it, I don't remember what she told me she had planned today."

"Call the police and tell them to do a wellness check on her." *God, I hope we are not too late.*

"She is supposed to pick up the kids in thirty minutes at the school."

"Where is that?" She put Omar on speaker phone and Ramit put the school name into his Google Maps. Mike called the surveillance team to give them a heads-up and to be careful about running hot into the school parking lot during dismissal.

"We are on the way. Omar, call the school and tell them to tell her to go inside and call the cops." Marsha and Ramit were running through the glass showroom doors. "Okay. Omar, what does she drive?"

"Black Ford Edge with a roof rack."

"Keep us in the loop."

"Will do."

* * *

Tamara loaded her groceries into the back of her SUV. She had already gone to the big box store and loaded up on sacks of flour, lard and sugar. It was then she realized she had forgotten her phone. She shrugged.

A couple hours without my phone isn't going to kill me.

* * *

I'm hoping that Kelly sticks to his routine or is long gone," Marsha said to Ramit as she temporarily suspended the Michigan motor vehicle law applying to a federal agents for the day.

They headed to the school with Dennis and Chance busting ass from the opposite direction. Lester would stay on the house until they relieved him. God forbid Kelly came home after spending a couple nights out with his girlfriend while the rest of the team was scrambling.

* * *

School protocols being what they are, the school secretary waited until the principal finished talking behind closed doors with a parent about a minor issue. The principal listened intently and set out to find the youngest boy's teacher, who then quick-stepped out the front doors to the pickup area.

"Mrs. Tabrizi. Mrs. Tabrizi!" she yelled. But it was too late and a school bus pulled between them, and by the time the teacher moved to acquire Tamara's SUV again, it had already pulled into traffic.

* * *

He didn't have much time. Tamara had entered the school parking lot from the other direction. He cut off an irate senior citizen as he drove back to his intercept position and then further back to where he had to enter the roadway to get a running start. He had to time it so that he could cross lanes on the straight-away adjacent to the woods and his moped.

* * *

Both of her boys told her about their day. It excited them that they had been both selected for an elite travel soccer team. Omar Jr. was getting noticeably taller and argued with his mother that they should allow him to sit up front. It wasn't cool to sit in the back with his little brother anymore. The conversation was good-natured, and she often made eye contact with her youngest, her baby boy, in the rear seat. It was her oldest who said, "Mom, what's that guy doing?"

* * *

Marsha laid on the horn to the Ford pickup that lurched out in front of her. Her eyes went to the license plate out of habit. That is when she saw the Fanner Ford license plate holder. The pickup then swerved into the oncoming lane. She saw the driver was wearing a fireman's helmet, and just before it picked up speed, she observed red plastic gasoline jerry cans strapped to the front grill with bungee cords and the final pieces of the four month jig-saw puzzle fell into place.

* * *

Tamara turned her eyes to the road in front of her as her son braced his arms on the dashboard. "Hold on." She jammed on the brakes and threw her right arm across his chest. She watched helplessly as the pickup headed straight towards them.

* * *

Marsha saw the Black Ford stay in the oncoming lane. "Hold on, Ramit!"

Marsha punched the accelerator on her subcompact rental and threw the steering wheel into a hard-left turn. She hit the pickup broad-side on the passenger-side door and saw the driver look at her in surprise.

Both airbags went off as she kept pressing her foot on the gas enough to nudge the pickup off course. Her car died in the middle of the oncoming lane and the pickup swerved into a parked mini-van head on.

* * *

Tamara and her son watched as, at the last second, a car smashed into the pickup truck like bumper cars at the amusement park. It threw the driver of the pickup against the driver's door, and in that moment, he veered to the left into a parked car.

A second later, the pickup exploded in a whoosh of flames. She felt the heat blast saturate her car and her air vents took in the fumes of burning gasoline. She threw her Edge into reverse, not caring who or what was behind her.

* * *

The female driver completely surprised him by broadsiding him and slamming him against the driver's door. The front-end impact was less than he expected, the fireball was more than he anticipated. He staggered out of the truck and fell hard to the ground. His suit became saturated with flaming gasoline shooting from the front bumper of the crippled pickup.

He staggered to his feet and wind milled around on the

sidewalk, trying to put out the flames. He dropped to the ground painfully again. He realized his left leg wasn't working. He began rolling to put the flames out, but they would come back as soon as fresh air hit the exposed parts of his suit.

He was heating up. It was getting intensely hot as flames licked at his exposed neck and chin. He would burn to death if he didn't peel off the suit. Getting onto his good knee, he ripped off his gloves and wriggled out of the suit that was killing him. The pickup was crackling and throwing off a furnace of heat now and had engulfed the unoccupied mini-van.

He had to get away. He screamed in agony as he made his broken leg bend so that he could pull down his suit. He pulled it back up to his waist and folded the top down over the bottom, smothering the last of the flames. The Black SUV sat staring at him like a bull at a gored matador. Tamara had won.

He dragged his bad leg behind him back to the moped. Thirty feet, twenty feet, ten.

* * *

"FBI! Kelly, it's over. Stop right there." Marsha held her Baby Glock steady from her knees. Her left arm was cocked at an awkward angle with her left hand cupping her right hand on the grip. She was teetering in her genuflect.

The nuns will be mad at me if I don't hold it steady. All those years in Catholic school are finally paying off.

* * *

Sean stopped and turned to see the woman from Sheeba's parking lot and his apartment hallway pointing a gun at him. "You crazy bitch." He turned his back to her and limped towards the moped.

* * *

Marsha summoned the last of her consciousness and steadied the gun on his torso, twenty yards away. *I can't remember the last time I shot right-handed.* She emptied her gun's magazine at the half-dressed man wearing a fireman's hat.

CHAPTER 42

"IS HE DEAD?" Marsha lurched upward, greeted by the incredible pain in her ribs taking her breath away. She saw stars.

"Whoa, pardner. Take it easy." Mike eased her back down on the hospital bed.

She had been in and out of consciousness for several hours. She looked at him and at her left arm in a splint. The throbbing in her skull continued unabated. "Is he dead?"

"Yes, you put at least four in him He was dead before he hit the ground."

"Oh God, I killed Ramit," she wailed as a nurse scurried in to see what the commotion was about.

Realizing the mistake, Mike was quick to soothe her. "No. No, Ramit is fine. He's fine, Marsha. Ramit is alive. He's banged up, but he is alive. Ramit is okay."

"After I slammed into the truck, I looked over at him and he wasn't moving. I thought he was dead. I thought that I killed him."

"Ramit's in the next room. He's okay, Marsha," Mike repeated and soothed her forehead with a moist cloth.

She relaxed her head against the pillow. "Mike, I thought I killed him I thought he was dead," she repeated. Relief swept over her, and she began to cry. He leaned over her and they embraced with their good arms for a long time.

Chance, Lester and Dennis stood by. The boys in blue were there for her, too, and wouldn't leave until they were assured she was okay. They stood silent witness to the woman that broke the case and solved their murders.

Mike released his grip and Marsha accepted the tissues to dry her eyes. It hurt everywhere when she blew her nose. "What happened?"

"I got to the school first and heard the explosion, looked that way and saw the fireball down the road. By the time I got there, it was over. He was down, you were down and Ramit was out cold," Dennis said, "A school bus driver behind you saw the entire thing. Told me what happened. Got the complete thing on video too. Within minutes, there were fire trucks, ambulances and cops everywhere. You know how to throw a party, Marsha." He grinned.

"If he got to that moped, he would have been gone," Chance said, "The school is in my bailiwick and my buddies said that he had a stolen getaway car stashed on the other side of the woods. Money, fake IDs, the works. If you didn't put him down, he would have gotten away."

"That's the last thing I remembered. I couldn't let him get to the bike," she said.

"Well, when you are up to it, there are some pissed-off FBI suits wanting to talk to you. They didn't take too kindly to us running around on their turf," Lester piped in.

"Fuck 'em," Marsha said.

"Fuck 'em is right," Mike said.

"Fuck 'em with a ginormous dick," Dennis added.

"Fuck 'em where the sun don't shine," Chance said.

"Nobody wanted to know nothing about this for years and they even tried screwing with the evidence."

"How did the press conference go?" Marsha had expected that it would have happened by now. She was thinking more clearly, even with the headache.

The guys all looked at each other, and through glances nominated Mike. "The six o'clock news is coming on in a minute, you can see for yourself, but there are some regular people waiting to see you."

The guys backed up to the corners of the room and Said and Farah walked in trailed by Tamara and Omar.

Farah asked, "How are you doing, Marsha?"

"This demolition derby stuff is not for amateurs; we have to leave it to the professionals." She winced. It hurt to laugh.

Said was next. "Ramit says that he has to drive from now on, no exceptions."

"How is he?"

"Concussion, sprained wrists from holding onto the dashboard, but otherwise okay. He's right next door."

Marsha took it in. "Go tell everybody who worked on this case what happened and how you all saved a life today. They can tell their classmates that tomorrow. I was just the wheel man. You have a lot to be proud of. Remember what you did on your summer vacation this year, always."

They nodded. "We will."

"That would be my life you saved. You saved my two boys too. They were in the car with me." Tamara reached out for Marsha's hand. "You were very brave. I saw everything. If you didn't stop him...." Tamara began to cry.

Omar placed his hand on top of his wife's and held Marsha's as well. "Thank you, Agent O'Shea."

"Call me Marsha, Omar."

"Marsha." He leaned down close to her ear and whispered, "The imam offers his thanks and apologizes for not being here. He will see you soon. There is a lot of fallout from what happened today."

She smiled back and nodded.

Chance reached for the tissues and passed the box around. It was strange how all the cops had fall allergies and watering eyes now.

"Here it is." Mike reached for the volume on the overhead TV and all heads craned to view it.

".... A car chase involving an alleged mass murderer ended in a fiery explosion today in Southfield. He is accused of preying on women in our community for years. With more on this we take you to the press conference held earlier today...."

Marsha was expecting to see the imam flanked by the mosque's attorney and other clerics, but more importantly, the families of the victims.

Like the pickup truck, she was about to watch her career go up in flames. Plan B was about to unfold. The media and the community would be told about each death and the killer's voice and DMV photo would be aired and displayed. Marsha promised them that she would do everything in her power to prevent another death. She had kept her word to the imam.

As the image came to the screen, she instead recognized Grayson Stanfield at the podium next to area supervisor in charge for the Detroit field office, Dennis Callahan.

"What the fu—?"

"*... The FBI conducted a long investigation into a series of murders spanning two decades in this community. We believe the killer acted alone when he preyed on women. He is now dead, his name is Michael Sean Kelly, formerly of*

Charlestown, Massachusetts and recently of Dearborn. A fast-acting FBI agent thwarted him from ramming his truck loaded with extra gasoline into a car driven by a local woman with her children onboard...."

The DMV photo of the killer was flashed on the screen along with pictures of golf outing foursomes and sales awards while Stanfield droned on about Kelly. No motive was given.

Stanfield handed the podium over to Callahan *".... As soon as we received tips from the community that a string of deaths made to look like accidents or suicides were connected, we worked tirelessly to bring this case to a—"*

"Bullshit," Ramit screamed from the adjoining room.

"—conclusion."

The station cut away to aerial footage of the scene showing the flames being put out by the Southfield Fire Department, followed by on the ground interviews with witnesses.

"...We will keep you informed on this continuing story..."

They broke to a Fanner Ford commercial of all things.

All eyes were on Marsha, all breaths held.

She looked at those assembled in her room and smiled, less from the relief of not having to resort to Plan B, but more to the truth. "There may be a greater good here that we don't see in this moment, but we all know how we did this with no outside help, plenty of interference and a ticking clock. We did this with our own brains and willpower. We had only each other to lean on my brothers."

"Damn right," Horton said.

"I'd work with you any day, O'Shea," Chance said.

"Same goes for me, Marsha," Lester chimed in.

Finally, Mike looked at her, and they squeezed hands.

"One of these days, you're gonna have to figure this shit out for yourself, Marsh."

During the previous week, he had told her that this case had re-energized him and that he accepted an instructor's post at the training academy and would teach until his arm healed completely.

"That's something Charlie would say." She grinned at them. "We know what went down. We never quit. We never quit."

She'd work with these guys anytime, and Ramit too. Poor Ramit. How would she make it up to him? He did good. Looking around so that a nurse was not present. "Do you think you can smuggle in some ice cream and my favorite Starbucks?"

* * *

"Ms. O'Shea. Ms. O'Shea? I am sorry to wake you, but you have two visitors," the nurse said.

"Send them in." She groggily sat up and took a sip of water. She looked at the clock. It was now after midnight of September 11. Mary Kelly died all those years ago and her death dominoed a rampage of vengeance by her now-dead husband.

Into the darkness of her room entered two suited men of equal height. One was trim and the other broader.

"How are you, Agent O'Shea?" Grayson Stanfield asked.

"Okay. How's my pen pal doing?" she said what she was thinking after recovering from the shock on seeing him in person.

"Very well. Thank you for asking," he replied.

"How was the funeral?" she asked.

"Funeral?"

"Myles Hanski's funeral. You gave a eulogy."

"Oh yes. Sad. Very sad. Exemplary man. Brilliant mind. He left such a legacy of work."

Looking at the beefier Callahan, she said, "Kudos on an outstanding job today. Good press is scarce." Marsha delivered the line without a hint of sarcasm.

"We got off on a wrong foot and that's why we are here to talk to you, O'Shea."

"Well, gentleman, it's late. Today was the day I had been dreading for months, but we solved it in time. The case is over. What more is there to say?"

"Plenty. There was more at play here than met the eye, Agent O'Shea," Stanfield said.

She dwelled on that. That had been the reason for all their secrecy and plausible deniability. "Well, if you don't mind, I'd like my partner in crime Ramit to hear what you have to say too."

The visitors looked at each other.

"A loyal FBI employee almost died in that crash with me. I think you owe him an explanation as well. That was some rough sledding you two put us through."

Stanfield nodded to Callahan, who left to fetch a nurse.

"You surprised me, Agent O'Shea. I wasn't expecting you to go public with your findings."

"Well, sir, when you didn't come down from the holy mountain with the tablets, I had to do something. I couldn't have Tamara Tabrizi's blood on my hands."

"I agree with you, but we both know with certainty that move would have ended your career with the bureau."

"Tru' dat." Marsha slipped into street slang to tweak the number two guy in the bureau as she sipped the last of her ice water.

"I don't know if I would have had the courage to do that," he said.

She shrugged. "It worked out in end." *He's giving a little to get a little. Hasn't forgotten how to interview subjects.*

"You put together a heck of a team of kids and former cops. I admire your ingenuity."

"Don't forget my old partners in crime, Mike Hollins and Charlie Akers."

"Duly noted. It was quite impressive."

Shaking off her second concussion in six months, she felt like a pro quarterback with a terrible offensive line. When was the next hit coming? With the painkillers coursing through system, she wondered if this praise was just a pleasant dream or maybe a set up.

Callahan walked in followed by the nurse wheeling in Ramit.

Ignoring her other visitors, he said, "Hey, pardner."

"Hey yourself. How are you feeling?" She could make out at least one black eye in the semi-darkness of her room.

"Head hurts too much to sing and I can't play the piano." He held up both bandaged wrists.

Ignoring their visitors as well, she asked, "What's the last thing you remember?"

"Horton pulling me out of the wreck."

"Before that."

"You deciding to plow into Kelly's pickup."

"Did you see how he had gas cans strapped to the bumper?"

"No."

"So, you only thought I was crazy and not completely suicidal, that's good." Shifting gears, she now turned to their visitors. "They have something to tell us."

"I can't thank you enough for stopping Kelly, before he struck again," Dennis Callahan said.

"You didn't make it easy, sir," Marsha said.

Looking at Stanfield for approval, he added, "But you made it easier for me to work behind the scenes when you ignored me and the field office. I could stay in role as 'one of the boys' when word came back that you were looking at the killings."

"Working on what?" Ramit asked.

Kind of ballsy, Ramit, Marsha thought, *but what the hell? He earned the right to ask.*

"That's a fair question, Ramit. I had to figure out who was doing the illegal bugging. It was some bad apples in my shop that played along with ICE and DHS to bug your rides, house and put keystroke-capture software on the kid's Chromebooks. You led them right to me and Deputy Director Stanfield. A few years ago, I was brought in to get a handle on the questionable sting operations, illegal wiretaps and harassment of this community. You were the straw that mixed the drink. I had to play the good ol' boy while you were the loose cannon that I couldn't control."

Stanfield was next. "Mr. Callahan here found the bugs at the mosque. He was able to catch the chatter about the last three years of 9/11 deaths of female members. It gave us the opportunity to work both cases — the mysterious deaths and the violations of civil rights of this community for two decades. We needed an outsider who could do the work and garner the attention of—"

"Georgie Boy Osterman," Marsha cut him off. *It's not often you get to interrupt a deputy director.*

"Yes, your good friend, George Osterman. You should have heard him rail at me about you and how I was weak and allowing you to run amok," Callahan replied.

"That must have been pleasant," she said. *This was the end game that Ramit saw better than I did. This was the reason for the hush-hush.* "Is he gonna get his?"

"Some more pieces still have to fall into place, but Dennis Callahan, working with a new team arriving tomorrow, is going work at warp speed to clean out the whole rat's nest."

"I have a question for you, Deputy Director Stanfield." Maybe it was the drugs pouring into her IV or the sugar from her Death by Chocolate triple fudge sundae that gave her the loopy courage to confront him. "I need to know why you never ever communicated with me."

"That's easy. I had to know how far DHS and some of their rogue contractors had penetrated the Bureau. Politics is still politics and shame on me if your investigation was uncovered and exposed prematurely."

"I see." She looked at Ramit and said, "You have good instincts, Kemosabe."

"If it's any consolation, I was your biggest cheerleader," Grayson said, "but I had to stay on the sidelines."

"You and Ravikant can work for me anytime," Callahan said.

CHAPTER 43

FOUR DAYS HAD PASSED since they were released from the hospital. Their excellent record keeping in *CaseSoft* was helpful to the agents gathered at an off-site location. These guys and gals selected from all over the country, by pre-design, had no connection with the Detroit field office. Search warrants at Kelly's apartment and his storage unit uncovered mementos from Kelly's conquests. They were able to connect him to most of the killings. They matched his DNA to both jumper's cars.

They found the bloody swatch and VHS tape in the police evidence room. Supposedly, the evidence had been "misfiled."

The board of trustees at the commuter college fired both their president and their Chief of Security when the proof of the switched incident reports and the missing statement were made public.

Chief Durkin got his visit by the Boston field office. They didn't play nice. They subpoenaed his file and dragged him into their offices for questioning. He got his phone call and the police union provided a former prosecutor as his representative.

True to her word, Marsha sent copies of *The Detroit Free Press* coverage to *The Boston Globe* and the story broke on the same day Durkin was being "interviewed" by the bureau. It was amazing how that timing worked out.

Fanner Ford filed for bankruptcy, but not before the mosque's attorney filed a dozen lawsuits on behalf of victims alleging negligence by allowing their salesman free access to the victim's cars and ordering key fobs without their knowledge.

Fearing adverse publicity, insurance companies did not seek reimbursement for payments made in good faith for "accidents" caused by Kelly.

Marsha and Ramit's LLC quit-claimed the deeds to the two properties tied to the building collapse to Tabrizi Masonry. Omar had ideas for affordable housing and maybe revitalizing the neighborhood.

"Hey, Marsha, are you ready?"

"Sure, Dennis. Let me fetch Ramit and I will meet you by the elevators."

It seemed so natural now to call Callahan by his first name. While they buttoned up the Kelly case, he had a unique group working on the more serious matter, which he spilled to her the night in the hospital. It was understood why he had to make it look like she was running rogue and that he had no parts of her investigation. That is why he acted like an asshole towards her, his words, not hers, during a lull in the action.

Other than the encrypted emails and payments for the AMEX card, Stanfield had successfully kept eyes in the bureau and outside off their investigation, There were spies and Stanfield was dealing with those issues as well.

"Hey, Ramit, you ready?"

He nearly jumped from his seat when she tapped him on the shoulder from behind. She loved getting the rise out of him.

They were both dressed in their Sunday best. His suit coat sleeves ran a little long to cover the wrist bandages. There was no way to hide Marsha's broken arm and sling, but at least she matched the sling with her beige blazer. His girlfriend Manju and Charlie Akers would be at the press conference with Lester, Chance and Dennis Horton, but they still had one more chore to attend to.

Callahan drove to the Rosa Parks Federal building where DHS kept their shop. It was another gorgeous morning for tourists coming to Motown. Dry with clear powder blue skies.

Ramit pointed toward the building of their most recent interest. They had been by there before, but certainly not in this context.

Callahan parked where he felt like and the three of them entered the building, badged their way through security and barged past George Osterman's secretary. They were followed by four additional agents for this timed entrance.

"Excuse me, Mr. Callahan, you can't go in there. Mr. Osterman is in a meeting."

"Like hell I can't. I've been waiting for this day for over ten years." He held Osterman's office door open for Marsha. "After you, Agent O'Shea, you have the honors."

"What is this? You can't just barge in here. Who do you think you are?" Osterman bellowed.

Those present and seated at the conference table backed away as stern-faced people with bright yellow vests with the bold print "FBI" on them circled the room quickly.

"Hi, Georgie," Marsha said. "These are for you." She pulled out her cuffs and held them to his face with her good hand. "You are under arrest. Do you want to go nicely, or do you want to give me an excuse, any excuse?"

His face flushed with anger or embarrassment. He leveled his stare at Callahan. "What's this about?"

"What's this about? It's about time," Callahan spit back. "Do as she says. I always told you she was a loose cannon, and I have no control over her."

"You will not get away with this. You don't know who you are dealing with." He seethed.

Marsha jangled the cuffs. "Now."

Osterman scanned the room one more time. There were no reinforcements on the way. He turned stiffly and forced his clenched fists straight down. Ramit grabbed one wrist and Marsha the other and snapped them tight as they had practiced before. Ramit had handcuffed no one before.

What a case to pop your cherry on, Marsha thought.

She handed him off to the yellow vests and followed Callahan out to his car.

"Before you get too puffed up, remember that people in my shop are going down too; agents I sat side by side with on hundreds of cases."

Callahan had first alerted Stanfield of the problems when he took over as ASIC and had to keep his cards close to his vest. These raids had to be done in the utmost secret at the FBI field office, ICE and DHS. They did the short drive in silence. The morning's indictments were to be revealed at a press conference.

* * *

Marsha and Ramit stood on stage next to the boys in blue. Callahan and Stanfield flanked by Assistant United States Attorneys. Ramit pointed out Manju in the audience. Charlie was on the other side of the room. The United States Attorney for the Eastern District of Michigan thanked the visitors and media for coming out.

The press release was then handed out, and he read from it. He thanked Agent Marsha O'Shea and Intelligence Analyst Ramit Ravikant by name for their efforts in bringing down Michael Sean Kelly. Their actions allowed the others on the dais to identify the persons responsible for mistreatment of the Arab American population in the Eastern District since 9/11 generally, but mostly for Civil Rights violations by illegally wiretapping or bugging Muslim gathering places, including mosques. They also brought obstruction of justice charges against higher-ups in DHS. He detailed how they attempted to thwart, harass or destroy evidence to impede Marsha's investigation.

What wasn't said for the cameras and reporters was something even worse. That is what Callahan told her about on the ride over to DHS. It made Marsha sick to her stomach.

Kelly appeared on the DHS radar in 2006 when their secret cameras captured Kelly entering the apartment building of Kamaria Aziz before the explosion. They had his image, and his car — and did nothing about it. A building explodes, a Muslim woman dies and no one connects the dots. That allowed him to operate unquestioned. Instead, DHS tried to stop Marsha and Ramit from building their case on him.

Osterman had said repeatedly to his minions that Marsha was bad for business.

After the press conference was over, Marsha mingled with Charlie, Ramit and Manju. The love birds were going back to Philly. She and Charlie were going to Clearwater, her home away from home. Their work in Detroit ended with cuffing Osterman; the rest could be done by email or Skype from anywhere. Her ribs were badly bruised, but not broken. Her arm would mend in seven weeks.

Stanfield approached them. "Marsha, I was hoping to have a word with you before I head back to D.C."

He could call her Marsha; she didn't have the balls to call him Gray or Grayson. "Yes, sir?"

"I liked the way this ended. We had a serious problem here. You did fine work. I have something else that I might need you for. Same ground rules. You operate alone."

"I will need another assistant as Ramit is going into the next academy for agents," she said without a hint.

"He is? That's wonderful."

"Especially when you tell him, he's standing right over there."

Stanfield was a little slow on the uptake and smiled. He walked over to them, slapped Ramit on the back and gave him the marvelous news. Ramit shook his hand profusely, probably aggravating his sprains.

Stanfield returned. "You are right, Marsha, he would make a fine agent, especially with my recommendation." He winked.

"What is it that you want me to investigate," she asked.

He told her.

"Where?"

"Reading."

"Like near my hometown, Reading?"

He nodded.

The End

Reviews are the life blood of independent authors. If you liked this book, please leave with your retailer. It's the best way for a reader to discover their new favorite author.

ALSO BY JOHN A. HODA

Also by John A. Hoda

Mugshots: My Favorite Detective Stories

Come ride along with veteran investigator John A. Hoda on his most memorable cases. He serves up them up like free refills at the 24-hour diner. His cases have headlined in the Philadelphia Inquirer and the New Haven Register.

My Book

Odessa on the Delaware: Introducing FBI Agent Marsha O'Shea

Book one of the Marsha O'Shea series

Can FBI Agent Marsha O'Shea stop a Russian Gang Enforcer on a murderous spree to take over the Philly mob scene. A mistake she made cost the life of a crime beat reporter and an innocent man is being framed for it. Uncovering the truth may get them killed in the final show down.

https://www.amazon.com/John-A.-Hoda/e/B00BGPXBMM%3Fref=dbs_a_mng_rwt_scns_share

Book two in the Marsha O'Shea Series: **Clearwater Blues**

Can disgraced and barely sober FBI Agent Marsha O'Shea prevent a deranged gun nut from shooting up a battered women's shelter? A perfect storm of domestic violence, untreated mental illness and lax gun laws come together in the final deadly encounter.

https://www.amazon.com/John-A.-Hoda/e/B00BGPXBMM%3Fref=dbs_a_mng_rwt_scns_share

Book four in the Marsha O'Shea Series: **West Reading Traffick**

Sixteen year-old Irina came to America to be a model or so she thought. Can an injured and burned out FBI Agent, Marsha O'Shea and a young patrolman find her alive or before she disappears in an international sex trafficking ring?

https://www.amazon.com/John-A.-Hoda/e/B00BGPXBMM%3Fref=dbs_a_mng_rwt_scns_share

DEDICATION

Matt Scudder, Tess Monaghan, Harry Bosch and Arkady Renko, figments of great imaginations, but no less inspirational to this humble investigator and author.

Acknowledgments
Beta Readers Extraordinaire: Kate Taussig, Jarod Topalian, Kasey Szamatulski, and Charles and Margaret Zeiders.
Editor: Rebecca Millar
Proofreading and copyediting: Zetta Brown
Cover Designer: Dominic Forbes
Consultant: Joe Koenig, Former Michigan State Police

ABOUT THE AUTHOR

John A. Hoda is an emerging author of crime thrillers. This is John's third book in the Marsha O'Shea Series. In 2019, he was feted as a debut novelist and panelist at the Mystery Writers of America conference in Dallas, TX. He was a judge at the Shamus awards for Short Stories.

John is a real-life PI whose cases have headlined in the Philadelphia Inquirer and New Haven Register. He coaches at www. ThePICOACH.com and has written several How To books on the business of private investigations. He podcasts **My Favorite Detective Stories** can be found at your favorite pod catcher or at www.johnhoda.com where he can be reached.

Coming Soon

Liberty City Nights: Marsha O'Shea Prequel Novella

Mr O'Shea wants his wife to settle down and start a family. FBI agent Marsha O'Shea is working on the Bank and Fugitive squad in Miami and is making a name for herself as gunslinger when the FBI was the federal alpha dog in the fight against crime pre 9/11. There is no compromising when the sparks fly.